Alex Keegan, like his fictional heroine, loves to run – he is a running coach and until injury halted his career, he was a UK top-thirty veteran sprinter. He has worked for the RAF, in direct selling and as a computer consultant. After being involved in the Clapham Rail Disaster he gave up his successful career to write full-time and is now the author of four previous novels featuring Brighton police detective Caz Flood – *Cuckoo*, *Vulture*, *Kingfisher* and *Razorbill*. He lives in Southampton with his wife and their two children.

Alex has been nominated for and won many prestigious prizes. He was a finalist in the *Cosmopolitan* Short Story of the Year Award 1994; *Cuckoo* was nominated for an Anthony Award for Best First Novel in 1995; he has won prizes from *Raconteur* magazine in 1995 and the Bridport Literary Festival in 1996. Alex will also have some of his short stories broadcast on BBC Radio in 1997.

Also by Alex Keegan

Cuckoo
Vulture
Kingfisher
Razorbill

A Wild Justice

Alex Keegan

First published in Great Britain in 1997 by
Judy Piatkus (Publishers) Ltd of
5 Windmill Street, London W1

This edition published 1998

A catalogue record for this book
is available from the British Library

ISBN 0 7499 3046 2 (pbk)

Set in Times by
Intype London Ltd

Printed and bound in Great Britain by
Mackays of Chatham PLC

When I wrote my first Caz Flood novel, still trying to find my way in the world of writers, my dedication took up a page! This one could too, if I named all the friends I've made on-line who read the first four books and commented on this one. My thanks to them.

And after a time spent "between publishers", I would like to thank: my agent, for hanging in there with me; and Kate Callaghan, my editor, for her support.

Those who have read my earlier books will know that there is a real Caz Flood – a real bobby whose name I use with permission. Needless to say, she doesn't do any of the things my Caz Flood does. But I mention the original Caz Flood because, as I finished A Wild Justice, she was at a police convalescent centre, undergoing physiotherapy, still trying to overcome injuries sustained on duty. So, Caz and all coppers, thanks.

William Kennedy once said that writers needed Faith, Hope and Charity. We find our own faith and we keep hoping, but reality, in the form of trips to Sainsbury's and dressing two kids, is such that, without the financial support from my wife over the last few years, I would have had to go back to real work instead of doing what I love.

So this is for Debbie. Thanks, love.

Acknowledgement

Extract from *Outlander* by Diana Gabaldon reproduced with the kind permission of the author.

If I can stop one heart from breaking,
I shall not live in vain;
If I can ease one life the aching,
Or cool one pain,
Or help one fainting robin
Unto his nest again,
I shall not live in vain.

EMILY DICKSON

The tyrannous and bloody act is done;
The most arch deed of bloody massacre
That ever yet this land was guilty of . . .
. . . we smothered the most replenished sweet
Work of nature.

SIR JAMES TYRELL

I

One

Moira Dibben was round and brown; wide and brown; gorgeous and brown. She was also at least eleven and a half months' pregnant, size-wise somewhere between an over-inflated Volkswagen Beetle and the Goodyear balloon. Caz Flood was in one of those moods.

"Moira, you are not just *big* – look at you, you're taking over the bloody flat! And can't you sit better? Close yer legs; you look like Les Dawson!"

"*You* try sitting better, Flood. You want some of this? It's all I can do not to pee all over your settee."

"You fancy a little glass of Il Grigio?"

Moira rubbed her belly, shook her head, and shifted her hips. Her knees went wider. "I think I'd be better off with a nice cuppa tea."

Caz groaned. "Bloody hell, first the DI, now you. Everyone is going soft on me!"

"Falling in love isn't going soft, Caz."

"No? Tom is walking round muttering Robbie bloody Burns, for God's sake. He's even sending Vaunda flowers with little poems attached!"

"I think it's kinda nice."

Caz was at the kitchen door. "Now, why doesn't that surprise me, I wonder?"

"Vaunda is sweet, Caz. I think *they* are sweet."

"Sweet? *Sweet*? Mo, I love Vaunda to death, but she's as mad as a hatter. It's not that long ago she was gonna blow me away cos I was a Russian or something. You do remember? I'll get the wine."

"Tea," Moira said.

Caz made a face. "Jesus, everything is so bloody *different*! I can't even get drunk with my mates or my boss any more. I wanna be so pissed my eyes bleed."

"You just need a decent case."

"I'll make your tea, dear."

Caz disappeared into her galley kitchen, clacked a kettle on, and dug out the corkscrew, leaving the good chianti and picking up the Ernst and Gallo Dry Reserve. She really fancied a glug, but she couldn't. She might be driving – she couldn't even get pissed on her own; she was *responsible.* Argh!

MeatLoaf was playing on the NAD and Moira grunted something over the music, something about a towel. Caz shoved the corkscrew into the E&G, then stuck her head round the door.

"What?"

Moira was grinning like a sick dog. "If that book you read last night was right, Caz, I think my water's just broken."

Caz had a bottle in her hand, the cork almost out. She looked at her mate. "You *what*? On my sofa? Well, I can tell you now, *Dibben*, I charge a tenner an hour for baby-sitting."

Two

Caz was driving her boyfriend's "Inspector Morse" car. Val had lent her the Daimler 250 a few days ago, in exchange for an orgasmic week or so thrashing round Brighton in her MX5. Caz didn't really want to do this but she knew Moira the Monster would never fit into the little Mazda. The swap was necessary, unavoidable – and Val knew it. He had grinned and held out his hand, but his eyes gleamed far too brightly. Caz had handed over the keys, but then explained to Val, slowly and precisely, what would happen if he scratched her car. What she said would have made a gladiator weep. He bleated.

"*Don't – scratch – the – car!*" Caz said.

Val had taken in the over-full, round, pressure-filled enormity of Moira. Mo had smiled at him sweetly.

"Then don't let *her* explode in the Jag!"

"Pregnant women don't explode, Valerie."

He looked at Moira to check.

"There's a first time for everything!"

Caz made two phone calls; the hospital and John Street nick. The desk sergeant was Bob Allen. He knew to pass on the message to Billy Tingle and Julie Jones who both had to-do lists. Billy was maturing fast now he was a dad, but when it really came down to it, Caz wanted another woman in on the act. Once a wanker, always a wanker, was Caz's motto. And Billy . . . She shook her head.

"How's Mo?" Bob said.

"Fine," Caz said.

"Give her my love then, would yer?"

"Yer luv?" Caz said. "That was what caused the trouble in the first place!"

"Not guilty!" Bob said. "But if she's not happy, she should've kept her legs together."

"That's what I keep telling her," Caz said.

Moira was shoe-horned into the passenger side of the Daimler-Jag OK, just as soon as Caz had laid out a few extra towels on the seat. As they set off for the maternity ward, Caz was trying to imagine Mo and the MX5. Maybe they could have taken the roof off and winched her in. But then they would have had to get her out . . .

She glanced at Moira as they turned out of Inkerman Terrace and on to Brighton sea-front. "So, bud, you OK?"

Moira was suffering quietly, just like a good Catholic should. She spoke with control. "Just get there, Caz."

Then Caz's pager started bleeping. She ignored it.

"No problems, mate. You're as good as in bed."

They arrived at the hospital, parked up and got into mother-mode; Moira in a wheelchair, being trolled down a polished corridor by a skinny angel called Jim who made it obvious he could land a 747 on a bowling green in heavy rain, steering with his teeth.

"This yer first, right? Yer one of Mister Jeremiah's?"

Moira urmed.

"'E's a great gynee, Jerems, and a good bloke. And sister Patel is in charge of your wing. With your luck, you c'd go dancing tonight."

Moira put her hand out for Caz. Caz's bleeper went again.

Three

Moira had said her Mum would fuss, Billy would faint, and her older sister had troubles of her own. So Caz had been elected; after all, what were mates for? So that was that, this was it. Caz wanted more drama, expected it; but the sister-midwife and the trainees were floating soundlessly by, soft-eyed and calming, whushing long vowelled words ending in "sh", done it all before, yes, yes, just get you out of these – clothes nurse – wash – a nice open gown – is there anyone you would like us to call?

The wall behind Moira was getting to Caz; stainless fitments, buttons, oxygen, gas 'n air, a mask; notices about cameras and videos. Moira was saying something . . . *Videos*! Yick!

"Caz?"

"You all right, Mo?"

"Of course I'm all right. How about you?"

"I'm fine, why?"

"You look spaced."

"Do I?"

"Yeah."

"Well, I'm fine. Just doing some research . . ."

Some woman let out a scream elsewhere and a rubber-flapped door closed on it. Moira smiled and Caz flinched. "Yeah, I'm fine, I'm fine. Just thinking of giving up sex."

Moira's smile was tight. She let her body settle about an inch. Her eyes lowered, almost as if she were looking inwards at the baby. Lines on her forehead disappeared and slowly she eased back out of it.

"Well, well, well, Flood," she said, "something you're afraid of!"

Caz was thinking about Val. "Piss off, Dibben."

Their door schlupped! and a dark little woman came in. Her race was not obvious. She had lovely, small teeth, shining eyes and long delicate fingers. She floated, with a saintly, controlling air.

"And you are Mrs Flood?"

"Miss."

"Also a police-woman?"

"A detective."

She nodded. Softly she said, "I am going to examine Moira now."

Caz was not quite in contact with the ground. Her usual grip on things was loose and slippery. All this was separate, odd, resonant, echoing like the lines of a Pinter play. The only time Caz had felt time working like this was once when she had faced a knifeman. But then her focus *was* there, on the muscles in his neck, the weight on the balls of his feet, the shine of the metal in his hand.

The midwife touched her. Caz felt what the faith-healed felt. All the woman's words were long and brown.

"You are tense, Miz Flood, but Moira is fine. Just hold her hand. She will tell you if she needs anything. See, look – she smiles at you."

Moira was smug, finally better at something than DC Flood. She smiled an even wider smile.

Caz moved closer; the nurse tapped Moira's knee.

"Come on Mo-Mo," Caz said, "open wide!"

Moira gave Caz a look. Caz expected her to hiss something back, but she glanced towards the foot of the bed and drew back her feet.

"Ah, that is good," the midwife's muffled voice said. "You are quite a way already."

Caz's bleeper went again and she ignored it again. Then she thought, grabbed it and switched it off. Moira was absorbing the pain of a big contraction, somehow managing a semblance of a smile. Her grip on Caz's hand was tight. Caz whispered to her to let it out.

"Are you being funny, Flood?"

"Just stop being so brave! There's no blokes here."
"*You're* here!"
"We're mates."
"Well, I'm not grunting, so tough."
"I'll bet you're praying under yer breath."
"Too bucking right, Flood! I'm on my ninety-third Hail Mary." She squeezed Caz's hand again.
"Another one?"
"This is going to be quick. I know it. My mum told me that start to finish I took less than an hour to come. It's the hips, y'see. The Dibbens were built for babies."
"Can't you grunt a *bit*, Mo?"
"No. What d'you suppose is up?"
"What?"
"Yer bleeper. What do you suppose is up?"
"No idea, Mo. And I don't want to know. There's plenty of other DCs, and none of 'em are holding your hand."
"You're all heart, Flood."
"No, I'm not. It's my night off. I want to be with my mate."
"Shucks, Flood . . . to look after me."
"Nah, to watch you suffer."
"You must wonder, though . . ."
"What? What's big enough for a bleep? Blackside's probably lost his keys and they wanna organise a search party. What's that smell?"
"What smell?"
"Oh, Mo, you coulda waited!"
"Oh, shit," Moira said, mortified.
"Exactly," Caz said.
An auxiliary nurse came in and Caz nodded at the bed. The auxiliary smiled. "It happens all the time. Pressure on the back passage. Two jiffs, not a problem!" She turned to Caz. "If you could just give us a minute?"
Caz was a bit slow. "Oh, sure. I'll be just outside."
Moira called after her. "While you're out there, Caz, why don't you ring in?"
Caz had already been wondering where was the nearest phone.
"Oh, yeah, good idea!"

Four

Caz dialled the nick and got through to the front desk.

"Caz Flood. Someone been bleeping me?"

"G-28, Flood. A pretty disgusting one. Some guy in Hove in little pieces, bits of 'im stuck all round the room."

"Bits?"

"Billy Tingle found it. Still there waiting for Scene o' Crimes and whoever's I-C the case."

"Bits?"

"Billy chucked up. This guy – his nose, his lips, his balls, his dick; all hacked off and stuck around the room. No fingers either. They're gone – at least Billy couldn't find them."

"Christ! And Moira's just about to pop her kid!"

"He knows, Caz, but you know the form; he can't get away until the team is assigned, and nobody's answering their bleeper. You any idea where DI MacInnes is?"

She lied. "No idea." Then she said, "Give me the address."

She rang Armando's; Armando himself answered. A minute later Tom came on the phone. She told him about the G-28, sudden death and the body bits. "That's all I know. I'm with Moira at the hospital. She's well on the way."

"And ah'm with Vaunda."

"I just thought we should be on the case, sir. If one of us doesn't get there pretty quick, it'll go to someone else."

"Ah shoulda retired when ah had the chance."

"You wouldn't know what to do, Tom."

"Try me," he said.

"I need to get back to Moira." Caz said, the words trailing off. "Anything I need to do?"

"Jest give me the address, Flood. Von can drop me off, an' gae on haem in ma car."

"And I'm on board, sir? I could be there in an hour."

"Ah'll do ma best, Flood. Y'dinnee desairve it, though."

MacInnes couldn't see, but Caz was grinning. "Thanks, Tom!"

As she put the phone down she was excited, almost sexual. Her fists were clenched. Then she remembered Moira, and went back to the delivery room.

Five

The G-28 was in a house in a grey terrace, one turn off the main road, one more turn away from the flapping sea. Caz arrived as the six blips of midnight were beebing on Val's radio. It seemed fitting.

The street was full: cars, lights, two barriers, one close-squared round the front door, the second further out to keep away all but the neighbours. Caz parked, pulled her warrant card and flashed her way past a young probationer constable. His pale boy's face was lit up by the blue-white field-light flooding the road and the victim's house. He was about nineteen. She didn't know him but clicked on a smile of support. She didn't think he'd make it through probation.

On the front step, a second PC, another kid. She grunted "MacInnes" at him and he opened the door. She walked through, into hell.

There was a long hallway, rich with the stink of blood and bowel and something else – bacon? surely not? sliding in between the waves of the other like a sick joke. Caz felt around for a tissue but then Tom MacInnes appeared, grey as the house, in casual clothes, shocked, breathing shallow mouth-breaths, frail.

"You made it, Hen."

"Quick as I could, sir. Moira—"

"Ah know, Hen." MacInnes looked behind him. "It's real bad."

"Billy, sir?"

"The garden."

Caz paused. What did the DI want her to do? The other

side of the door was horror – but it was the job, experience, promotion. She leaned slightly that way. MacInnes seemed saddened. His eyes flicked towards the room and he half-shook his head. "Not just yet, Hen. Plenty o' time for that. Go hae a word with Billy. He'll be wanting to know about Moira and his bairn."

"Where?" Caz said.

"Through the kitchen," MacInnes said. There was disappointment in his voice.

There were footsteps above them; someone fell and swore. The DI looked up and moved to shout something. Caz turned away. A voice, sounding like Bob Saint, muttered an apology from the head of the stairs and MacInnes gave a resigned reply.

Scene of Crimes were taping off the kitchen and the gas stove was covered in a wax-paper lid protecting whatever was underneath. Caz wondered but didn't say anything, stepping out instead into the bright rear garden, the click-clack and buzz of electrics, and the guys in white carefully searching the garden. Billy was at the far end, behind the lights, one side of him darkness, the other reflected silver. He was flopped on a garden bench, limp as a rag doll. There was a mug of tea in his hands, undrunk, hanging in the balance with half long since dribbled away, the rest cold. She took his hand and the cup. When he looked up it was with empty eyes.

"She's OK," Caz said.

There was no answer.

"Billy, Moira's done it. You're a dad."

"How heavy was 'e?"

"*She.*"

"No, it's a boy, Caz. Moira had the scan done. They told us. We're calling him Timmy. How big was 'e, d'you say?"

"Eight pounds, a couple of ounces. But she's a girl, Billy, and she's long and skinny, just like you."

"We saw the X-Ray thing. He had a dick 'n' everything . . ."

"Sorry, Billy. No Willy."

It almost worked. Billy looked up. There was a flicker, as

though his personality was trying to restart, but then it slipped away again.

"Bastards said it was a boy, Caz."

"Hey, Billzebub, no big deal! Next time, eh?"

"We never thought of a name."

"Moira has."

"It was definitely a boy. We called him Timmy . . ."

"You want to go home or to the hospital? Moira will be asleep."

Billy glanced towards the house. "I want to get a shower."

"It was bad, huh?" Caz said. Billy drooped again.

"Very bad?"

Billy came alive. "It was fucking *evil*, Caz. Nobody, nobody could ever, could ever . . ."

"OK," Caz said. "How's about we get you home, then? You can get out of your uniform, get a shower and some sleep. How about it?"

Billy looked up, still only half-focused. He zeroed in on Caz's face and his eyes sharpened, went cold. For the briefest, perverse second he looked like a rapist. Caz shook her head.

He mumbled, "Yeah, home. Good idea. The DI said . . ."

"Come on then," Caz said. She saw his eyes again and Billy saw her see. He laughed. As he stood to his awkward six-foot three, his face shone with artificial light, the imagined evil flickered and then it was gone. He was just Billy Tingle again – Moira's feller, a bit of a wanker, but OK. Caz was thinking: would she be lumbered or could she get someone to take Billy in an area car?

Six

On the way to Moira's mother's, Caz told Billy: their girl was called Titania. Moira had made her mind up.

"Titania Tingle-Dibben," Billy said. "Yeah, cool."

Caz bit her tongue. She could smell vomit, somewhere on Billy's uniform and had wound down the window. She was leaning ever so slightly away.

"Or should it be Titania Dibben-Tingle?" Billy said, looking at the dashboard clock.

"I think you should let Moira decide," Caz said.

"It was fucking *horrible*," Billy said. "I've never seen . . ."

"Get a shower," Caz said. "Get some sleep." She smiled. She was thinking "*Titty Dibben-Tingle*". "In the morning you can go see Mo and Titty-Ann. She looks great. I think she's gonna be a model."

"It was fucking horrible," Billy said.

Seven

Caz drove back slowly, not in so much of a rush now to see all she would have to see. She had the windows open to the night, washing away the taint of Billy's accident, and when she stopped on King's Parade to step out and stare at the sea's faint nap, smell its salt-light air, she ached. Nothing, nothing was as solid as she needed.

The surf was luminous, maybe it was green, and here, as it broke on the shingle, it hissed and rushed among the stone, a little soft, left-over light from the promenade adding a dirty, unsure yellow.

It had been quick for Moira, but quick and brutal. And Mo had been angry, and had bitten Caz, and when she had called out a man's name to call him "bastard", she shouted "Mason", not "Billy".

And her beautiful round-brown face had contorted only twice; once just as the head threatened to emerge, the second time, later, when the midwife produced a huge hypodermic needle to use before the stitches. In between, the boy-girl had come, so long and purple and so flecked with a dried, alien white that Caz was frightened for Moira. But Titania – it was Titania straight away – was fine, even when curled and red-blue, so long and awkward she had to be Billy's.

Then Caz had kissed her friend, squeezed her hand once more, pulled back the blanket to see the crusty tight-eyed thing that made Moira so happy, not understood, and made her excuses. It was something heavy down in Hove, she told

Mo. She managed to forget that the father of Titty was the poor bloody copper who had found the carnage, the copper who had been alone with it until MacInnes arrived.

Eight

Caz got back to Hornby Terrace a little before one o'clock. It was darkest dead of night but the street was day, lit by the arc lamps outside number seventeen and the glowing front-room windows and bedrooms of people too wakened now to sleep, tinkling their cups of Ovaltine or stirring big pots of tea for the uniforms outside. One curtain tugged nervously as Caz pulled up. She looked, but all she saw, behind a mask of lace, was a gaunt, sexless face.

The young PC looked like he was beginning to feel the cold but his face brightened when he saw Caz. She made some remark about the weather and he grinned. Caz felt sorry for him. There wasn't anything worse than this; no drama, no involvement, just a long, long, cold night and nothing to do but think and freeze.

She went in. As she did so, she heard the deep voice of the Detective Chief Superintendent. Blackside was speaking, gently, respectfully, but in the hush of the death-house, even his muted speech seemed to boom. Then the lighter, now accentless voice of the Detective Inspector answered and she heard her name.

They were in the kitchen. She knocked. Blackside said, "Come!"

She went in, nodded to MacInnes but spoke to the DCS. He was in a dinner-suit complete with red cummerbund, gleaming shoes. "Sir, I took PC Tingle home. A bit of shock, I think, sir, but he's with his mother-in-law. I left him downing a cup of tea."

"Busy night for you, Flood."

"Sir?"
"WPC Dibben."
"Oh, yes, sir! She's fine, sir."
Blackside glanced at the white cover on the stove and took a short, uncomfortable breath.
"Has Flood been briefed yet, Tom?"
"Not yet, Norman. Ah thought it best to get rid of Tingle. There's never a rush to see something like this, is there?"
Blackside turned to Caz.
"Strictly speaking, Flood, you could skip going in there. S-O-C have been in and we'll have plenty of photographs in the morning."
"Is it that bad, sir?"
"It's bad."
"Then I'd rather see, sir. See the crime, know the criminal."
"This is one to be excused on, Flood."
"I'd rather see, sir." She nodded apologetically, but left the weight in her voice. "If it's OK with you, sir . . ."
"Up to you, Flood."
"Thank you, sir."
"I'll leave you with the DI, then, and get off home."
MacInnes shifted his feet and Blackside glanced again at the white covering the stove. "The morning, then. Tom. Flood."
Caz backed into the hall to let the DCS through. As he stepped out, the big man paused, looked Caz in the face, went to speak, then changed his mind. He stepped past, then changed it again.
"Flood?"
"Sir?"
"You courting, Flood? Seeing someone?"
"Engaged, sir."
"You love him?"
"Sir?"
He paused, as if what he was about to say was weak.
"I mean it, Flood. Nobody will think the worse of you. Nobody. You don't have to take stuff like this home. There's really no need . . ."
"I understand, sir."

Blackside almost wobbled.

"No, you don't, Flood."

MacInnes was in the doorway now. Behind him was the shrouded stove and behind that, the floodlit back garden. His hand rose as if he was going to touch Caz's shoulder, but it came to rest on the door-jamb. He was tense and his accent was coming back. He flicked a glance to Caz.

"We'll hae a talk before we go in, suh."

Blackside took another funny little breath, looked at them both, shook his head and walked away.

MacInnes shouted after him. "I'll be in at seven, suh!"

The DCS raised a hand and stepped out into the night.

Nine

The DI pointed to the street-door and Caz walked ahead. Outside was sharply cold but sea-fresh and Caz took her first deep breath in minutes. They walked across the road. Another curtain twitched and Caz glared at the face. It disappeared quickly.

MacInnes seemed older, sadder, ever more frail. He had his hands in his pockets and shrugged his shoulders forward against the cold.

"We have a male Caucasian, about fifty years old, naked. He's been tortured and badly mutilated – partly disembowelled. He has no fingers, ears, lips, and he's been castrated: testicles and penis. We won't know for sure until after the PM, but the doctor thinks the victim was still alive when the cooking began."

"*Cooking*?"

"You smelt it?"

"I wasn't quite . . ."

"The doc thinks it's the poor bastard's penis. He thinks the killer cooked it, tried to make him eat it. There was stuff in the mouth but for sure, we don't know yet."

"Jesus!"

"Blackside meant it, Caz. There's no need."

"I think there is, Tom. I could be where you are in ten years time. When it happens, am I going to send for someone else?"

"Thissun is different, Hen. It's wuss than anything ah've seen."

"Are you ordering me not to go in, sir?"

"Ah'm jest saying there's no need."

Ten

Caz got into the Daimler. MacInnes opened the passenger door and slid in wordlessly. At the far end of the street, the undertaker's white van blinked its headlights on-off, dipped them, then pulled away left. The young PC was talking through the open window of an area car. He was nodding. Another cop got out, touched his arm and moved onto station for the werewolf shift. One by one, lights were going out.

"Are you OK?" Tom said.

Caz started the car. "I'm fine," she said. "What time do you want me in tomorrow?"

"You mean the day?"

"Today."

"There'll be a briefing in the War Room at eight. Best be in before that. Ah'll see if you can get a break in the afternoon. You sure you're OK?"

"I'm OK."

They drove slowly, first to Tom's flat near the Grand Pier, the night amber and windswept now, the streets glistening, not even foot-stepped. When they stopped, before MacInnes could speak, Caz said it again. Yes, she was OK. There was a light on upstairs.

"You've a light on."

"That'll be Vaunda," Tom said. He touched her arm, clicked open the door and went as quickly as he could. Cold slipped in.

Caz waited until the street door re-closed and Tom was swallowed up. Then she checked her mirror, sat more upright, took a sharp breath and drove slowly away.

She swung the wrong way; not towards her place – it would be empty save for her stuffed pigs; not to Valerie's – not at nearly three in the morning; and not the nick. For sure someone there would say the wrong thing.

She went east, past the Dolphinarium, out towards Rottingdean, the cliffs, past the marina, white-sliver masts tinkling below her, even the harbour lifting and falling. She floored it a bit once she was out of the town, the window open, the wind cold, painful, the slick-slick, slick-slick-slick of the Indian tyres, the phwah-phwahwah of the night air slapping her face.

Caz was thinking about Moira. She was proud of her. Knees up, undignified, but human; braver than she had expected, and only the one moment, the worst one, when she had bitten Caz and cursed out Peter Mason's name.

"You're all right, Moira," she whispered.

Titania or Titiana. What had she told Billy? Poor misbegotten kid. Blood. Shit. Who the fuck could even think of such things, do such things? What were they looking for – a sea-side ripper? Moira's face, oh, Mo! She was so simply sweet. No doubt Titty would be too. And if she was tall and thin like Billy and as beautiful as her Mum, Jesus, she'd win prizes. Even when, even when it was gone, it was there, the death aura, the filth, the . . .

One day a Paris catwalk. If ever, *ever*, someone touched her . . .

"So Caz, you'll be T's god-mum, yeah? I wouldn't want anyone else. Me and you, we go back, and T couldn't get a better one."

"You've fucking lost it, Dibben."

"No, I haven't, Flood. Look at her. You try telling me this isn't what it's all about."

A purple monkey covered in white gunk? Caz was going to say yes? She looked again. Yes. Big scene – but time to go.

"Hey, buddy," Caz had said, "I'd love to be Titty's godmother." She had looked at her watch, stood up. "Now look, I gotta go. Hove."

Moira sighed, closed her eyes, opened them.

"So Caz, be careful out there . . ."

Eleven

Kings Parade, silent, amber; Inkerman Terrace, silent, amber; the sea, a funny rush, wish-away, just out of sight. Her door-key, as quiet as she could; the dark hallway; then bright light, the stairs, the door to her flat, light, and then a hand out onto the landing and the switch, and then her bright, white, kitchen, the *Il Grigio*, not the Californian, fuck the coffee.

Elton John. *Love Songs.*

She sat on the sofa and cuddled Pink Vincent, the biggest of her piggies, fat-bellied and wonderfully stupid. She offered him Chianti, talked to him, tried to cry when "Blue Eyes" came on, failed, and tried to sing along, looking into Vincie's beady, pug-nosed face, not getting it right.

There had been no need, Blackside said.

There had been no need, Tom MacInnes had said.

She had said. She had thought, different.

There had been no need.

II

Twelve

Monday, 08:00

When DCS Blackside and DI MacInnes came into the War Room, the squad hushed straight away. They all knew the DCS by now.

He stood at the lectern and waited, the odd stripes of louvre-rippled light down his side like camouflage make-up. Caz glanced very quickly at the windows creating the effect and thought it was about time someone sorted it.

"Gents," Blackside said. He looked directly at Caz and nodded. "Gents, a particularly nasty murder. Victim as yet unknown. PM in progress."

MacInnes nodded to someone at the back and the lights went down. The reading light from the lectern now shone up under Blackside's chin making him look like a ghoul. There were a couple of clacks at the back of the room and finally a picture appeared up on the wall – the victim, upside down. Immediately, three-quarters of the heads in the room automatically swung left and down to look.

Blackside hissed, "Jesus!"

"Sorry, Sir," Jim Greaves said, then the screen went white and then, after another *sc-lack!* the dead man re-appeared. The synchronised rush of breath said it all. Someone muttered, "Fucking Hell!"

Blackside let them all take it in then stretched taller. "OK, lads – Flood – that's enough of Mr Hornby. Photos will be available." He nodded and the lights went back up. The mutilated body washed out against the wall until Jim realised and switched the Kinderman off.

"Right. On the ground: IC, DI MacInnes, Detective Sergeant Reid, DS Moore. Sergeant Moore will do the rosters as usual. And we have a guest; where are you, DS Sweet?"

Next to Caz a hand went up. She'd not noticed him before. A medium-to-large guy, pleasant enough, but a fade-away face, quiet, forgettable. His most noticeable feature was boyish, curly blonde hair, vaguely like David Gower, the cricketer. With that, and a name like Sweet, it must have been tough before he made DS.

"Sergeant Sweet has just transferred. Before this hit the fan we'd arranged for him to ease himself in. Things will have to be a bit quicker now. Welcome aboard, Sweet. You'll be with the DI today – and DC Flood, DC Saint and DC Greaves."

The hand went back up.

"Sweet?"

"Permanent, is this, sir? Only I thought I was marked up for CP." The accent was northern – Lancashire, maybe Manchester.

"Child Protection can wait, Sergeant. When you've seen a few more pictures, I'm sure you'll understand."

"Sir."

Blackside nodded to Tom MacInnes. The DI stepped forward.

"Our first problem is a name. Door-to-door today, tomorrow. We had four different names and half a dozen don't-knows last night. The house was rented – cash up front, no references, for six months. I'd like a name today and we need to know where the victim lived previous. For now he's John Hornby. The place looked temporary – we'll be having another look at it today. Questions?"

"Are we holding stuff back, sir?"

"Yes. And we're pulling the *Argus* in to ensure their co-operation."

"What about the nationals, sir?"

"It's just an ordinary murder."

There was a cough. MacInnes continued. "There's an

absolute blank on the mutilation. It goes out as a savage, senseless attack – nothing more." His voice raised. "When you get the details, I know the jokes are going to start, but if they get into the public domain, I will personally make sure that the man responsible gets his card marked. This is a very, very bad one. We do *not* want the tabloids crawling all over us. Those of you who remember the murders, November, year before last, that was kid's stuff compared to this."

Blackside was shuffling papers as if he'd had enough and wanted to get on. Tom MacInnes spoke quickly.

"OK, lads, Bob Saint could do with some help setting up in here. Meanwhile I need Jack, Bob, and DS Sweet in my office." He glanced down at a piece of paper. "Jack, is it? Another one! That'll help lots. You gotta nickname by any chance, Jack?"

Sweet stood up.

"Two, guv. One I don't mind."

Chairs were moving, people coughing. Caz was probably the only person who heard Sweet saying he didn't mind being called Angel. Saint and Greavsie were moving towards the front and Caz offered to go get the coffees in. Greavsie grinned at the new DS.

"So what's the nickname you *don't* like, Sarge?" Sweet moved as if he hadn't heard. "Do we get to guess, Sarge?"

Sweet turned round. "Jim, isn't it?" Greavsie nodded. "Jim, don't even think about it. You use my other nickname, we have to go outside; you won't like me if you get me angry."

Caz caught the eyes but Jim didn't. Greavsie thought Sweet was joking. "Something to do with cricket, is it?" he asked.

Sweet stopped and looked right into Jim's face. There was a man's sizing up and Sweet won. He spoke slowly. "I'm Jack, or Angel, Sergeant until you know me better, OK?" He was about to break away but he turned back and leaned close. "And no, nothing to do with cricket. You'd best stop guessing." Then he was gone, following MacInnes and the others through the door.

Greavsie was awkward, smitten. "The fuck's with him?" he said. "How to make friends and influence people, right?"

"I think he's right," Caz said sensibly. "Why bother guessing?"

Greavsie laughed. "You're joking, right? There'll be a sweep started on the name by coffee-time. I guarantee it."

"He doesn't want it used, Jim, and he's a DS."

"Oh, it won't be *me* starts the sweep, Caz. As if!"

Caz shook her head.

"So Bob, you want some pikkies stuck up?"

Thirteen

On one wall they tacked up a dozen pictures of Hornby: close-ups of the strapping, his blackened, flattened face, the stumped feet, hands, the crusted groin, hair plastered black with rusted blood.

Space was left for a plan of the house, a PM summary, and the blow-up street-maps: X marks the spot for every successful door-to-door. When Caz came back with a dozen coffees she helped finish off with a few pikkies of the sitting room. One thing she had not registered the night before was the bookless white, the lack of a TV. The room was more like a cell than part of a house. She could see the edge of a pile of magazines on top of a wall-fitting. They'd be porn mags.

They stopped for coffee. "So Mo managed it then, Caz?"

"Twenty to twelve, a girl, eight pounds."

"What they calling it?"

"I can't remember."

"I thought Billy said it was gonna be a boy," Greavsie said.

Saint laughed. "Billy still believes in Father Christmas!"

Caz looked at the photo-wall.

"Not any more," she said.

The other teams started filtering through, sidling sideways past the pictures like browsers in an art gallery. The first few had grabbed a coffee; the rest had a good excuse to leave. Caz was used to jokes but no one cracked any. Then DS Moore came through with the pictures from the kitchen and stuck them up. Then someone said did anyone fancy a hot-dog or a sausage-roll and a dam burst.

"Plenty of ketchup for me, Dick!"

"Check mine for hairs, Willy!"

"So Caz, you recognise it?"

"Hey, Greavsie, mine shrinks in the bath, but—"

Bob Moore turned round.

"Very funny, lads, but remember, some shit actually did this and when the nutters start coming in to confess, we need to have held something back. If this gets out and it's down to me or mine . . ."

"Just letting out some air, Sarge."

"Yeah, sure."

"So Caz, *do* you recognise it?"

"Caz?"

"Caz?"

She got up, walked over, peered, studied the split-meat. The pest was a new DC, a weasly-faced guy called Ken Mitchell. She turned to him, thought, looked at his groin, turned back to the picture.

"Short, bloated, cut-off; no fucking use to anyone."

She turned round.

"Not yours is it, Ken?"

Fourteen

09.30

The DCS had decided he wanted another look and feel at seventeen Hornby Terrace so the DI drove him down there. Jim, Bob, Angel and Caz went down together in a spare Sierra.

Saint and Greavsie were in the front, Caz and the DS in the back. Before they were out of the car-park Caz had snapped at Greavsie. She was thoroughly pissed off with penis jokes.

The other teams were dealing with the area door-to-door, but Hornby Terrace had been left to the DI's unit. Caz and the new DS started at the sac end of the cul-de-sac, Bob Saint and Greavsie down near the main road. It was an old trick Caz had picked up from an encyclopaedia salesman. Every door-knocker works *into* the street; most get pissed off before half-way and give up. At the top of the street people are hostile, cynical, or don't answer their doors. At the street's stub-end they are rarely questioned and therefore far more interested in books, new windows and satellite TV. DS Sweet thought she wore a lucky charm. Caz kept her secret secret.

Even at the street's arse-end there were plenty of no-accesses. For every one they left a printed card asking the resident to contact the station. At number twenty-nine, a Mrs McDermid told Caz that the man at number seventeen had had a few visitors. No, she couldn't say when, or what they looked like. Oh, but they were men, did she say? Name? No, she had no idea. She kept herself to herself.

At number twenty-three, a single, harassed Mum, barely twenty years old and two under-fours. There was a faint smell of pee and one of the kids was crying. She thought maybe the man's name was Jack Brown, but no, she couldn't remember where she had heard it. Wouldn't the postman know?

"John Bourne," the old dear at number fifteen said. "Yes, I'm sure. I took a parcel in for him about a month ago, J. Bourne. I've got tea on if you'd . . ."

Caz looked round and stepped in. Over tea she asked Mrs Barker: she hadn't heard anything last night, no noises, perhaps the sound of a fight?

"I wasn't here, luvee. I play bingo Sunday nights, and stop at my daughter's. I don't like to come home late."

"Oh," Caz said.

"I asked him about the J. Mr Bourne told me, for John. I can't say I really took to him. My daughter didn't either. Something about the way he looked at you. He wasn't particularly nice-looking, sort of grey – until he started tanning."

"Tanning?"

"Those sun-bed things. The blue lights, you know. My daughter tried to get me to try one once, but I didn't like being closed in, you know, or the funny smell."

"How about visitors? Did Mr Bourne have any?"

"I can't say I ever saw anyone. Mostly, I sit in my back room with the telly. I'm not one for poking my nose in. Not like some. I only knew his name because the postman asked me to take a parcel in."

Caz finished her tea. "You've been very helpful, Mrs Barker."

"I heard, his head was smashed in with a hammer. Is that true?"

"It'll be in the *Argus* tonight," Caz said.

10.42

They got two John Browns, Caz's John Bourne and a James Brown – but no one *knew*. Caz suspected it was a committee decision after an early morning doorstep conference. What else did people do with no work? Yeah, he may have had visitors, late-on mostly. No, no idea what they looked like. Why should they care? Men or women? Oh, men, yeah men. Men? You mean often? No, maybe once, could've been twice, but a man, yeah. Last night? No, I was watching telly; No, I went to bed early; No, I was out; No, I tries to keep myself to myself, you have to nowadays, don't you? Was it drugs, then?

The DI's car was still there. Caz had a word with DS Sweet and then they knocked Hornby-Bourne's door. The PC who should have been outside answered it.

"I was just having a slash," he said, faintly embarrassed. "The DI said it was OK."

"Mr MacInnes still here?" Sweet asked.

"Upstairs."

The sergeant looked upwards and moved to go that way. Caz quickly said she'd take another peek into the sitting room. She said it quietly. Sweet coughed as he mounted the lower stair.

"Middle bedroom," MacInnes said in reply.

Caz pushed open the lounge door.

"*And* you, Flood!"

"Yes, sir!" she shouted. "Right there, sir!"

Then she went inside.

Look and feel. Know the crime, know the criminal.

Bare white.

Bare white?

Fifteen

"You walk slow, Flood?" Blackside said.

"A note in my note-book, sir, sorry."

"So what d'you think? What d'you think you know that a DCS and a DI and a DS can't work out on their own?"

"Me, sir? Nothing, sir."

"No female intuition, Flood?"

"No, sir."

"What about in here?"

"What about in here? In *here*, sir, or in the house, sir?"

Blackside showed his teeth.

Caz gestured towards the bed. "May I?"

Clean sheets, very clean sheets, clean pillow-case, the sharp touch of starch. Blankets, not a duvet. Good quality. She pulled back the unmade bedding.

"Sheets are laundered, sir, not home-washed and ironed. Same for the pillow-cases."

"Yes."

"And the bed's been rustled-up to make it look like someone has slept in it."

She leaned down and sniffed.

"But these sheets haven't been slept in. There's no body smell and I'll bet no skin residue, hair, anything, when we check."

"The pillow-cases?"

She checked. "Same, sir."

"So we have what?"

"I don't know, sir. Maybe the murderer wanted the place not to look so tidy, so anal."

"Anal?"

"Anal-retentive, tidy-desk syndrome, creases in pyjamas."

"I have a tidy desk, Flood."

"Yes, sir. So does the DI, sir. Mine is immaculate, sir."

"Why the murderer?"

"Well, why the victim, sir? Why *start off* tidy, and then fluff everything up? Downstairs is very tidy too. Almost clinical."

"We wondered about that. So what do you think?"

"I haven't the faintest idea, sir. It's just odd."

MacInnes spoke. "There's some porn magazines downstairs."

"Do you mean the *Fiesta's*, sir?" She nearly said Tom.

"On top of the bookcase."

"The last ten issues, consecutive. It's just a wank-mag, sir. Silly stories and gynae shots of women, but there's a hell of a lot worse. I'd hardly term it porn."

"You approve?"

"Not at all, sir, I didn't say that. But this day and age, what's called porn is a bit heavier than that, wouldn't you say?"

MacInnes cleared his throat and caught Blackside's eye.

"Oh," Caz added, "They were in order and they've never been in the bathroom."

Blackside. "*What?*"

"Crisp pages, sir, never in a damp environment. They hardly looked read."

"Meaning?"

"I don't know, sir. Right now I'm just here for look and feel."

DS Sweet spoke for the first time.

"Ten months' magazines. Do we think this Bourne chap has been here all that time? Only the door-to-door suggested three or four at most."

"*Bourne?*"

"Sorry, guv. Bourne, or Brown, or Boon, is favourite according to the neighbours. Lady at number fifteen says categorically he was John Bourne. She took a parcel in for him. DC Flood—"

"It's four months. House belongs to Raymond Patel, let it for cash first of April. To a James Brown."

"Sock it to 'em JB!" Caz said.

Then she said, "Sorry, sir."

"Thing is, guv," Sweet went on, "the place is very clean, very tidy, right? Even the dirty magazines are very neat. But where are the guy's suitcases and stuff? Are there clothes in the cupboards? What?"

"Shirts are laundered, in that drawer. Usual stuff – socks, underwear. He was a thirty-eight-inch waist. One dark blue suit, spotless, college-stripe ties, four or five different ones. Two pairs of shoes, so shiny you could use them as shaving mirrors."

"Anal!" Caz said, half to herself.

"Thank you, Flood," Blackside said.

"Sorry, sir. Should I go downstairs, sir? I wouldn't mind looking in the sitting room again."

"Didn't you just do that?" Blackside said softly.

Ooh, touché, you clever sod.

"Only a second, sir, the magazines. I noticed them on the War Room gallery and I just wondered—"

"Hmmm. Bugger off then, Flood. You know the score. No fingers." As soon as he'd said it, he flushed. "I mean, don't leave fingerprints all over the shop."

Sixteen

It was cleaner now. No blood, no shit, no vomit, and no screamed-flat ripped and battered face staring; no neck-straps, no wrists leathered to the kitchen chair, no opened belly. But still Caz had her arms wrapped tight about her, still she spun round slowly, continually, as if she preferred not to stand too long with even the possibility of anyone or anything behind her.

Know the crime.

There had been no screams. A gag? How had Bourne been overcome? And if the poor bastard was alive when his penis was cut away, why hadn't he bled to death? How much pain would there have been? Was this a sex thing? Was this like a Mafia thing? Didn't they stuff genitals in the mouth of those who had broken the code of silence?

Perhaps, but they didn't hack off the nose, the ears, the lips. They didn't choose to paint a bizarre oval on the wall and fill it with pieces of the victim, re-mouth the mouth, re-nose the nose, super-glue ears to the wall like some gross potato-man, like some sick joke, so very, very, deeply sick, as if the devil had come to Hornby Terrace and showed the Bundy's, the Dhamers, the amateur rippers how a real expert worked.

And then cooked the poor man's cock? Not to eat it himself but to make the man eat it? Why? How could this be sex, how could this be thrilling? And if it wasn't sex, then was it revenge? And if it was revenge, a paying back, why was the victim kept alive, deliberately tended, nursed, made to feel, not allowed to die? Why?

But there was nothing here, nothing to show why, nothing hidden, half-hidden, no secrets, no evidence of a bachelor seediness, no dark satin sheets, no videos, or dirty books. Just ten top-shelf newsagent magazines, crude women in crude poses, stupid letters made-up by bored university teens; the day I came home and my two luscious cousins were on the bed! And then . . . There had to be *something*. They would have to gut the place, find the whips or chains, the pictures with animals. There had to be *something*. Stuff like this didn't happen to ordinary men, to average, blue-suit men, chaps who polished their shoes and had their sheets and shirts laundered.

She went into the kitchen. The refrigerator had five cans of coke in a ripped-open six-pack, seven eggs, bacon, sausages . . . Oh, shit!

She closed the door.

There were new dinner plates, new cups, a couple of mugs, all for Scene of Crimes to work painstakingly through; tea-towels, an iron, candlesticks, a jar of chocolates, Quality Street, still sealed. Coffee, and tea-bags, sugar, a tin of Marvel dried milk. She went back to the refrigerator; no fresh milk but a half-pound of butter, some cling-wrapped cheddar. In the bread-bin a loaf with today's date after "sell-by" and above it, in a cupboard, two tins of tuna, baked beans, Heinz spaghetti. Someone lived here or someone stopped here? Somewhere to snack, stop briefly, almost like a safe-house. Surely not? Even a safe-house, a flop, would have a TV, or at least a radio, or a ghetto-blaster. Could someone simply sit here, no books, no music, no TV, not even a newspaper, just ten cheap girlie-mags, ten unread, untouched, far-too-crisp wanker comics? But not in the bedroom, not in the bathroom. No, in the lounge, delicately placed so they could not be missed. Left to be found.

Or just very tidy.

Maybe Bourne wore white gloves.

So clean, so neat, so cleaned. *Cleaned*.

Did Hornby, did Brown, Bourne, did John Doe have a cleaner? He didn't have a washing machine, he had his shirts . . .

Caz went back into the lounge, no table – no table in the

kitchen. So a tray? How did Brown eat? Where were the cleaning things; mops, J-cloths, scrubbing brushes, Flash liquid, Domestos, blue-loo, toilet-paper? Apart from when he died, did Brown shit? Mr Lilywhite laundry-pressed, pin-sharp college-boy, did he crap, did he have a bath? People in books never pissed and shat, but people in Hove terraces did, even dead ones, as and before they died.

She checked the kitchen again. No round-cornered melamine with flowers on, no lip-edged rectangle, wood, inset-wood, no silver fancy present, not even a bread-board to rest a plate of beans on toast.

No washing-up liquid either, but in the bathroom, when she went, baby-oil, baby-bath lotion, Johnson's soap, Johnson's talc, a plastic duck, a tube of KY. A fucking plastic duck!

And there was loo-paper; there was a toilet-roll, Andrex, light green rather than a matching pink but still unrolled, still sealed shut on the first-last dotted line, the one that drove you fucking mad while you sat there, until in the end you tore the bloody thing in frustration, ended up with a jagged, repeated mistake, round and round. No one lived here. It was sanitised, too clean, a showhouse? No, too old. Just over-clean, cranny wiped, nook-safe. No-one had lived here. Did someone live here? What did he do, do at night, re-iron ironed shirts, eat off the too-clean floor?

A plastic duck, KY, Quality Street. No tray.

Caz needed treatment. Time to wake up.

She went back into the kitchen.

Seventeen

Brighton General Hospital, 15:07

Moira was sitting up in bed, in the middle of 2,000 pillows, a tilted episode of Knots Landing on a ceiling-slung TV above her. Titty was asleep, swaddled in a wheeled crib at the side of the bed. There were half-a-dozen cards already, one huge bunch of flowers, a card from Billy – signed by his Mum. Caz and Moira kissed.

"The DI let me sneak away. Last night it was nearly four o'clock, after I'd taken Billy home. It's a really yuck murder, Mo."

"How's Billy?"

"Hasn't he been to see you? I thought—"

"Maureen said he was really poorly. Affected."

"So when's he coming?"

"Tonight, she said."

"I can't believe he hasn't come. Is everything OK?"

Moira looked across at the baby. "Oh, sure. Maureen said Billy felt funny about the G28 and he hadn't shaken it off. She said he didn't want to let his troubles spoil things for me. And anyway, he'd been there for the important bit, he said; it wouldn't matter if he didn't come. It'd give me a chance to talk about things with my girlie friends."

"The flowers from him?"

"My sister."

Caz went to have another look at Titty. Her face was much less screwed up now and she'd been bathed and looked as lovely as her Mum. The first tint of jaundice showed in her soft face.

"Isn't she gorgeous, Caz?"

"She's my god-daughter – what d'you expect?"

"And she's passed all her tests, there's nothing wrong. She looks like Billy, too. She does, doesn't she?"

"She's long enough," Caz said.

"D'you want to pick her up?"

"She's asleep."

"It's all right. I don't care if she wakes up. I'm bursting with milk already." She leaned forward and whispered, pointing at two empty beds. "Those two, neither of them have started yet – me, I could feed a football team."

"OK, how do I pick her up?"

"Stick a fork in! Just use yer common sense, Caz."

"Like this?"

"Yeah, not bad. It suits you."

Caz held the bundle. Madonna and child, not the Virgin Mary, Madonna-Madonna. "It's weird, Moira."

"It's bloody lovely, you mean! Haven't you held a baby before?"

Caz sat gingerly on to a chair beside the bed.

"Nope, twenty-eight and a bit years and I've managed to avoid it. Nothing this young. Will I start clucking now?"

"Knowing you, I doubt it, but I've heard rumours of you being human. I heard you helped an old lady across the road once."

"Who told you that?"

"The old lady."

"She exaggerated. I took her to a zebra-crossing, that's all."

You ligature the penis close to the body, very tight, as tight as you can. Use a neck-tie, flex, or stout string. Then a sharp butcher's knife, a scalpel, even a Stanley-knife, or a modelling blade. A good pair of scissors might work. If he's still unconscious, he will stir; there'll be blood, but not that much. Then take the flat-iron, it's already hot, press it on the exposed stump. Does it sizzle? An ancient method of cauterisation – but sometimes the old ways are the best, eh?

"Wake her up so I can give her some milk."
"Hang on, Mo. I'm enjoying myself."

Use smelling salts – he'll come round. Now ask him things, tell him things – he'll hurt, sure, but the fear will be the real thing. Don't tell him what you're going to do to his face, don't tell him what pretty pictures you plan for the wall. Just a little cooking. Offer him mustard, ketchup, let him know how disappointed you are. He can't see; not the way you've strapped him up. He may not even realise. Get him to eat something. When you take the tape off, he won't scream, not now, but be ready. Be ready just in case.

"No, it didn't really hurt. Even though you probably thought it did. The contractions, the worst bit is not having any control. When they happen, they're a bit frightening. You can't do anything."
"But when she started to come out – that hurt, yeah?"
"No. Only the contractions."
"I was trying not to look, but when you, when Tee's head was just about to break out, just before it did, when it looked like you couldn't possibly expand any more, you looked like – as if your – as if you were just going to be ripped open. That was the worst bit."
"It didn't hurt, Caz, really it didn't. It's like you're deadened, but very full. The contractions hurt, they've weird. You'll be worse than me, cos you're always in control, but down there, well no, it didn't hurt. At least I don't remember it hurting."
"Once Tee's head came, she just went shlupp! It looked easy."
"That's how it was when I was born, so Maureen says. And then I was like spaced out, and proud, and serene. I think that's the word. Then they gave me her. Caz, you couldn't buy a feeling like that."

She had told MacInnes. The iron in the kitchen cupboard had made her think of it. Why an iron when you never iron anything? The end has something sticky on it, sir. It's not plastic, is it?

"So how does your – how do you feel now? Are you very sore?"

We don't know what word to use. How funny.

"It's more odd than sore, Caz. I don't want to make any sudden movements, you know what I mean?"

"So you and Billy won't be at it tonight, then?"

"Ha! He'll be lucky if he gets near me before Tee goes to school."

I'd've said, "my pussy". Funny how we only half-talk . . .

"But I have to admit, Mo, you look made to be a Mum. And this little tyke is just plain gorgeous."

"Apart from being tired and having a numb puddy-wuddy, I feel great, too. Having a baby's not as bad as getting a kicking off a yob."

Puddy-wuddy?

"She's waking up! D'you want her?"

"Oh, yeah. Relieve the pressure. Which side you reckon?"

Caz stood up. "Does it matter?"

"I guess not," Moira said. "Stick her on this one."

Eighteen

War Room, John Street, Tuesday 08:00

"A string of aliases. House was rented in the name of James Brown, mail went in there to James Brown, James Bourne, John Bourne, Brian John, Leighton Richard. We're talking to the PO and Parcel Force, seeing where trace-back takes us."

A hand.

"Sir – these guys late at night?"

"Maybe only one guy, if at all. It wasn't so regular that it became obvious to the neighbours."

"So we don't think a knocking shop, sir?"

"Completely wrong. Too clean, too neat."

"Drugs?"

"We don't think so. We put dogs through last night. One of them got a bit upset – there may have been something there once, may have been, but the handler doesn't think so."

"IRA, sir?"

"Special Branch are coming down today. We don't think so."

No other questions.

"OK," MacInnes said. "The floorboards come up this morning. S.O.C will be there and DS Sweet and company will do the honours. Meanwhile, we continue the leg-work. We should have some more photo-fits today, but James Brown musta had one of those faces. All the descriptions so far have been next to useless."

Canteen, 08:33

"I coulda done without carpentry duty," Caz said. "Look at these nails, they took months!"

Greavsie fluttered his eyebrows. "Iss awright, Caz, I'll do all the heavy lifting for you."

"You're a treasure, James. What can I do for you in return?"

Greavsie grinned. "A quick bonk'd be 'andy."

"You wish!"

"Well, yeah . . ." Greavsie said.

Angel brought the tray over, four coffees, three sticky buns. Caz was trying to be good.

Bob Saint hunched forward. "So what do we think this is, guys? Is this not the weirdest case ever?"

"I think it's aliens," Greavsie said. "They were doing tests and this was one that went wrong. Like we're a free-range farm and they were just checking us out, it went wrong."

"Jesus, Jim," Sweet said, "what are you on?"

Greaves seemed to not hear. Then he looked at Caz.

"It's love," he said.

"So," Bob Saint asked, "we think we're going t'find anything under the floorboards?"

"Like what?" Greavsie said.

"Drugs, guns, skeletons, used notes – I dunno."

"I don't think we'll find anything," Caz said, without looking up from her drink. "I don't think anyone was living there. I think it was a meeting place."

"For what?" Sweet said.

"Don't ask me," Caz said. "You're the sergeant."

17 Hornby Terrace, Hove, 10:42

A Pickfords van finally arrived and its two passengers dropped down from the cab. One was young and skinny, ginger; the other one fifty-ish, fat and bald. Both wore light grey dust-coats.

Caz came out. "Nice easy day for you, gents. I hope you brought plenty to read."

The driver appeared. He looked like an undertaker.

"We're to report to a Detective Sergeant Sweet."

"He's just inside," Caz said.
At least it wasn't raining.

The sitting-room carpet had been lifted – less the bits Forensics had already whipped off to Aldermaston. It was now sealed in polythene, taped up, labelled four times and loaded into the Pickfords van. Before this, the removals men had unloaded their tea-chests.

DS Sweet had come out and shook his head.

"But they's what we always use," the driver said.

"Sorry," Sweet said. "Has to be new boxes. Contaminants, y'see."

An executive decision was made and the kitchen stuff, as they stripped it, was stacked in the bathroom. That way they could keep working while they waited for a Pickfords transit to arrive with fresh fold-up cardboard boxes. They stacked things neatly and the DS supervised, marking each square of the floor with its kitchen equivalent. By one o'clock the cupboards were bare and the sitting room was empty. They were ready to have a go at the floor.

"Lunch-time!" Angel Sweet said.

So far, they hadn't found so much as a receipt.

Nineteen

Three of them went to a back-street pub a walk away, a free-house Bob Saint knew, Caz, Bob, and the DS. Someone had to stay behind. and keep the crime scene free of hob-nailed boots. They were going to draw lots, but then Sweet remembered that he was the Detective Sergeant and he didn't like Greavsie all that much. They had stepped out of their overalls, given the Pickfords men an hour's break and slipped away. Jim had sat on the doorstep and sulked.

The DS really didn't mind being called Angel. "Call me Angel," he said, and no, he wasn't married any longer, no, no kids, and he'd come down to the south coast for a fresh start. He didn't much like going armed and in Manchester's Moss Side, cos've the drug scene, that was getting to be standard.

"And I don't mind the sea air, either. It's OK here."

"So yer found a place yet, Sarge?"

"A bed-sit, till I've sold my house up there. And I said – call me Angel."

"It takes some getting used to."

"Angel, please."

They were still dry. "Christ!" Sweet added, "I thought Saint knew the owner? How long does it take to get three Carlsbergs and three packets of crisps?"

Caz grinned, waited for him to calm down.

"So, Sarge, Angel, Jack. Did I hear you say you've come down here to work in Child Protection?"

"It was the only place open."

"You'll get out as soon as you can?"

"I dunno. I suppose so. It's a bastard that everyone thinks it's a farm, nowhere to go, but they do, one for the girls an' that."

Caz lifted her eyebrows.

"Well, you know what I mean," he added quickly. "T'be honest, I think there's some real police work to be done in CP. What pisses me – and, I guess, why it's seen as a dead end – is the low conviction rate. Who the fuck wants to lock away one animal for every coupla thousand offences?"

"Shit, Sarge, it's not that bad."

"Oh, no? You've checked the numbers, have you? You got any idea exactly how hard it is to put one of these low-lifes away? Do you know Jill Bartholomew?"

"I know of her. She's a bit older than me."

"You go ask her about the numbers, Flood."

"You don't want to tell me yourself, then?"

"No, Flood. It makes me too damn angry. Ah, at last!"

Bob had brought a small round tray and he'd only spilled a little bit of the lager. "They were changing the barrel. Sorry."

Angel lifted his glass. "To Greavsie," he said.

"You know we're mates, don't you?" Saint said.

Angel was grinning, "Yup!"

Bob had his hand on his beer-glass but hadn't picked it up. Caz grabbed hers. "To Greavsie!" she said.

Bob's face finally broke into a smile. He lifted his drink. "Silly bugger's always picking the wrong bloke to upset." He sipped, held his drink up to the light.

"To Greavsie!"

Twenty

They got back at five to two. It was overcast but Greavsie was pretending to sunbathe. There was an empty plate and cup beside him. Sweet grunted something and stepped past with Bob Saint but Caz paused when Jim spoke to her.

"Hey, Flood, you lot did me a favour," he said. "Young bird from a coupla doors down came out and we had a chat. She made me some tea and gived me a plate've Jaffa cakes!"

"Number twenty-three?" Caz said.

"Yup."

"So Jim, how long you been divorced now? Two years?"

"'Bout that, why?"

"Just, number twenty-three, she had a couple of nippers in tow when I spoke to her yesterday."

"Yeah, I know. They're in nursery, private, just started. She's a nice kid. She was living with a bloke, he pissed off and left her in it. She had a good job 'n' everything – solicitor's clerk – but she had to jack it in when the dad did a runner. Now she's found a nursery for the kids so she's starting back. Her firm is going halves on the fees."

"You found all this out in an hour, Greavsie?"

Greavsie flashed a silly grin. "I'm a detective, in't I?"

"I've heard rumours. So y'going to be sniffing round?"

"You've seen her, Caz. What do you reckon? And you know I like kids. I hardly ever get to see mine, since me and Jackie split up." Jim's boy-grin was gone. Caz felt vaguely guilty. "Yeah, sorry, Jim. What the hell do I know? Police marriages, eh?"

"Tell me about it," Greavsie said.

She smiled, quite softly. "So, you going round there now? I mean, it's yer lunch break, isn't it? And you'll have to take the dishes back, yeah?"

The sun broke through and the doorway lit up. So did Greavsie's face.

"Sounds good to me, Flood! I'll be back fer three."

Caz stepped inside.

She heard the first sckrenckk! of jemmying wood, then another.

"Hey," she shouted over the second one, "Sarge, I just sent Jim off to speak to a woman down the street. I told him to be back for three – that OK?"

The DS looked up, sweat on his face, heaving his crowbar.

"It's Angel. Ain-Gel."

There was another sckrenckk!

"Shite!" Saint said suddenly, "Fucking splinter!"

Caz tutted. "Language!"

Saint was waving his hand, then touching it to his lips. Caz managed to stop herself saying, "Diddums" and offering to kiss it better.

"So," she said, "who wants coffee?"

Twenty-One

Underneath the lounge floor: chocolate-wrappers, cement scrapings, runs of thick white electrical cable, some older wood, some new, cross-pieces for added strength; copper piping traced back to the radiator, dust, the cobweb bog-end of a long-gone spider's empire, a few nails; all crap; but all bagged, along with the bits of newspaper, a page of another porn mag picked up by Angel, all junk, but better safe than sorry, in the bag, let the DI be the one to throw it away.

"OK, upstairs next," Angel decided. "I get the distinct feeling this is all a waste of time, but let's go get it done before it's dark. When Greavsie gets back he can work with Bob. Flood, you and me, we'll take the front bedroom. I'll sweat, you look pretty."

"We going to do the hall, Sarge?"

He traced a big A in the air.

"Sorry!"

"Yes, we will, but we'll leave it to last thing. We don't want to make life any more difficult than necessary. No point in climbing back and forth over big holes. Tomorrow morning."

They went upstairs. Bob was still moaning about his splinter and the side of his thumb was red already, swelling very nicely. Caz offered to needle it out but Bob said his missus would do it for him when he got home.

"Well, soak it in a bowl of Dettol, dear!" Caz old-ladied at him. "Now don't forget, Robert, can't be too careful . . ."

Bob was not amused. "Don't give up the day job, Flood."

By three-fifteen they could get a head and a torch under the floor of the front bedroom. Greavsie hung down, looked around and said there appeared to be nothing. His voice echoed.

"Get the rest up," Angel said. "I don't want to screw anything on my first job."

By quarter past four they were sure; a complete waste-of-time. Nothing under the floorboards at the front either, nothing on the landing, and now, getting on for six o'clock, there was just the hall.

"The hall's for tomorrow, right?" Saint asked. He was holding up his thumb. "We're not going to – are we? Only if—"

Angel smiled. He was tired too. "No, that's enough for today, lads. You've all got homes t'go to, I guess. Piss off back to the nick. I'll ring for an area car to drop some poor sod of a PC on the front door and bum a lift back myself. There's no one waiting for me."

"You sure, Sarge?" Greavsie said.

"Jesus!"

"Ain-jel."

"Yeah, I'm sure. I'll make a start downstairs. You just bell me up a woodentop to look after Chez Nous overnight."

Saint shook his thumb. It was so big now, it lit up the landing.

"See?" he said to Jim. "It's not true, what you said about Angel, is it? His mum and dad *were* married."

The DS was as impressed as Bob had been earlier. "What was that about the day job, Saint?"

"Yeah, all right," Saint said. He put his throbbing hand under his arm and stood up, speaking to Greavsie. "Take me home, James." He started for downstairs. Greavsie got up to follow.

"And you, Caz," Angel said. When she looked at him, his smile was full of warmth. "Just make sure they phone for a PC."

Twenty-Two

Wednesday

Caz woke to her alarm breeing. 05:45. She hadn't run for days.

She rolled out of bed, went through, peed, threw cold water onto her face, ran fingers through her hair, pulled it back into a ponytail, and sighed at herself in the mirror. Last night she'd been drinking alone. Vaunda had stopped at Tom's Sunday, Monday, Tuesday. . . .

She went out dressed in her usual running stuff, mostly ASICS, the same stuff she'd roughed round the flat in last night, playing Simply Red and U2, sorry for herself, wishing she wasn't on this murder, wishing Valerie would hurry up and get back off his course, wishing that her mad lodger would lodge just, say, one night in two. That'd do. Southern Comfort and Coke.

It was light already but white, sea-misted, cool; the shingle beach indefinite to her as she jogged, the hacked-away West Pier a vague fade-to-grey ghost to her right, the soft sea-front apartments to her left dull-glassed and soulless, cream-into-sky. Ahead was the Palace Pier; but utterly dead; not even a beeping one-armed bandit alive there yet, not a flicker of Frankenstein current anywhere. No organ ground, the ghost train was de-railed, and the Helter-Skelter, coconut matting piled at its base, the top two turned over against the night air, was dew-damp and miserable, gloss fogged to pastel, sharp to soft. If the sun ever came up, the mats would dry quickly.

Caz was intending to run hard but she didn't like not seeing.

There was a peculiar moment as she strode Grand Junction Road, passing close to the DI's mahogany-dark flat – not jealousy exactly, but an oddly-deep, "I miss you" feeling tinged with a sad happiness for Tom and Vaunda. She couldn't imagine them – it, – like parents, Tom awake again after fifteen, sixteen years, Vaunda still trying to find herself a personality that would stay with her for more than forty-eight hours, and both of them knowing that years back they'd been two sides of a triangle, (or the vertical and horizontal of a square if you bothered to include Norman Blackside's wife).

Past the Sea Life Centre, pick it up on the rise to Marine Parade.

Would they soften, would MacInnes finally ease off the pedal? Was he soon to say, "It is too dark. Enough is enough, I have done my penance; I don't need to discover any more secrets. I want to grow roses now." Would it be like that?

Did Caz imagine it, but weren't both he and Blackside already a little vaguer, misty like this, the sharp edges blurred, less brick-solid, not so brilliantined dark, their suits hanging looser, their heels no longer clacking so loudly down corridors?

Along the top road, the sea-sky so white it was disturbing, eyes front, just steady seven-and-a-half-minute miling, heading towards Rottingdean, Telscombe Cliffs, and, somewhere off to the left, the place – Vaunda's place – where Caz had welcomed, pointed into her, the dark sexy mouth of a gun; where she had looked, thought about it, and then carried on. Months later, Caz had killed someone, and she had been pleased. They made Vaunda better.

Her watch finally beeped, forty-five minutes, a little short of six cold miles. Twenty to seven. She turned. Four six minute miles now, and then a long warm-down. She'd be in the shower for twenty past, in her jeans and T for twenty to and at the nick for ten to eight.

She had gone to see Moira and Titty straight from work, as soon as Saint and Greavsie had dropped her off.

Tee had been asleep – *again* – but Moira was brighter, her light brown face full and sure, her dark eyes sparkling as Caz's did not. They kissed, chatted. Moira asked about the Hove murder and Caz fobbed her off with bullshit. Then Caz picked up the baby. She told Mo she hadn't noticed the dark hair before. Billy was due at half-seven, coming in with Maureen, so Moira said. Caz said, if it was all right, she'd get off at quarter past, only she hadn't run Sunday *or* Monday and if she hung around, they'd come, she'd get talking, and Tuesday would be down the tubes too.

In the car-park she had seen Billy with Moira's mum. It was easier not to shout hello. She went home slowly, got into a hot bath with a glass of wine, the rest of the bottle on the toilet seat close by. She'd stayed in until she started to wrinkle, got out, got dressed with the vague thought that she'd work out, put on the U2 instead, and started on the Southern Comfort. Then the alarm went. It was fifteen minutes to six in the morning, foggy outside.

07:58

She dropped in alongside Angel Sweet in the corridor leading to the War Room. He looked skin-deep cheerful. Inside there was the usual CID murmur and they stepped in, one conversation suddenly stopping. Caz spotted Saint and Greavsie; Billy over by the photo wall. Angel saw him too, then looked quickly at his watch.

"Just made it!" Sweet said.

They sat down next to each other, front row. Behind them metal chairs scraped; someone laughed. Then near as could be guessed, it was eight o'clock and, like the hush before rain, the banter stopped. Billy loped along the front, last to sit down two seats away from Caz. At 08:01 the doors opened, Tom MacInnes and Bob Moore.

The team was working steadily through missing-persons: London, Home Counties, Hants, Berks first, then Glasgow, Liverpool, then the rest. With no good ID they were going on height and weight alone, males of course, and any refs to South Coast from those originally reporting the misper. It was a waste of time, Moore said.

MacInnes was sitting down and letting Bob Moore run things. There'd been persistent rumours going round that Bob was going to be made up. He'd done enough courses, so maybe it was true. He never looked at Caz but he owed her a huge one. She wished he didn't. If he ever became her DI they'd have to talk.

"And we got nowhere with the Post Office. Last six months the walk's been covered by temps and newbies. Apart from the names we've already got – nothing.

"We've had a long talk with the landlord, Ray Patel. He's fine. Round Table member; bit of an entrepreneur – buys, does up, rents and sells smaller terraces like Hornby Road. All his other places are being checked out but everything seems to be kosher.

"Previous occupants? Mr Patel bought the place just under two years ago. About fifteen months ago, he says, Bourne saw it being done up, asked the builders who the owner was, got in touch and asked about renting. The place had already been promised for a long let which finished in April. Bourne came looking again in March with cash in hand."

Someone asked about the PM. The results had been a bit slow.

"Yeah," Moore said.

The *post mortem* had given the cause of death – the actual final rubber-stamp moment – as heart-attack, but yeah it was murder, no other way of looking at it. Stress due to torture.

What about the fingers and toes, the amputations?

"That's what's taken the time, Bob – working out the sequence of events. The pathologist now gives us what's up on the board:

"One: Victim rendered unconscious, strapped into chair;

"Two: The castration, while unconscious;

"Three: Wound cauterised with the iron found in the kitchen;

"Four: A time elapsed;

"Five: Some fingers removed while the victim conscious: mouth was taped. Face showed signs of tape being applied, removed, and re-applied. May have been another time lapse.

Most likely scenario is that then the victim fainted. Traces of ammonia in the nostrils suggest use of smelling salts.

"Six: The rest of the fingers, the thumbs, the toes, were removed after death. Ditto lips, nose and ears.

"Seven: Some sort of large pruning shears, curved blade used for the fingers and toes, something like a Stanley knife used on the face and the belly. The belly looked liked a few swipes, like this . . ."

Caz shifted in her seat, accidentally touching Angel. Torture for information, then? So drugs, serious crime . . .

"And DS Sweet and his team are stripping the house. Most of it's done already."

He held up a plastic bag.

"And no surprises, so far."

What about the garden? someone asked.

What about teeth, dental records?

"The garden will be down to Mr Blackside, but at this moment in time, it's not going to be signed off. Same with dental records. We follow up all possibles first and keep the expensive stuff for when we get desperate. You all know the score."

That was it. DS Reid's team would be looking to speak to the builders, speak to Ray Patel today. Forensics were doing a rebuild and plaster cast of the face, and there'd be a poster soon – probably Friday. Other than that, and a few people to walk by and nod to Billy Tingle, it was coffee and then back out into it.

Billy was just sitting there. Caz leaned over.

"Must've been really shitty, Billy. How are you doing?"

"OK."

"I was up to see Mo last night. She was looking well."

"Yeah."

"When's she coming home?"

"Tomorow. Maureen's picking her up."

Caz felt Angel tap her shoulder.

"I gotta go," she said.

"Doan worry about it," Billy said.

Hornby Terrace, 9:15

Over coffee Caz had got the low-down on Greavsie's latest feeble attempt at finding a woman. Jim was one of those guys who tried too much, *yearned* too much, and frightened women off – and he had told her Janice James was twenty-two, nearly twenty-three, and, yeah, he'd be seeing her again.

"Sooner than you think," Angel said.

Saint had driven and Angel had been in the front passenger seat. Bob had managed OK, but with his huge, bandaged, cartoon-sized wound thumbs-up above the steering-wheel, he looked like an over-enthusiastic boy scout. Caz and Greavsie had sat in the back and Caz had turned side on, her knees half up on the seat while she made a big thing of sussing Greavsie up and down. Something was different.

"You're not that ugly, Jim. Sheesh even me, if I was very pissed, I could, on a dark night . . . But you look—"

"How pissed?"

"Oh, it'd have t'be *very, very*, Jim. And I was gonna be dying in the morning . . . but you're not fat, you're not spotty, and you don't wear glasses. There is hope."

"But I smoke."

"No-one's perfect."

Now they were at the death house and no one seemed to be in a hurry to start working. Angel had produced two pump screwdrivers for the hall floor – one-inch chipboard – but they all knew it would be a pig to get up, and once they'd done it, chances were they'd be knocking more doors. No need to rush.

Caz still felt playful. "So come on then, Greavsie. Did you have to play with the kids, or were they in bed?"

"In bed – what's up with you, Flood? You not getting enough?"

"None. I thought you knew. Val's away until late Friday night. He's learning about the analysis of behaviour in group interviews. Fun, huh?"

"She's all right, Janice. She's twenty-three Christmas week; I'm thirty-three. Not a big difference. And she thinks I look about twenty-eight."

Caz looked. "That's it! You've shaved off your tash!"

Bob Saint was just about to try one of the screws. He looked up. "Well, bugger me, so you 'ave!" He pumped and the shiny screw came out, sweet as a nut. "Hey, magic! So what d'you shave for?"

"Dunno. Just did. It was a spur of the moment thing. Hey, Sarge, you wanna pass me the other screwdriver?"

Angel slapped the red handle into Jim's palm; Jim made much of looking down at each screw as he unzipped it. Caz was smiling, her arms folded. Jim was "concentrating" even though the screws were coming out easily.

"You look so much *younger*, too," she said mischievously. Angel was grinning but Greavsie kept his head down. Zzzzrrrrrrrrpppp!! Another screw. "Why, James – Jim – may I call you Jim? You could pass for, what, I'd say, twenty-six, maybe twenty-seven . . ."

"I was just fed up with it, that's all!"

"And she's twenty-two next Christmas! That right?"

"Twenty-three."

"Twenty-three, eh? She looks much younger, wouldn't you say? Like nineteen maybe or maybe twenty. Looks are funny things, though, aren't they?"

Jim looked up. He'd run out of screws. So had Saint.

"Flood," he said, "everything they say about you is true."

23 Hornby Terrace, 10:20

It takes a while to develop the skill of eating up time, but Angel was good. Underneath the hall at number seventeen: bugger-all, not a fag end, not even a decent cobweb. But then the DS produced four large measuring tapes and a pad of graph paper.

"Right, internal measurements," he said. "We need to check this house against one similar. I vote for Mrs James's."

"Sarge?"

"False walls," he said.

They had traipsed round, knocked the door to twenty-three. Slightly red, Greavsie had explained. Behind him, the other three detectives put on matching beatific smiles.

Janice James looked pretty good, actually; as if she was feeling really up today and had tried a bit harder that morning. There was a vacuum cleaner at the foot of the stairs and the smell of lemon airfreshener. All the windows were open.

"So you need to measure my rooms, you mean? Like an estate agent?"

"Yes," Jim said.

"OK," she said. "Who fancies tea?"

Angel spoke first. "Well, that would be *wonderful*, Mrs James."

It didn't take very long, or rather, it didn't need to take very long. Greavsie was very keen to be working so he did the kitchen and back room while Janice kettled about, Caz did the lounge, Angel and Bob did upstairs. Then they sat down to tea.

And Jaffa Cakes.

"So," Caz said pleasantly once they were all sitting. "I believe you know Jim here. Did he say, he's one of our top detectives?"

Caz, Angel and Bob Saint left number twenty-three. It had been necessary for Detective Constable Greaves to stay behind and discuss witness-counselling with Mrs James.

"If you could get back by eleven-fifteen, detective?" Angel asked.

"Of course, Sergeant!" Greavsie said. To Janice he said, "I think you should sit down, luv. Let's just chat. Events like this . . ."

The others left.

Back at number seventeen, Caz and Saint worked the bedrooms, straddling beams to lay the metal tapes wall-to-wall, writing down numbers, tapping the walls for the sound of hollowness. A while back, in Nottingham, a house had been stripped and the police had missed a secret cupboard. This wasn't going to happen to DS Sweet.

When they got back downstairs, Angel was scclapping his retractable tape into its shell. All his numbers tallied too. They'd take a slow look at the garden, but it looked like they were going to have to go back to the nick pretty soon.

Greavsie got back at 11:14 and counting. There was light in his eyes and his cheeks were pink.

Twenty-Three

Val's coming home tomorrow

It's 08:00 Thursday. You sit still like a good girl, front row of the line of chairs, in the War Room. You get the first whiff of "scale-down" and it's only been four days. Instead of six by six chairs there's five rows of five and Angel's not here, Billy's on a day's compassionate leave and Bob Saint is off sick: you heard a short-sighted pilot tried to land a Jumbo on his thumb, attracted by the flashing red light. You end up with Greavsie and Greavsie is in love.

"Janice, she's got an older sister, nearly as good-looking, 'bout thirty. She came round with her two and baby-sat for us. It was great, Caz. We went into town for a drink, went walking on the beach and ended up on the pier, like a coupla kids."

"Any idea where the DS is?"

"Probably been hauled back into CP. They've got a big case-load. You ever been on the big slide on the pier, Flood? The wiggly one?"

"The helter-skelter? No, I bloody haven't!"

"Well you should, Flood. It'd do you good, loosen you up some. Me and Janny, we went on three or four times, and we weren't even pissed."

"Are you sure she's not under age?"

"Ha, bloody, ha!"

The doors open. Jack Sweet, DI MacInnes and DS Moore half a flap behind him. Angel sees Caz, mouths "over-slept" to her, ducks to the nearest chair. His face is red.

"OK, listen up!"

It's not shit and fan time but oh-bollocks, grind. They are getting nowhere. They listen to Bob Moore.

"It's still a blank on the victim. Clothes, Marks and Sparks, all bought London or south coast, nothing bought more than fourteen months ago, conventional as you get. Collar size sixteen-and-a-half, waist thirty-eight and forty, chest forty-four, inside leg thirty-one, foot size eleven.

"Mr Bourne should be renamed Mr Bland. No one can give us a fix on the face except "not young" and "not thin" and the builders, well the two we've caught up with, just remembered him as some tidy bloke with pasty skin. He may have had a London accent – our first clue. We're down to about ten million people.

"Knowns so far haven't been a lot of good either. We've talked to all our ABHs and GBHs, even though we've nobody with anything like this on file. Details have gone nationwide, with a separate note to head of CID about the castration. Not a whisper back and nothing even close from Region Intelligence or the Yard. Anyone got any ideas, now's a good time."

Caz raised her hand.

"Yes, Flood."

She almost stood, then lowered herself.

"Sarge, this guy was tortured, right? That's what we think? It's just that I've never heard of or seen anything like this – nothing so over-the-top, and you're saying that Scotland Yard has no similar MO. Where are we going with the why of all this? I mean, if Bourne was tortured, and if the tape was coming on and off, it sounds as though someone was after information."

"And?"

"Well, Sarge, I was wondering what kind of information. You don't cut a bloke to pieces, and get covered in blood—"

"There was very little blood, less than you'd expect."

"OK, you don't go to all that trouble, that weirdness, unless something matters a whole lot; so are we any closer to deciding if this was a sex thing, a revenge thing or someone desperate to find out something the victim knew?"

"Get to the point, Flood."

"Well, Sarge, I just wondered what was being said on the street. Are the snouts coming up with anything? Couldn't we maybe blitz them? If this guy was tortured for what he knew, then it's got to be something reasonably heavy. Is there anything missing? I dunno, like cash from a robbery or some drugs?"

"Not that's raised its head. Anyone?"

There was a voice from the back; Ray Carver, ex-Met.

"Ray Carver, Sarge. I've been sniffing round my snouts. No-one knows a thing, but one o' mine was as edgy as Trap One. He went down for under-age when he was twenty, flashing way back, and since, a few burglaries and receiving."

"Edgy? As in a suspect?"

"Christ, Sarge, no chance. I gotta nickname of my own for this guy – I call him Kay. He'd blow away in a strong wind. Scared of his own shadow half the time. No, he just reacted that's all, something about him or one of his mates trying to disappear for a while."

"Y'didn't think this was important?"

"No, Sarge, and we were busy. I told you, Kay, he's like a rabbit. And there was the raid on the bookies in Victoria Road and we were called out – remember?"

MacInnes spoke. "Find this guy today, Carver. Bring him in."

Bob Moore waited, but that was it from the DI.

"OK. We're fucked on this one lads. Get out there and lean on your snouts. Any lead is a good lead right now. Do it, else this is going nowhere and half a dozen of you are gonna be legionnaires shoved out back somewhere."

There was a slight, room-wide groan. This was a real threat. A case like this couldn't be dropped easily. If they got nowhere, soon it would be "A hand-picked squad actively pursuing any new leads". What that meant was shit street. The Legion's Last Patrol. Six, eight of you, going nowhere, round in circles, no hope. One by one there's less of you, Beau Geste, the staring desert . . .

Chairs started to scrape.

"Oh, and one more thing."

Everyone looked up, but this was just for Angel.

"DS Sweet is off our hook. He's needed in Child

Protection. He was only with us a few days, but a thorough job. Thanks, Jack."

A couple of mumbles went Angel's way and he nodded.

"Oh, and one more 'one more thing'. Flood?"

Caz looked up. Despite the hubbub, Moore didn't shout but she was looking directly at him.

"Stay," Moore said. Behind him, MacInnes nodded.

Twenty-Four

Caz got up, walked over to Angel. He managed a smile, but when she offered her hand he seemed awkward. He was sweating slightly.

"I'd just like to say, Sarge – last few days, it was almost all right. I'll buy you a pint some time. Hope you like it in CP."

Angel seemed uptight. Caz guessed it was because he didn't fancy being temporarily out to grass.

Caz offered her hand again. "Well, anyway."

He was still distracted, but then he came back into gear. "Oh, sure. Sorry, Flood."

His hand came out and Caz shook it. It was a little limp. She heard Moore cough.

"The Ayatollah wants me . . ." she said.

"See you around," Angel said.

Twenty-Five

"Hands up everybody who wants to go to Manchester?" Moore said.

Caz blanked him.

"Hands up, Flood. Don't you want a coupla days oop north?"

"I'm not with you, Sergeant."

Moore grinned.

MacInnes spoke as he stepped down off the stage. "Flood, two of the builders are up in Manchester. We don't expect anything, but we have to send someone. You got elected."

Wonderful.

"It's not so bad, Flood. You'd rather be knocking doors?"

"No, sir."

"And you're not been to your desk yet, have you?"

"No, sir."

"Ah had a phone call from yon Trevor Jones, your half-a-snout in Southampton. Wants you t'ring him. And DS Mason down there, he wants you to ring, too. Coincidence, huh?"

"So do I have any appointments in Manchester, sir?"

"Not exactly, Flood."

"And what exactly does 'not exactly' mean?" She added the sir.

"Well, these two builders. They're working on site somewhere and stopping in digs. All we know is it's a nursing home conversion."

Double wonderful.

"And if you have t'go to Southampton, there's a train direct from there. It went at seven o'clock."

08.42

"DS Mason?"

"Ah'll get 'im." Clunk. "Simple! DC Flood, Brighton!"

Dum-de-dum . . .

"Caz?"

"Caz Flood."

"Hiyah, Caz." A slight pause. "I was wondering – Moira Dibben . . .?"

"Wondering what, Peter?"

"Well, I checked my diary and . . . Isn't Moira due about now?"

"No, not so soon after her first. She's only just had her little girl."

"Wha?"

"A girl, Peter. She's fine. She's not yours."

"Oh," Peter said.

"You sound disappointed."

"No. I'm back with Ann. Did I say? It seems to be going OK."

"Good. Did you ring just to chat?"

"No."

She waited.

"I got a bell from Trevor Jones. Did you know his Mrs has just had a sprog?"

"I didn't know, but I can count to nine, Sergeant."

"Well, yer boy, *our* boy, he wanted to speak to you. I told him if he was after money, officially he was my snout, not yours. He said he just wanted to speak to you."

"What about?"

"He wouldn't say, something about when he was on remand."

Caz made some calculations.

"Look, Peter, I gotta go to Manchester this afternoon on a case, and if I come to Southampton there's a train right through. Can I leave my motor at your nick?"

"Don't see why not. You wanna lift to the railway station then?"

"Yeah, but I figured if you could contact Trevor for me, we could both see him before I got off up north. Maybe we could have a chat in the station buffet or something."

"When are you going to get here?"

"Not before eleven. There's an afternoon train goes right through. Two-something. I've got to get a warrant and book a Hertz car at the other end, but I should get to you before eleven-thirty."

"All right."

"All right I can park, all right you'll give me a lift to the station, or all right you'll get hold of Trevor?"

"Yeah," Mason said.

"I gotta rush, then," Caz said.

"Just one more thing," Mason said.

"What?"

"What's the baby's name?"

Twenty-Six

Caz picked up her rail warrant, and the name of the DS she was to liaise with when she got to Manchester. Off her patch she wasn't allowed to use a pool car and she wasn't supposed to use her own. Using Valerie's car was probably breaking rules that hadn't been written yet. She could have got a Hertz hire-car and gone Brighton-Southampton, but after meeting Trevor Jones she would have had to drive to Newbury, then to Cirencester, Gloucester, and Birmingham and *then* another ninety miles. Sheesh, that was pushing being keen a bit too far.

She was home just after nine and out the door at twenty past, another pair of jeans and bits and bobs thrown into a Nike bag and a quick kiss for her piggies. At the last moment she thought about something to read and grabbed a paperback of Vaunda's. If Von came back and missed it, tough. She left a note for Valerie just in case, "In Manchester, back Friday (I hope)."

She thought about lots of things as she drove. About Moira and Titty, about Billy's flatness, how cold he seemed, about Angel Sweet and about Greavsie and his new girlfriend. Everyone she knew seemed to be getting paired off, having another try or settling down: DCS Blackside, staying in the sticks for the sake of his marriage; Mason the medallion man; Billy and Moira, and baby makes four, even Vaunda the mad lodger and Tom MacInnes. And now Jim.

And she was engaged! Hah! To Valerie Whatisname.

Jesus, that was Portsmouth. Where did the road go?

Shirley Police Station, Southampton, 11:42

At the desk, a female civilian clerk, blonde hair and green eyes, the same as Caz, about the same age but the eyes with no light shining. Boyfriend or negative equity, Caz wasn't sure. She asked for Peter Mason.

"Is it personal or—"

"DC Flood, Brighton," she said.

"Oh," the woman said, relief in her voice? "I'll buzz him then."

Mason came out through the burrzz-cluck of the security door. He looked like he'd put back on a couple of pounds after Caz's advice and his marriage problems had taken off ten. Caz upped and downed him. He was avoiding the receptionist.

"MacDonald's?"

"Home-cooking."

"And let me guess," Caz said. "You got your 10K road-race time below forty minutes in January, but you can't seem to do it again."

"A psychic."

"A cynic."

"I couldn't get hold of Trevor Jones."

"Oh, what!"

"He works for Dixons, now. He's on a one-day course somewhere."

Another course! She had come all the way to—

"His girlfriend says he's a changed man, Flood. Looks like that was one you got right."

"I wouldn't have put money on it," Caz said flatly. "And I don't like burglars. But his missus was all right. I thought half a chance wouldn't cost that much. Jeez, it's not twelve o'clock and my train is at quarter to three. I'm not going to have to have lunch with you, am I?"

The receptionist was sitting up, a fraction too stiffly. She was looking at Mason's back. Caz ached for her, but it was none of her business.

"You can afford it?" Mason said.

"If you were worth it, I could."

A door went: the blonde, the toilets. Suddenly Caz wasn't so sure about lunch.

"You got many mispers, Peter?"

"*Got* or *had*?"

"*Que*?"

"Well, we *get* lots, but they're cleared up pretty quick. Wanna look at the index? On this patch alone we get one or two mispers a day, but most of them are from the children's homes, 'specially in the summer months. They go off to Gran's and don't come back. Happens all the time."

"How many are we talking? You've got hundreds of lost kids?"

"Christ, no. Usually they come back the next day. We get so many all we can do is log it, ring the usual places. Sometimes they're back before we've had a chance to do anything at all."

"Show me," Caz said.

Since the beginning of the year, three-hundred and eighty misper informants. Outstanding, there were just nine; four of them kids' home runaways, three fourteen year olds and one kid of twelve, four middle-aged men and one woman of thirty. The woman and one man worked at Pirelli, but one husband and one wife, both from Totton, were in denial. Most eloping couples didn't get reported.

"So these three?" asked Caz.

Ristorante La Lupa, Southampton

"It's different if it's a kid that's under ten say, or there really are suspicious circumstances. Then we click into action. But Shirley and Freemantle is a pretty stable community, Caz; we don't have people disappearing mysteriously every day."

"Except that once every few years we discover a Dennis Nilsen."

"I shoulda said people aren't getting *reported* as missing, then. Young men and women are far more mobile now. People aren't so close, and they don't take such an interest."

"And serial killers don't get caught."

"We catch 'em in the end."

"In the *end*? You mean when they've *become* serial killers, when they've killed five, six, a dozen? And anyway, how do we know we catch them? How many are never caught?"

"Oh, Christ, don't start that, Caz. I have enough trouble sleeping with the stuff I know about. Don't ask me to speculate."

The food came, well the garlic bread and a bottle of Valpolicella.

"You know, this is very unfair, Flood. I'm on duty. I have more than a glass and a half of that, I'm in trouble."

Caz grinned. "It takes practice. I'll sleep on the train."

"So," Mason said, his voice suddenly softer.

"So?"

"Moira. How is she?"

"She's fine, the birth was OK, the baby's healthy." Caz upped her voice and firmed it. "And mother and father are very proud."

Mason paused. He had a glass of wine cupped with both hands like a chalice. "Just tell me, Caz."

"I did. The baby is called Titania – and it's definitely Billy's."

"You know this?"

"I know this."

Mason rolled the wine round his glass.

"It feels funny, Caz."

"Well, forget it. Get your own life sorted out."

"Yeah, I know. But I wanted to send something, y'know. A toy or something; or a little silver-egg cup."

"Forget it, Peter."

Mason sighed at his glass.

"Yeah, yeah, yeah."

Twenty-Seven

Manchester, 20:00

Welcomed by summer rain.

Caz picked up her rental car and drove to the hotel. She was feeling sluggish and dirty and not a little tired. And she was bemused; amused too. Vaunda's book, when she had looked at it properly, had been a bit like a romance but had time-travel and Scottish history and stuff. She had read the prologue which began; "People disappear all the time. Ask any policeman . . ." and decided she was hallucinating. She put her head back to sleep off the wine and the next time she looked she was rattling into Birmingham. Never drink at lunch-time.

A run would have been good but she couldn't quite make herself do it, not in the rain, so she settled for the hotel pool, fifteen yards up and down, chlorine, chlorine, chlorine, until she felt human again. Dinner was late and light and she cut back to half a bottle, a good French red. In the morning she *would* run, rain or shine.

In the night, she dreamed about Valerie, about Peter Mason and about the room in Hove with just a chair.

Twenty-Eight

The DS Caz had to speak to was called Puzo. He had two nicknames too: "But you call me Mario," he said, a wide eye-full smile. He was early thirties, gorgeous, and worked out, and, he decided to tell Caz, "I am 'appily marry-ed." He had got her a list of major sites in the Central Manchester area, some in Cheadle. Unless she was lucky, she had a day's work already, but he would have her somc morc addresses by one o'clock. His mix of Lancashire and Papa-Mama cheered Caz up. She had been annoyed with herself and miserable. Not only hadn't she run this morning but she'd eaten a full English breakfast and felt like a beached whale. Mario smiled again when she told him.

"Here, an A to Z," he said. "Let me 'ave it back before you leave."

The first two sites were blanks and a couple of guys were nervous. Caz had to explain to the foreman that she was interested in nowt else but putting a face and name to a body in Brighton. Still no go; but a plasterer called Tony Harper thought that there was a chippy called Ernie King who lived down South somewhere, and was up here with his mate . . .

At the second site – a church destined to become a sixty-eight bed rest home, Caz got a bit closer. She would have liked the place as a way-out house. "Yeah, Ernie King and his oppo," one of the electricians told her, "they're from Brighton. Last I 'eard, they was working on an 'otel in Stockport."

The next two sites were duff too, but then, just off the M63, she got lucky. "Ernie King? Yeah, sure, he's in. He's up on the second floor with his butty. You want me to get him?"

"No," Caz said, "I'll go up."

"Well, stick this on," the foreman said and passed her a yellow plastic crash-hat.

"Does it suit me?" she said and went up the stairs.

"Ernie King?"

"Yeah, that's me. Summat up?"

"Not exactly. It's about Brighton."

King went white. "Oh, Jesus, not Betty, not Cheryl or Chester!"

The young man close by stopped and turned.

"No. If you mean your family, Mr King, they're fine. This has nothing to do with them."

He was still pale. "Jesus, you frightened the shit out of me."

"I'm sorry about that, Mr King. It's about some work you did for Raymond Patel just over a year ago."

"There's nothing wrong, is there? Only I done a lot of work for Ray. He's a good payer and he wanted the job done proper. You can't be worried about him."

"It's about Hornby Terrace, in Hove."

"Little two-up, two-down, bathroom and kitchen in the extension on the back?"

"That's the one. Number seventeen."

The young man was standing close now. He was grinning. "That smart piece from nummer twenty-free, 'member? Jaffa cakes!"

King turned back to Caz. "We were there about a month. What's it you want to know, exactly?"

Twenty-Nine

Caz was back at Bootle Street Police Station, Alpha Three Division, before the one o'clock when Roberto Puzo was supposed to have the rest of her addresses. She couldn't believe her luck was running so sweetly. As she went into the two-hundred-year-old white-fronted building – (calling it a "lived-in nick" was about as kind as you could be) – she thought about Ernie, "I can draw a bit" King.

"I remember him. Too right, I do. Sam here, he had little Sammy with him, he was off school, and this Mr Bourne you say his name was, he took quite a shine to 'im. He seemed like a real nice bloke."

Ernie's oppo wasn't so sure.

"Well, I didn't take to 'im. 'Ee was a bit smarmy for me."

King nodded. "Maybe, but you can't blame a bloke for being well-spoken, Sam."

"Well-spoken?" Caz said. "Did he have any accent at all?"

Ernie King thought a second. "Well, he was a bit 'BBC', you know, sounded all his haitches and all the gees on the end of his words. It wasn't so much he was posh as he was careful."

"Any accent?"

"Londonish? I'm not sure. He wasn't cockney, but sort of London, Home Counties."

"And a bit lah-dee-dah!" Sam said.

"Yeah," Ernie said. "And a bit lah-dee-dah."

Someone shouted there was tea up and Ernie asked Caz if she wanted some.

"Oh, sure," she said. "That'd be great."

"Go and get three mugs, Sam," Ernie said to the younger man. He looked at Caz. "You take sugar do you, luv?"

"No thanks," Caz said. She tapped her belly.

He sent Sam off. "The girl's no sugar, got it?"

As soon as his oppo had left, Ernie leaned forward. "Sam's a good chippie and he's an OK plasterer, but he's as thick as two short planks. If he wasn't with me . . ."

Caz smiled. "I didn't think he was in Mensa."

"But his heart's in the right place, y'know? He's my son-in-law, married to my Cheryl. He may be a touch slow sometimes, but he dotes on little Sammy. Cheryl could've done a lot worse."

"We are trying to identify – "

"Mr Brown?"

"We're not sure. We think maybe his name was Bourne."

"Well," King said, "I'm sure he called himself Brown. John Brown. He didn't, like, say, 'My name is Brown, John Brown', like in the films, but when he spoke to us, he said his name was Brown and then, when he was talking to Sammy, he said his name was John."

"You've got a good memory."

"Well, it was just he came back a few times, that first day and the next few days. He was quite keen on the house and we gave him Ray Patel's number."

"We'll need you to do a photo-fit. We need it to try and discover his identity."

Ernie laughed. "A bloody photo-fit! You ever seen anyone who looked even remotely like one of them? Look, I'll do a picture for you. I can draw a bit."

And now Caz had the face of John Brown, a fantastic, detailed, too-real picture of the man they'd found in the room with no furniture.

"This is brilliant, Ernie. What a talent! But I know already what my bosses're going to say: 'How do we know Ernie King's any good at faces?' "

He was scribbling on a second piece of melamine, rushing a little.

"There," he said. "Just show them that." He looked at his sketch and then at Caz. "You're a bit thin in the face, little lady, but you take a bloody good picture."

Caz took it. "Oh, *me*! Oh, Ernie, I think you're in the wrong job."

If they'd had paper, Caz wouldn't have had the two sketches on these boards, two chunks of white plasticised chip-board, both a bit bigger than a sheet of A4. But when she left Ernie and Sam – and she did linger, did drink her tea with them – she went carrying her two boards, feeling something like Moses with his tablets of stone. This was a coup and she knew it.

"I'd like to send this to Brighton now, Mario, give the investigation a bit of a shot in the arm. If I could just maybe get a photo-copy? Only I don't think this lump will go through the fax machine."

The DS was impressed, and laughing a little. It made him sexy. One day Caz would meet an Italian who wasn't cute. He smelled her interest and laid on the accent and the hand-gestures. "Mama-Mia, Senorita Flude. Si, this is easy, this I can do pronto!"

Caz groaned. "Just a photo-copy, Mussolini! I gotta train to catch."

"You doan wanna talk about our misseen pair-suns, Caz?"

Caz looked at her watch: enough time. "Go for it!" she said. The way her luck was running she'd probably get a match first misper.

Thirty

The Inter-City train sloughed out of Manchester on time at 16:17 and Caz settled down to try and read Von's *Outlander*. She read again:

People disappear all the time. Ask any policeman. Better yet, ask a journalist. Disappearances are bread and butter to journalists.

Young girls run away from home. Young children stray from their parents and are never seen again. Housewives reach the end of their tether and take the grocery money and a taxi to the station. International financiers change their names and vanish into the smoke of imported cigars.

Many of the lost will be found, eventually, dead or alive. Disappearances, after all, have explanations. Usually.

She was going to get into Southampton just after nine o'clock in the evening and then she'd be driving to Brighton, so when the buffet trolley came by she was a good girl, buying just the one whisky and ginger, plus a jumbo packet of crisps. She had missed lunch, looking through the Alpha 3 misper files.

It wasn't a very likely place for disappearances, at least at first glance. Mrs Baird's was like a thousand other Highland bed-and-breakfast establishments in 1946 . . .

By Stockport, Caz had settled into the book, finally managing to drown out the four slurred Glaswegian voices on the next table, a merry quartet she hoped wouldn't have to drive when they arrived.

By Birmingham New Street, Claire had wondered vaguely about her husband's fidelity, and then wandered, less vaguely, into a stone circle. Caz was hooked. But then, somewhere between Birmingham International and Coventry, she sighed and slowly let her eyes close. Comfortable books always did that to her, especially fat ones.

Leamington Spa – the best bit about it was the name, then Oxford already, then Reading, Basingstoke's glassy new-town look, then Winchester, Eastleigh, Parkway and Southampton. Above her, her Nike bag, her running shoes dangling by the laces and two strange slated pictures sticking out through the half-zipped top.

She was awake now, *Outlander* open, but not quite seeing it. She was smiling oddly. Up there, the white slates, the two pictures – all these people, the four skinny Jocks on the next table playing cards and knocking back McEwan's – all of them – who knew what Caz knew, what Caz had above her?

It was an odd, somehow sordid secret, an odd triumph, a peculiar specialness, and for a moment, Caz wondered, was this gloating the same as that of Bourne's killer, was this why they did what they did? Like art-collectors who hid stolen masters in their cellars, never to show them but just to know them?

The train was in darkness, in a brief tunnel, and then stopping. Caz saw a rainbow-lettered toy store across a road and then she was in station gloom, then de-training, stepping down, and passing a closed news-stand. Outside, black on white, behind wire diamonds, was a splash: LATEST. HORROR BODY FIND IN BITTERNE. She left to get a taxi, get to Shirley, get the car, get home.

It took a while for them to release the car, even when she had flashed her warrant card, explained, and dangled the Daimler keys. And there was a message, too, from DS Mason: not a yellow Post-it note but in an envelope. She tucked it away, determined not to read it until tomorrow. She wanted to get away. If she was lucky, she'd be in the shower for midnight – *if* she was lucky. Whatever it was would have to wait until the morning. Anyway, the envelope was probably a wind-up for the green-eyed receptionist.

Peter Mason might be "settling in back at home" but, unless Caz could no longer read tea-leaves, the DS was still playing away.

Thirty-One

And now the long drive home. She cruised out to the M27, thinking about the other times she had criss-crossed the south coast looking for villains – like the time she had chased murder-suspect Trevor Jones and faced him down in an archaeological dig, or the time, when hunting for a serial rapist, she had had to be up and around in the dead of night, 4 a.m!, finding out how thc mail mailed and postmen got it pat.

She drruurrmmed past the airport, past Fareham, down the hill towards the lights of Portsmouth, then out past Chichester, Bognor, and then the single-figure miles into Brighton, right, down towards the sea then left, along the promenade, and then, why? but slowly, slowly, slowly, almost stopping as she reached the street where she lived, where Val would be, where her man would be.

It was twenty to midnight, the street amber-quiet, the sea placid tonight, a distant, hushed, whistle-blue. Her house was not quite in darkness; a low light, the one under the telly, glowing, cracking out through the curtains. Her home. She couldn't remember.

She went in, carrying her sports bag and shoes, the melamine man and her own felt-on-white image. Quiet again at the door, quiet on the stairs, but no longer, yes!, afraid of the dark, no longer held whisper-tight by the man in the straps, in the chair in the house. No longer, no longer, no longer, what?

She opened her flat door. Elton John, low. Val asleep on the sofa.

She slipped in, dropped her bag, took off her shoes.
Valerie was good at being asleep, so good she let him stay that way; unbuttoned her Levis and let them fall, pulled out of her tee shirt, skipped into the bathroom and quietly closed the door on the dribbling bath.
When she slipped into the water, the grey of the train meeting Matey-pink and losing, she aahhed silently, felt the silk heat slide over her, oozed, stretched, washed quickly, then got out, into a rough towel and then into a long white bath-robe. She was surprised to be randy but she was. Before she woke Valerie she went through barefoot, ballet-light, and poured herself a Baileys. *Now* she would wake him.

Thirty-Two

Caz touched Val as gently as she knew how, as softly as she knew how, thinking of how it would look on film, as tenderly as she could imagine, holding his denimed arm, holding his late-night hand, then gently, gently, gently, touching his light brown hair and whispering his name. Eventually he moved, ever so slightly, off his side and onto his back, and, as his unconscious creatured legs were splayed, his buttocks tightened and he lifted up his front, before relaxing, groaning, settling down again into his deep, whatever dreams.

It was late and so, Caz decided, Valerie was excused. She smiled not for any reaction, but for herself and she stroked his head some more. Asleep, Val seemed smaller, softer, gentler and she loved him, no excuses, loved him. Fuck the bastard, but she actually loved him.

She finished the liqueur, a wine-glass full, rolling her red tongue around the slippery fawn, the soft taste of the alcohol, the delicious, sensuous, decadent cream. She was torn for a moment, fancying another, but then, feeling sadly giving, she put down her glass, and, two-handed, undid the clasp of Valerie's leather belt.

He groaned again, his head turning away, and Caz slid her hand inside his slowly unzipped fly. He wasn't hard, but meatened, his body more aware than his mind, and Caz stroked him, through the pale-blue linen of his shorts, her head turned slightly and rested, ear-pressed, against his belly. And he rose, came hardened and still refused to wake, and she rubbed, through the cotton, until his hand came from behind her and softly, ever so softly, touched her neck.

"Caz?"

"Hello, babe."

"Caz."

She sat back. "Hello, babe."

"I didn't know if. I thought I might as well stay. Mad Von's not."

"She's been stopping at Tom's all week."

"I stayed awake as long as I could. I was watching telly, then I put on 'Love Songs'. I'm sorry, love."

"Sorry? What for?"

"Well, just, you have to go away, and then you get back and I'm fast asleep."

"It's past midnight."

Valerie sat up and leaned round to kiss Caz, only to find it was impossible. She moved.

"Hey, welcome home," he said.

"Let's go to bed," Caz said.

He touched her face, paused. "Oh, Tom MacInnes rang you about nine o'clock. He says, if you get back, can you ring him at John Street as early as possible in the morning."

"Oh, wonderful," Caz said. "Like I really need to have to go in on a Saturday."

"It's Saturday already, Caz."

"So it is," Caz said. "And I'm knacked. Take me to bed."

Thirty-Three

Saturday

You can go for a run, you can slip out of bed, get into your Lycra, go out and hammer five miles or so, it'll do you good; or you can wake around six-forty, realise that your mate is here with you, smell the faint musk and sweat of last night – wasn't it amazing? – and roll closer to his back, baby yourself around his buttocks, put your arms around him, your fleshless hands against the rise of his chest, pull him into you, feel the warmth in you slowly rise, and as he stirs, you slip your hand lower until you hold him and he pulses, you want him so much. You're so wet he must know, and you kiss his ear and you whisper, "Are you awake?" and he rolls over.

"DC Carver went to see this snout, the one he calls Kay, real name Robert Foster. He's got a hovel in the back of one of the squares. Kay is freaked and Carver begins to get suspicious. Kay is obsessed with standing in front of a bread-bin, so Carver says, 'Let's have some toast, Kay.' And Kay tries to make a run for it."

"He got away?"

"No, of course not. Ray gave him a little tap, took him back inside and got him to open the bread-bin."

"And?"

"Two pictures. Before and after shots of one John Bourne. Colour photo-copies."

"Jesus!"

"So he's pulled in. Suspicion of murder, complicity, conspiracy – whatever we need to hold him."

"I thought Carver said Kay wasn't capable, sir?"

"He did, and I think he's right. This chap is a weed, a pathetic thing. If *he* could do that to a man, even a man strapped down, it's time I retired."

"You keep saying that."

"What?"

"About retiring."

"Mebbe it's because I'm thinking of doing it, lass."

"Maybe," Caz said. "So you need me in?"

"Bit o' luck, it's jest for the morning."

"OK, sir, give me thirty, forty minutes."

Hard against her back Caz could feel Valerie again. She could have rushed off to work but then she could've gone for a run earlier.

Thirty-Four

Kay, Robert Foster was an unpleasant little man, skinny, sallow-faced, his mousy hair badly cut, with a fringe he nervously kept flicking back. He had a huge, swollen, yellow-headed spot on his chin. Even across the widest table they had, Caz could smell him; unwashed clothes, stale water, old sweat, fear. The tape was running.

"So, Kay," MacInnes said quietly, "You tell me again, where did you get the pictures?"

"I telt yer already, Mister MacInnes. I found 'em."

"And *I* telled *you* last night, didn't I? If y'can't come up with a better answer than that, you'll be down for murder. A little guy like you in Parkhurst, Dartmoor, Kay . . . a lifer . . ."

Kay's hands were on the table, filthy fingernails, white skin. When he paused, the hands went to fists, opened again, then closed again. "Mr MacInnes, I swear, they was in my flat when I got 'ome. Through the letter-box. I found 'em on the mat."

"You want a ciggie, Kay?"

"I don't smoke, Mr MacInnes. Look, they was just there, on my carpet. I didn't know what to do and I stuck um in the bread-bin."

"Who is it, Kay? You know, don't you?"

The fingers fisted.

"No, Mr MacInnes! I never! I never seen anything! I mean, what is it? I mean, why would you, I'm not like that, I mean, why."

Caz cut in. "Robert, take your time."

Foster flicked his eyes Caz's way then obediently back to the DI. MacInnes nodded. Foster turned slightly. Caz smiled.

"Mr MacInnes, he . . ."

"Slowly," Caz said. "It's OK."

"I'm not that – I wouldn't do – something like, I'm not that kind of person, Miss. Whatever the person was 'oo done that, I'm not like that. I wouldn't never 'urt someone."

MacInnes had a brown folder in his hands.

"Except little girls, eh, Kay?"

"I've never 'urt no little girls, Mr MacInnes. You know I hasn't. What you take me for?"

"Under-age sex. It says here, you were eighteen and you were having sex with a girl of twelve. You did time in Lewes for it."

"It wasn't like that, Mr MacInnes. Tracy was a big girl, she was my girlfriend and we – I thought she was older, fifteen like."

"Fifteen?"

"Sixteen."

"OK, it says here, seventeen counts, exposing yourself. Let's see, Preston Park mainly, and Borough Cemetery; twice at the paddling pools off Kings Road."

"I was having trouble with my nerves. I'm better now."

"And two counts of a lewd act in a public place? Waterloo Road?"

"That wasn't down t'me, Mister MacInnes. I was going fer a walk. I jest went for a pee and this big bloke, he ast me to, you know, and I was too scared to say anything. I'm not queer, Mister MacInnes."

"And receiving, all the burglaries?"

"That was when Sheila 'ad jest left me. My nerves. I couldn't work and I got in with the wrong blokes."

MacInnes leaned forward. He spoke slowly, coldly. "If you don't help us, Kay, then these wrong blokes you talk of, they'll soon seem like angels."

"You don't understand."

MacInnes drew back. He was about to speak but Caz interrupted.

"Sir?" she said. "I think that Robert is telling the truth. It's not his fault if he's in possession of these pictures."

"Oh, you do, do you, Flood?"

"Yes, sir. Perhaps a word, sir?"

Foster looked up as they stood. His mouth was open and his teeth were yellow. MacInnes banged the door. It opened and he stepped out with Caz. They left the door open, and stopped just across the corridor. Kay was still visible, his hands still fisting, relaxing, fisting. "What is it, Flood?"

"Sir, Kay's scared, right? But he's been inside for lots of things, so it's not the nick is it? And he's not so stupid that he could really think we'd pin this murder on him."

"So?"

"What's he scared of? Going down for the murder, or what's in the photo itself?"

"The murder," MacInnes said definitely. "DC Carver told us Kay was thinking of disappearing for a while. My guess is he's involved in some way, knows the dead man, maybe, or at least why he was killed. He didn't want to talk to us, he wanted to drop out of sight."

"But he told Carver, sir. Why would he?"

"What?"

"I was just wondering, sir. Wondering whether Kay *wanted* to be pulled in. I mean, why do a runner on Ray Carver when you know you're going to get a smack and at least one night in the cells?"

MacInnes went with it. "To get off the street?"

"Could be, sir. Because you're scared of what's out there! I mean, if he was involved, would he have a picture?"

"These types do, Flood."

"But not lying around almost in public view, surely? Kay already knew Carver was interested. He had to expect another visit. I'm just wondering if he *wanted* a bit of drama and the picture found, and himself locked safely away."

"So what are we thinking?"

"Tell him he can go, sir."

"Just like that?"

"Well, we could try him with the Bourne drawing and, if that's no go, then we could tell him to piss off. If I'm right, he won't want to go, will he?"

"Or he could walk out and then disappear."

"So we put a PC either end of the street and stop him."

MacInnes hesitated. "You really think he's that clever?"

"He's not stupid, sir, but no. I think he's just very, very, scared. You get that scared, you freeze, you run, or you get devious. Our friend I think is the sly type. He wants to stay alive. Maybe Ray Carver can suss him and offer him a really good deal."

"Like what?"

"Like, give us a name or two, somewhere to look, and we can get him a month or three on remand and then drop all charges."

"Or?"

"Or this."

Caz walked back through the open door. Kay looked up. She was smiling. "OK, Robert, party's over. You're off the hook. DI MacInnes says you can go home."

Thirty-Five

Give Foster his due, he tried.

"I should fink so 'n'all!" he said.

He was standing.

"Well, off ye go, lad," MacInnes said.

"Right!" Foster said.

He was walking out of the interview room when Caz wished him luck. There was the faintest stutter in his walk.

"So Robert, be careful out there!" she said.

He leaned back slightly but kept going. Caz bit her tongue.

Then he was gone and MacInnes didn't look too happy.

"Well, Flood?"

Caz didn't know what to say, she wasn't wrong often. "Er, well . . ." she said slowly.

She was rescued by a cough: Foster at the door.

"Yes?"

"The security door?" Foster said. "I can't get out."

"DC Flood will take you," MacInnes said. He turned away, barely hiding his disgust.

Foster nodded. "Any time, Mr MacInnes, you want some help, you know me, ay?"

Caz touched his elbow and pushed him away. Even finger-to-coat-sleeve she felt too intimate. "The DI's not a happy bunny, Robert. You'd best keep your mouth shut and get off home."

"I can't. I got my tape stall to worry about. Up the North Lanes."

"You're worried about a market stall?"

"Yeah, course I am! I gotta work."

They were at the door into reception. Caz shook her head. "Oooh, not such a good idea, Robert. Not such a good idea."

"What'cher mean?"

Caz looked sad as she paused. She looked as if she might tell him something, then she said, "Sorry, Robert, can't say." She pressed the button and the door buzzed. "You'd better get on."

And Foster left.

Thirty-Six

The last time Caz looked, Foster was paused in the station's main doorway, looking up at the weather above John Street as if it was about to rain. Caz was trying to stop herself swearing and trying to think of an excuse not to have to rush back to see Tom MacInnes. She thought about going to the War Room to check her messages and turned away. Half a second later, Foster turned away from the street and went to the front desk.

The War Room was empty. There were just the two notes: one from Moira – "I'm home, with baby, come on over," – and another one from Peter Mason asking her to ring asap. Both should have been marked with a time. Neither were. She went to pick up the phone just as one of them rang. "Flood? The guy you just escorted out? He's back, wants to talk to you or the DI."

"Foster?"

"How many blokes you escorted from the building in the last five minutes, Flood?"

"I'm coming out," she said.

"I was jess thinking, this photo that was there on my 'all carpet. D'you think one of my mates mighta stuck it through my door?"

"Oh, sure," Caz said. "Happens all the time. Bloke gets a picture of a corpse through his door, then he plays pass the gore and sticks it through someone else's letter-box. All the time."

"Well, I just think, you know. It was for a mate of mine."

"Will y'give us a name or no'?" MacInnes snapped.

Thirty-Seven

Foster was banged up for the weekend until they could decide what to do with him. The man they wanted to talk to was John Rayner. "From up Cheshire way", was the best previous address they could get out of Foster, "this and that" for how he made his living.

So how tall?

"Biggish."

Build?

"Average, you know."

Hair Colour?

"Well, brownish, I fink. Light or dark, and not that long. But it's not short eever."

"Rayner, J for John, aged twenty-five to forty-five, height medium, hair brown," the DI said when he rang through to control. "Last known address . . ."

Foster touched his arm. "Oh, an' 'ees got a limp, did I say? And a shiny purple jacket."

Caz watched Tom's knuckles whiten. He picked up the phone.

"Bill? Add a limp would yer, and a purple jacket."

"With a dragon on the back."

"Bill? With a dragon on the back."

"And he rides a motorbike. Issa Kawasaki. Big."

MacInnes picked the phone up again. He put his hand over the mouthpiece and took a great deep breath.

"Flood. Take this bloody idiot out back and shoot him, would yer? Bill? Yeah, I know, sorry. And a Kawasaki motor bike, 500 cc plus."

Caz and Kay exited left.

Thirty-Eight

Tom MacInnes let Caz away just after twelve 'clock. As she left, down the stairs, past the canteen and out into the car-park, she passed the face of John Bourne postered up and saw it for the first time: a good face she didn't like, the smile of a false priest, a crooked accountant, a nice man, but.

She walked in the half-dark to Val's car. After they'd made love in the morning and she'd left it late, she had rushed out, and without thinking, had got in the boyfriend's car again.

She didn't think he'd complain; he liked thrashing the MX.

MacInnes had surprised her; he'd not been his usual hard, hard-edged self, nor had he worn his classic interviewing officer's dark-blue suit. It might have been he wasn't in the mood; more likely, though, love was getting to him and he was losing his cutting edge. As she drove out through the up-and-over doors she was trying to remember the words to an old Everley Brothers song. "The Price of Love" . . .

When she got to her flat and went upstairs the NAD was on – Malcolm McLaren and she went in, trying to think of a sarcastic remark. The first time Val had heard this album he had taken the piss, but months later she had screwed him to "*The House of the Blue Danube*" and changed his mind. Actually, they'd made love to that, "*Something's Jumping in Your Shirt*", "*Waltz Darling*", "*Shall We Dance*", "*Deep in Vogue*", "*Call a Wave*" and a slightly rushed bit of "*Algernon's Awfully Good at Algebra*". Val had been miffed. He'd thought he could last the whole thirty-six-something minutes, but Caz hadn't let him. That had been a Saturday afternoon too.

Thirty-Nine

"Moira rang you. She said she's home with the baby. I think she said Titania?"

"Yup."

"She's home with Titty-Anna and she wondered if we'd go round."

"Go round?"

"As in, drop in, Flood, as in visit, as in go there and say hello and take a prezzie for the kid and tell Mo she's looking well, you know, like people do."

"I think I know what 'go round' means, Val. I meant do we have to? I thought maybe we'd go out somewhere or go to bed."

"You want a coffee?" he said.

Caz had licked her lips as she came in, but Val had rolled up off the sofa, turned down the stereo and dropped his *GQ* on the floor. The peck on her cheek would have left a sister expecting more.

"I've only been up half an hour," he said. "I was out like a light."

"Perhaps you were tired," Caz said; just a hint there, just a test.

"I guess," Val said, and then he mentioned the phone call. Caz was thinking. Obviously sex was off the menu and it didn't look a lot like they were going hang-gliding, or for a run.

"It's half-twelve," she said wistfully. "D'you fancy going out to Armando's or Donatello's and then some shopping?

I'd quite like some garlic bread, a nice bit of fish, to look into my lover's eyes . . ."

"We ought to watch the money, Caz. You know, put some away."

"What for?"

He looked at her ringless finger. She'd refused the engagement ring; the commitment was enough.

"What?" Caz said. Her voice was a touch too high. "You don't mean bottom drawer, white dresses, honeymoon, all that bollocks, do you?"

He looked again.

"You *do*? Val, you're thirty-something, I'm nearly. We've both got a place, neither of us are virgins, what have we got to save for?"

He looked from her hand to her face. "OK, then, maybe for once I'd like us not to drink at lunch-time."

"Oh, fucking *great*!" Caz said.

Forty

"There was a man, Val. I've seen a picture of what he once looked like. He looked like a parish-priest or your bank-manager or maybe a teacher. I've seen this guy, Val, I've seen him naked, with his balls ripped off, with his dick cut away, then cooked, then some of it stuffed in his mouth. I've seen your priest, your neighbour, with his belly opened up – do you know what colour intestines are? – with his ears cut off, with a hole where his nose had been and with a fucking great mess where he used to have a mouth."

She was shaking, despite this huge whisky.

"I drink, Valerie, and I really don't care. And I don't care if you care, and I don't care if you don't care. I don't talk to you about these things, I don't talk to anyone. And I drink. And I'll drink what I like, when I like and as much as I like. So fuck you."

"Let me know when you've finished," Val said coldly.

"Bastard," she said.

Caz turned away, unpretty, her neck burning. She walked stiffly into her kitchen. She must have put the drink down because she found herself staring out of the window, her fingers on the stainless sink, staring out and down at the clumsy backs of the next street, fire-escapes, windows, drain-pipes, gutters, grey slate, distempered walls. That was what Val saw, things; she saw ways burglars got in, rapists slithered, she saw curtains behind which abusers abused, killers sometimes killed, fornicators fornicated, cheats planned.

"I'm going for a run," she said.

She came out of the kitchen. Valerie was sitting on the sofa, pretending to read his magazine.

"I'm going for a run," she said again. "A long one."

"You want me to come with you?" he asked.

"I mean a long one, fifteen, sixteen."

"Oh," he said.

"Look, two hours," she said, "OK? Then I'll be OK, We can go and see Moira and Billy."

"We don't have, to, Caz. She's your friend, I just thought."

"I can manage that myself, Val."

"Where are you going to run? I can come out and meet you if you'd like."

She thought a moment, then she said, "I'll go towards Shoreham, from here out through Portslade, over the Adur bridge and onto Shoreham Beach, that's three miles round. I can go out steady, hammer it round the island and then wind down on the home leg."

"I'll jog out from here, meet you at Portslade or something, then. Six or so is fine for me, and you'll be reasonably knackered by then."

"That's one way of putting it," she said and disappeared into the bedroom.

She changed quickly. It was hot out, so lightweight nylon SubFour stuff, white ankle-socks and some heavier shoes, Nikes for a change. When she came out, Val was in the kitchen. The stereo was on again, one of his jazz things, and he was making a lot of obvious noise, clattering through preparing a light lunch. She watched his back, then quietly she said, "Don't try to change me."

He turned round, "What?"

"I said, I'm off. Portslade-by-Sea."

"I'll jog out to meet you," he said.

Free! There is nothing like this! See the sea, sniff the salt, drop down on to the shingle and clunsh through the wet falling pebbles, tease the wave-edges, feel the sun, climb up steps, down steps and up steps again, take a detour out past the paddling pools and the toy yachts, dads with kites, grass, old ladies in summer frocks, laugh when some teens give you a whistle, grunt when you see a runner in black circling the other way.

Out! Out! There is nothing, nothing to touch this! Let the body come to terms, the muscles settle, let the breathing find its balance, the juices even out, the tensions, all the tensions, all the sad, sad diamonds, ease away.

Until that shlapp-shlapp rhythm arrives, the perfect pace where you know you can run forever, your heel-strike toe-roll, heel-strike toe-roll, bedded in now, the sweat more the sun's than from your effort and now, as always, the thoughts begin to line up.

MacInnes is going to retire. He doesn't want to die in harness. He's Vaunda's. He's losing it already. And Moira won't come back to work. She talks of creches and of nurseries, but she won't come back to work. Greavsie will be talking "forever" by the end of next week, he'll be saying how great Janice's kids are, how a ready-made family is brilliant. At best it will last a couple of months.

Portslade.

And Peter Mason will continue to play away, of course. He'll hurt receptionists, hurt his wife. And then one day he'll move out into a small bed-sit or into the bedroom of an old flame, recently divorced.

And DCS Blackside, him too. The successful senior copper, pillar of the community, settling for safety, to be fair to Mrs Blackside, thinking of the kids coming up for their GCSE's, then A-Levels, Uni – then their careers, and here we go round the mulberry bush again.

Caz climbed up and crossed the chain-bridge over the Adur, the multi-colours of the house-boats down to her left, the tide right out. She knew a couple in one boat, Claire and Tim, and in another she'd once met an American.

And what about me and Val? Me and Val? Me and Val?

She hooked left past shops and through houses. Here it was flat and fast, here she should really push it.

Me, Val, me Val, me and Val.

She picked the fourth lamppost and kicked very hard, 800-metre pace, the thrill of her body, lamppost, lamppost, lamppost and yes! Then she dropped to a jog.

Us. It can't work, can it? What's love got to do with it?

She picked another, two lights away and another four further on.

Ready to kick?

What's love matter if you have to do something and the love stops you? What if you must paint, and your woman hates oils? What if you have to write and your partner hates words? What if you must do better than your Dad, and what if your man, your lover, the only person left in the whole of the world who can make you cry, what if Valerie doesn't like the dark?

And kick! This time hard!

Harder, harder, harder, post, post, post, post.

Jog.

She came to the turn, a long grey sea ahead and then to her left, then on her shoulder, then behind. *Oh, Val, isn't there a way? Can't I be a bitch Monday-Friday, a woman weekends?*

She knew the answer to that. She worked weekends. Even when she didn't, the smell of evil still lingered.

Lampposts. Lampposts. Hammer, hammer, hammer.

Forty-One

Val had come out to meet her and she knew, when she saw his shape, his easy miler's lope, that she loved him, that she didn't want to lose him, that she would have to find a way in a place where she knew before she searched, that there wasn't, there never was, a way.

"Hi-yah, babe! Hurting yet?" he said.

"Nah," she said. "Super-cool, me. Shoulda seen me on the island. Right now I think I could give Kelly Holmes a run for her money."

"You wish," he said.

They were settling now, into a matched, comfortable stride.

"I could. If I got serious. I was doing 2:03 back when I didn't have a clue what I was doing. I could be back there by the end of this season if I really wanted it."

"You don't?"

"Well, I do and I don't, you know? It's the commitment, the diet, the no booze, training twice a day. We hardly see each other now."

"I could train with you. I like the fast stuff."

She laughed. "Yeah, but there's still giving up the booze!"

"I know," Val said. "But it's your last chance."

She looked across but he was looking ahead.

"What d'you mean, last chance?"

They must have been speeding up because now his speech came in short gasps.

"You're twenty-eight, right?"

"Yeah?"

"Well – next season – and a hard winter – could you break two minutes? You'll be twenty-nine."

She'd thought that he'd . . .

"I thought you were suggesting—"

He puffed out, "What?"

"The booze . . ."

"What about it?"

"That I was in trouble."

They were passing the lawns and the paddling pool, the small white sails, the serious, blue-eyed child-faces watching. When she stopped looking, she realised Valerie hadn't answered. They slowed right down.

"It would be nice to have just one more season, one or two serious cracks at going sub-two," she said.

Valerie was smiling. They were almost home.

"I think you could do it," he said. "The job will make it extra hard, but if you really want it, if you don't get injured."

They stopped and waited for a gap in the traffic.

"Oh," Caz suddenly said, "that thing I told you about the murder victim, it's not public. Forget I said anything."

"Forgotten," Val said.

They skipped through a gap in the traffic. He took her hand.

"You really think, sub-two?" Caz said softly.

He squeezed her. "Yes, I really think."

"Yeah," she said, but there was a long slow ache in her voice,

They walked together up Inkerman Terrace and Val's hand grip was firm. He waved to Mrs Lettice, a neighbour at her window.

"But giving up booze, Val . . ."

He squeezed again. "Nothing good comes easy," he said.

Forty-Two

Val drove them to Moira's; like a man, not a trained police driver, lots of brakes, the Mazda sports car rrammpping!! and racing, but more huff than puff, more show than A-to-B efficiency. Caz loved it, anyway, just as she had loved it earlier, grape-vining up Valerie's body in the shower, slipping up and over and on to him, not so much for the great sex – it's not that great in the shower – but for the sheer *fun* of being able to do it.

Maureen answered the door, big and full and confident, her dark hair curled and bobbed and short, her eyes deep and brown, as lovely as her daughter's.

"Kathy! How lovely to see you! Valerie! You too!"

"Where's Mum?" Caz asked.

Maureen smiled. "She's got her feet up on the settee in the front room. Titania is asleep."

Caz almost asked, "Billy?" but on a sudden instinct didn't.

Maureen showed them through to the lounge and whispered that she would go and make some tea. Caz and Valerie stepped in gently, respectfully, feeling slightly foolish, as if entering an invalid's room. They needn't have bothered. Moira was sitting up, a flowered duvet over her, watching someone swashbuckling in smudged colour. She looked voluptuous, and tired.

"Caz," she said.

"'Ello, Mum!" Caz said.

"Hello, Moira," Valerie said.

They sat down. "So, Mo," Caz said softly, "how are you feeling?"

"A bit tired, a little bit low," Moira said. She glanced down at the duvet. "And uh-hum . . ."

"Y'sore?"

"A little bit, yeah."

"But babe?"

Moira brightened a bit but it wasn't quite heart-deep, "Oh, Tee's fine, she's wonderful, and she *sleeps*, Caz! It's great, she wakes up, has a feed, and falls asleep again. It's Heaven."

Caz raised her eyebrows.

"He's in work," Moira said heavily. She tried to lift the voice, her head, tried to smile, but didn't manage it.

"Overs?"

Moira nodded. "Standing in for Bob Saint. Blood poisoning. He's not very well."

"For Bob?"

"Yeah, he got a splinter or something. They had to take the nail off. It's a bit sore, apparently. I know he's not very happy."

"Billy's not actually standing in for Bob?"

"Dunno. Not exactly. It's these two betting-shop robberies. Spread things a bit thin, so Billy went in. I don't know what he's on exactly. Can't say I'm that worried. But he's in work, he's working, and he's picking up overtime."

"Well, the money will . . ."

"Oh, I know the money's handy, Caz."

But you want him home . . .

"Maybe he had to go in."

"No," Moira said. "He didn't."

"Shit," Val said. "I've left the Mazda open."

Caz stood and watched Valerie walk to the car, open it, close it, go round to the boot and rummage.

"Is it really bad, Mo?"

"I don't know, Caz. He's like, so cold; like he couldn't care about me, Tee, anything. He's almost nasty, Caz. He frightens me. To tell you the truth, I don't mind that he's in work; when he's here, you could cut the atmosphere with a knife."

"It'll pass, mate."

"I thought I was the one who was supposed to get depressed."

"It'll be the G28 in Hove. Billy had to stay there for three hours, the best part of two on his own. It wasn't nice, Mo."

"He won't talk to me about it."

"I won't either. You don't want to know."

Caz was still looking out the window; Valerie looked up and Caz flashed him a spread hand: five minutes. He nodded and got in the car.

As she turned round, Caz laughed. "I think Val's listening to the football results, the bugger."

"Typical," Moira said, just as Maureen came in with the tea.

Forty-Three

Tea, but no sympathy. It was rarely the best thing for Moira and certainly not when Maureen was floating about, smiling, tinkling her teaspoon against her gold rimmed tea-cup, nodding like a toy dog in the back window of a Cortina.

"Mum!" Moira said the third time Maureen had asked about Caz and babies.

"I don't think so," Caz said politcly.

"Oh, really?" Moria's Mum said. "I'm glad Moira doesn't think like that. Wouldn't seem natural for me, if she didn't want – "

"That's up to Caz, Mum!" Moira said.

Maureen fluffed, picked up her spoon again, stirred some more.

"Oh, I suppose so, but things – "

"Are different now, Mum. That's the point."

Caz gave the faintly embarrassed Maureen a tiny warm smile.

"It's just I want my career, Maureen. I want to be a sergeant by the time I'm thirty and Inspector as soon as I can after that. Thirty-five and I'll think I'm slipping. Then I'd like to go for DCI. Val says he'll wait. Thirty-eight, forty, these days, that's not so late."

"But life begins at forty, Kathy."

Caz smiled again. "Life begins when I've made DCI. And that's just the way it is. Once they label me 'mum' I can kiss the fast track goodbye. Maybe if I'm a DCI when it happens, I can change that."

"Oh, it seems so, so – calculated."

"We prefer to call it choice, Maureen."

It might have gone on, both sides digging a nice big hole, but Valerie came in and beautifully thespian he said, "They lost *again*, can you believe it?"

Caz took the opportunity to change the subject.

"Did I tell you, Mo? We got called out – some dog had gone wild in a pub up by the Albion ground and started biting all the customers."

"What?"

"By the time we got there, the owner had it under control. He apologised to us and to the customers. Apparently the dog was a fan of the Seagulls and whenever they lost he went mad, biting people. If they drew he just howled."

Moira and Maureen were taking it all in. Valerie had heard it before. Caz continued.

"So I asked this guy, 'What happens when they win?' 'Oh, I dunno,' the guy said, 'I've only 'ad 'im four years!'"

"Oh, my dear," Maureen said. "Did the dog have to be put down?"

They got away about six and Caz drove. She had managed to get the keys off Val with a display of diplomacy at least as impressive as that shown in the company of Maureen and Moira. She hadn't once talked about Frank Dibben (last seen in October 1991 heading due west with the barmaid from The Lost Ferret on his arm), and hadn't even opened her mouth when Maureen queried her son-in-law's behaviour. As they left, Caz kissed Moira and whispered to her that she'd get to Billy, soonest and see what she could do.

They drifted back, Val's hand loosely on Caz's jeaned thigh and as they got near home, Caz thought "Wine", went to speak and stopped herself. There were spaces near the house. They parked, went in, up the stairs. Just as Caz was opening the door she "remembered".

"Oh, bloody hell!" she said. "We've got no plonk for tonight!"

"That's OK," Val said brightly, "we can just shoot round the offy."

Caz pouted, a little sexual hint in her face. "I was going to start the food . . ."

Val grinned. "Hey, no problem! I'll go get it while you start in the kitchen."

"Thanks," Caz said. She was a very smooth liar.

Val went back down the stairs as Caz unlocked the front door. As he went into the street, she slipped the chain on the door to the flat. By the time he had edged out into the traffic on the parade, she was on the phone to Southampton.

Forty-Four

"Hello?"

"This is Ann Mason. Who is that, please?"

"Oh, Ann. This is Caz Flood. We met once, you might remember, at the Stubbington 10K? DC over in Brighton . . ."

"I remember you, you took Peter round."

"That's right, then the bugger out-sprinted me at the finish."

"That's Peter, always grateful. Is this business?"

"I think so. Peter left this number, asked me to ring him."

"He's not here, Caz. Did you hear about the murder in Bitterne?"

"No."

"On Friday, pretty horrible, I believe. Peter won't talk about it."

"He's at the station?"

"He's at work. I don't know exactly where he is."

"I'll try Shirley, then."

There was silence.

"Right, then," Caz said.

Another beat. Caz thought she heard Ann Mason swallow.

"I'm sorry," Ann said.

"I'll try Shirley," Caz said.

Bastard!

She put down the phone.

"DC Flood, Brighton, speak to Peter Mason."

"He's out, but he's on a mobile. I can get him to ring you."

"Please," Caz said.

She put down the telephone then looked at a piece of paper and dialled another Southampton number. It rang five or six times; then another female voice.

"Jenny? It's Caz Flood."

"Oh, hi, Caz! You must be busy. Trevor's been trying to get hold of you for days."

"He's there now?"

"Er, yes, but he's busy."

"Trevor is *busy*?"

"You're not going to believe this, Caz, but he's upstairs changing the baby."

Caz chuckled. "You're right, I don't believe you!"

"Really, Caz. You wouldn't know him. *I* hardly know him." There was a pause, a hand over the phone at the other end, Jenny Wilkinson, checking over her shoulder, then she came back, hushed. "Caz, I'll *never* be able to thank you enough. Trevor's a good bloke, really. I know it's hard for you to believe, but he's a changed man. Having the baby, well, it's turned him round. That, and you giving him a break."

Caz was embarrassed; it wasn't *that* much of a big deal. She had spoken up for Trevor Jones in court, just that once. No, she had said; Jones hadn't resisted arrest or threatened her; and yes, she did believe he thought he was being pursued by debt collectors until she had cornered him in a muddy trench. She'd lied, yeah, but it was only a little lie. It hadn't cost her much.

"OK," she said. "But I still don't believe he's changing nappies."

Before Valerie got back, a brown carrier bag with four bottles, two Ernst & Gallo Dry Reserves and two Il Grigio's, Caz had undone the flat door, rushed into the kitchen, thrown a few saucepans round, stuck some frozen prawns in a bowl of water and quickly massacred an onion. Val was a bit slower than she'd expected and she had just started malleting the steak to death when she heard him. She went out and kissed him, smelling of onions.

She thanked him for going. Val shrugged and put the wine down. "You know, you don't deserve me," he said.

"Hah!" she said.

She turned to the second onion, a strong one which made her cry.

Val was opening the Chianti when the phone rang.

Caz turned round, chemical tears on her face. "Can you?" she said. Val went. She had tossed two lumps of garlic out when he called her. "DS Mason for DC Flood," he said. Then sarcastically he added, "*Returning your call.*" She sniffed and went through. Valerie wasn't particularly happy and she tried to head him off at the pass.

"D'you want to fry the onions and chuck in the garlic?"

"Are you staying in," he said.

"Not too much butter," she said and picked up the phone.

Forty-Five

"Peter, what goes?"

"You rang me."

"Yep, but you left a message for me, John Street. I rang you back, and spoke to Ann. She said you were on a big case."

"Too right."

She pulled the phone from her ear and groaned inwardly. In the kitchen, Valerie was clacking around.

"Peter. It's Saturday, you know, my day off?"

"Yeah, I know, Saturday, all day, change at midnight."

"Peter . . ."

"Yeah, all right. Coupla things. Wanted to tell you about our murder and our friendly Dixons man."

"Trevor Jones."

"Yeah. He'll be home all day. You might want to try him there. It's a bit weird. It's not him but a mate of his who wants to talk. A guy in Parkhurst for rape."

"A mate of Trevor's is a *rapist*?"

"Figure of speech. You know when Trevor was on remand for those burglaries that the Crown Prosecution Service eventually dropped? He shared a cell with some bloke waiting trial for rape. Bloke said he didn't do it of course."

"Of course."

"This bloke. He's written to Trevor."

"And?"

"And nothing. Trevor won't say anything to me. I tried leaning on him, but he just grinned. He says this bloke will only talk to him and what he knows is serious."

"What kind of serious?"

"Trevor wouldn't say. I think he's holding out for more money."

Caz thought a second. She could hear Valerie.

"I don't think so."

"Well, anyway, Trevor wants to talk to you. So get in there and fill yer boots, Flood."

"Thanks, Peter. That it?"

"Well, if it's something on my patch, we can go halves?"

"Go round there and give him fifty, and it's a deal."

"What? How am I supposed to swing that, Flood?"

"I should care? Yer good at lying, Peter. You'll think of something, I'm sure." She stopped, listened for Val again. She was thinking of Ann Mason, and the miserable receptionist at Shirley nick. "I think you're fucking mad, Sergeant."

The line was quiet for maybe five seconds; then, change of subject.

"You heard about our murder? On Wednesday night, Thursday, the blow-torch thing?"

"Not a dickie. I was up in Manchester, remember? I came in for an hour this morning but I only spoke to the DI."

"OK. On Wednesday night, about three to four a.m. is the best timing, some guy in Bitterne was done in, unbelievable mess, burned to a frazzle with a blow-torch."

"Yick! What's that got to do with me?"

"Nothing, probably. It's just funny, you came on to us checking out our missing persons cos you had an unknown stiff and now I have to ask you about *your* mispers."

"What, you're saying your burned guy is unidentified?"

"Right. Well, so far, anyway. The poor sod was really worked over. Hair burned off, face, hands; it was not nice. Made me think of your boy smacked about in Hove."

"Anything else you can tell me about this? Was he tied up or anything? Was there any other mutilation?"

"Like what?"

Caz was getting angry. "*Was* there, Peter?"

Mason's voice changed. He'd probably stood up. "Are you holding something back on yours, Caz? You *are*, aren't you? D'you think ours is the same MO or something? Look,

I was only telling you because it struck me as funny that we were criss-crossing, asking each other to check out our misper files. Our Force Intelligence would have told yours by now if there was anything more. No big deal."

"Was there any sexual mutilation, Peter?"

"Like what?"

"Please!"

"No. The guy's hair and face was severely burned, so were the hands and feet and one of the arms. But our man wasn't tied up. Yours was, right? And no, no sexual whatever. You telling me there was your end?"

"Our Intelligence will have told yours."

"What are friends for, eh, Flood?"

"It's not that, Peter. We're supposed to be sitting on some bits. We need to hold something back for all the nutter confessions, and we don't want the extras getting as far as the tabloids."

"Come on, Flood."

She gave in. "Are you on your mobile?"

"Yeah."

"Analogue or digital?"

"How do I know?"

"It's analogue, then. You'd know if you had digital. I thought it was a shitty line. Ring me on a land line and I'll tell you."

"You should be in Special Branch, Flood."

"It's been offered, Sergeant."

"I'll ring you back," he said.

Forty-Six

Caz went into the kitchen. Val was wearing a silly plastic apron covered in pigs. "I'm sorry, Babe," she said.

He smiled, eyes too. "I opened a bottle of red. Want to pour two?"

The gas was low, then off, and the two fat steaks, poxed with peppercorns, were on a chopping board to the side, ready. She smiled and turned to the window-sill to grab the wine.

"The baked potatoes will be ready in twenty minutes," Val said. "Is that going to be all right?"

"Pete Mason is just about to ring me back."

"How long will that be?"

He seemed tense. "No time," she said.

"Good," he said and came to her. She managed to get the glasses down without spilling any.

She didn't know what it was – unless it was love – but Val only had to touch her, touch her, and she was there; it didn't matter what her mood was, on or off, any one of thirty-one days, he had the key. As he kissed her now, hard up against her front, then behind her, unbuckling her belt, running his hand round her hip, over her pants and then inside, a little voice said "pheromones" and another one said "who cares?" as she wriggled so he could get at her.

"Oh, Jeez!" she said, just as the phone rang again.

She coughed as he let her go, swigged a glug of the wine, leaned to kiss him and then went to answer. As she went out of the door she said, "Wash yer hands."

*

"Peter!"

"Is that Caz Flood?

"Yes."

"It's Trevor, Caz."

"Oh. Hello, Trevor."

"I was changing the little 'un, otherwise I'da . . ."

"Forget about it," Caz said. "What can I do for you, Trevor?"

"It's this bloke I know, Caz. I met him when I was on remand. He didn't seem that bad a bloke, just burgling mainly, same as me, but he was in for rape. I – uh – well, this bloke, he went down for it, six years. He's in Parkhurst, over on the island."

"I know where Parkhurst is, Trevor."

"Sorry, Caz. This bloke, 'is name's Jimmy Munro. Thing is, he sent me a letter. He 'ad to smuggle it out, pay money, like, and in this letter he was talking about this bloke, celled up with 'im, in fer touching kids up. He says he's gotta tell someone what this bloke's been telling him."

"So what did he tell you?"

"He didn't. He means he wants to tell a copper."

"Tell a copper what?"

"I don't know, Caz, but he thinks he knows something. He used 'is phone card to ring me and he was *scared*, Caz. But he was sick, too. I don't know what it's about, but someone ought to talk to 'im."

"Why me?"

"DS Mason, he'd fuck things up. Jimmy's not up to dealing with people like him. I thought of you. He's too scared to go to one of the screws – you never know with screws. The way Jimmy was talking, whatever it was it sounded pretty serious. This isn't snitching, Caz, it's summat else. Big, maybe."

"So what are we talking about, Trevor?"

"Jimmy's going to ring me again this week. I was going to suggest he had a chat with you. He doesn't know you, Caz. He'll think, young bird, yeah, nice one, no problem. I didn't tell 'im it was you arrested me."

Caz was beginning to think about Valerie again, with a bit of luck getting at him on the lounge floor. She was thinking of dinner, too and maybe getting at him later on, say about ten.

"OK, Trevor. See if you can get it sorted. If there's something to talk about I can get over on to the island."

"Yeah?"

Caz had a final thought. "But I'll need a hint of some kind, Trevor. It's a whole day, Brighton to the Isle of Wight. Don't leave me pissing in the wind."

"OK," Trevor said. Then he said, "So what d'you think of that murder, eh? Not far fr'm 'ere, you know. You 'ear what was done to the poor sod, burnt all over, even up 'is arse."

"Where did you get that crap, Trevor?"

"You telling me it's not true?"

"It's not true," she said.

She said goodbye and put down the phone. As soon as she'd put it down she realised she hadn't asked Trevor about his kid. She shrugged and shouted through to Valerie that she was putting Malcolm Mclaren on. She felt a little surge of heat go down through her. Ten seconds later, the phone rang again and she cursed. In the kitchen Valerie growled and she heard the gas going on full.

Forty-Seven

"I'm putting the steaks on *now!*" Valerie shouted.

"Caz Flood," she said into the phone.

"Caz, Peter. So what's the gen?"

"In a second, *Sergeant.* What about *your* body? I just heard he had a few more burn marks than you told me first time round."

"You show me yours and I'll show you mine."

Jesus!

"OK, but there's a very heavy lid on this, Peter. Our man had lips, nose and ears cut off, super-glued to the wall. He also had all his fingers and toes cut off."

"I know all that. It's on the intell report."

"And his balls, Peter, and his prick. When we got there his prick was half-cooked in a frying pan in the kitchen."

"Oh," Peter said slowly.

"Oh, what?"

"Ours had nothing actually cut off but his scrotum had been badly blow-torched and it didn't do his John Thomas a lot of good."

"Cause of death?"

"Heart failure."

"Two minutes!" Valerie shouted.

She shouted back. OK.

"What?" Mason said.

"I was talking to my fellah."

"Oh."

Caz was trying to think fast.

"Peter, your Super should know about our guy having his three-piece suite removed. Didn't he make a connection?"

"Caz, I'm not sure there *is* a connection. We're seeing this as general burning, torture or something, maybe drugs. The fact that this guy had no ID and nobody seems to know where he came from fits with that."

"Too much like ours, Peter."

"Maybe. I'll talk to the DCI on Monday morning."

"Don't mention me!"

"I'll just say I heard a whisper and ask about the Brighton case. It's easy enough. You spoke to Trevor Jones yet?"

"Just now."

"Anything worthwhile?"

"You gonna take him fifty round?"

"Yeah."

"Y'promise?"

"I *promise*, Flood."

"OK, then I think what he says is bollocks, but I'm going to follow it up next week."

"Unfortunate phraseology, Flood."

"What is?"

"It's all bollocks."

"Ha, bloody ha!"

"It's ready," Val shouted.

Caz put down the phone.

Forty-Eight

The concoction was an invention of Valerie's, so he said, presumably it was an ex's; the prawns finally creamed with peppercorns after they had been cooked with the garlic and onion, then the whole lot poured over the rare, flash-cooked, peppered fillet steaks and served with the baked spuds, a little butter, *mange tout* cooked *al dente.*

They sat opposite each other at the tiny kitchen table, even a candle and napkins; and a second bottle, this one *Il Grigio*, ready.

Val was smiling, "Flood, what am I going to do with you?"

She smiled back. "Are we talking, short, medium or long-term here, boss?"

"Caz, are we going to have to spend every weekend away, or are you going to learn to leave the phone off the hook? I was getting randy there and, well, it would have given me an appetite."

"What!" Caz said indignantly. "Exactly what sort of girl do you think I am?"

"Over-sexed?" Val asked as if looking for help here.

Out of the blue, a thought, "*You're rushing, trying to take what you can before he goes.*"

"That's me!" Caz said after the slightest beat. "That's what the *Waltz Darling* was for."

He groaned, not quite all show. Then he stopped, and he looked. She thought he was going to burst into tears.

Then she thought *she* was.

"Caz," Val said, and the way he said it melted right

through to somewhere she had thought dead a long time ago. "Caz, I don't know how to say this."

Oh, no! She grabbed her wine and shlupped some, her shoulders high. Her eyes were wide, blinkless.

"Caz, I love you to death."

She should have been happy but this wasn't happy.

"Caz, I *love* you. It's fucking boring, I know it is, and it's two point four kids shit and it's Marks & Spencer's and all the crap you don't want to hear, but I love you. I don't know another way to say it."

"Say what?"

"Just that I love you."

She was terrified. She grinned idiotically. "Is that it? Do we get to finish our steaks now?"

"Oh, Caz," he said.

But Valerie couldn't understand. She was really frightened, *really* frightened, like once locked behind a trap-door, like once a child in a cellar. Not like facing a knife, all that could do was kill you, not like being in a storm-dark ship, searching for a body, trying to find the light. Those were *choices*, those were *head* things. She could walk away, close her eyes, shut the door; but *this*, this wasn't hers to decide, this was her body making it's mind up, hormones and babies and love and being out of control. And she was very frightened.

"It's not that I don't..." she said, but suddenly she couldn't see

And then she heard Trevor Jones, and Peter Mason, Billy Tingle. And Moira screeching "Bastard" as Titty's bloody little head swelling into the world; and she thought, "*responsibility*". And then she re-saw a picture of a man in a chair in a house, and the contents of a frying pan, and then she smelled the smell of burning flesh and she looked down at the plate before her, a one-by-four inch cut of beef, the blood oozing, butter, and she thought it would leap up and bite her, lick her, slobber over her face, a huge rasping pink-purple cow-tongue and foul cow-breath and and and...

And she was standing, her hand to her mouth, and retching into the hand, her face and her chest filling with heat as she rushed through to the toilet, crashing into there, vomit spraying as she slipped and her lights turned briefly down.

And then, as she came back into the light she realised; all this wet, this smell, and then something perverse made her think "*And they say romance is dead,*" and she was giggling and crying and Val was there, trying to pick puke-stuck hair off her face, but gagging because, like her, he couldn't out-think his body.

And she pushed him away from her, but her eyes were kind, and she whispered, "It's OK, now, baby. I'll be OK. Really. It was just the prawns, and not eating, and I'm a little tired . . ."

He didn't want to go.

"It's *OK,*" she said again, tenderly, like she'd heard it done in some film. "I'm fine now, really I am. I'll just – get out of these things, and, I'm fine, really, and I'm glad you love me."

And she closed the door.

III

[illegible]

"Today [illegible] all be [illegible] to the hot-dog man. You've heard, and I don't need to remind you what happens if it gets out. I want you out there hitting the markets, [illegible] restaurants and pubs plus [illegible] Greaves DC [illegible]

[illegible]

Forty-Nine

John Street, Monday 08:05

Twenty-something guys in the War Room, Caz. DCS Blackside was in Lewes with the Chief Constable; Bob Moore and DI MacInnes were going through the motions, the sergeant doing the honours.

"An IC-One male, medium to large build, height anywhere from five-nine to around six feet. No known employment, no fixed abode, possible northern accent. Name we have is John Rayner. Hair colour brown, average length. May walk with a limp, last seen wearing some sort of shiny purple jacket with a dragon pattern on the back. May ride a large Japanese bike, probably a Kawasaki."

"You didn't give us an age, Sarge."

"Twenty-five to forty-five."

There was a quick murmur and the slapple-snap of two dozen plastic pocket books closing. The DS raised a photocopy of Bourne's face, and it stared out, benign, dead, discomforting still to Caz.

"Today you'll all be trying to put a name to the hot-dog man. Yeah I've heard, and I don't need to remind you what happens if it gets out. I want you out there hitting the markets, shops, restaurants and pubs plus DC Greaves, DC Flood, you can door-knock round Hornby Terrace with PC Banks, and PC Tingle."

Another mumble.

"Yeah, I know. But I don't want any of you pulling your plonkers on this one. Let's get a name today, and see if we can find Rayner. Talk to your snouts. Flood, you need t'speak to Mr MacInnes?"

Caz nodded.

Tom MacInnes stood up. "OK, my office, fifteen minutes."

Caz recognised the signs; the jokes half-hearted, DCs and PCs slow to rise, slow to race downstairs for coffee, the two poor sods due to type reams of nothings into Holmes keen to re-tie their shoe-laces, adjust the already straight pictures on the wall, tidy a tidy desk – anything but sit in front of the computer. This one was a "going-nowhere" and they all knew it; an instinct, nothing more, but one of those cases. Shoe leather and disappointment. If it didn't rain it would be a miracle.

Caz didn't have time for coffee, but she told Greavsie, Billy and Gordon she'd be down soonest and not to eat the last sticky bun. Then she turned to the wall, the charts, the pictures; the image of John Bourne's face. She stared at it, trying to understand how she could dislikc him so much on no evidence, not anything in the face, at least nothing she could point to and nothing anyone else saw. The general reaction had been, "Could be any poor bugger!" and a shrug. But something, something . . .

She glanced at her watch – nine minutes – and nipped across the hall to Child Protection just to say hello, see who was round. She tapped the door apologetically, and then went in.

"Caz?"

"Jill. So how goes CP?"

"Are you taking an interest, Caz? I thought you reckoned this was a place for old duffers?"

Jill talked like an old school-teacher but was large, ever-shrinking on a long-term diet and with a frizz of dyed-blonde hair, more like a barmaid at first glance than anything else.

"Not me, Jill. It's just I get the feeling maybe that's what the force thinks."

"Maybe. Meanwhile we just try to help kids. There's coffee . . ."

Caz said yes straight away. Jill was like that, disarming, likeable. So what if she was a few minutes late for the DI?

They sat down and Jill said she understood that Caz knew Jack Sweet.

"Angel? I worked with him for a coupla days. Nice guy, quietish."

"Quiet, yes, but keen. Jack works all hours. He's on his own, isn't he? Got a bed-sit?"

"That's what he said to me. Hasn't he told you?"

Jill Bartholomew smiled. "Caz, I wouldn't pry."

"He's divorced," Caz said. "I think. I'm sure he is. No kids."

"Oh?"

"What d'you mean, 'oh'?"

"Oh, nothing. He just seems to be so good with the kids. Not many male officers have the knack. You have to be a bit of a kid yourself for them to take to you. Jack is very good."

"I can't say I'd thought about it, Jill. I don't know much about CP. Jack was saying I should chat to you."

"He was?"

Caz laughed. "Well, come on, Jill, who knows more about it than PC Bartholomew?"

Jill laughed back, a huge, unrestrained guffaw.

"OK," she said, "I know a bit. What d'you want to know?

"Just is it a farm. Career-wise, is it a dead-end?"

"Do it for a month and you won't care, Caz. Trust me."

Fifty

08:30

Caz walked down to Tom's office. This was a peculiar sensation. For the first time she could remember she felt lifeless, ageing. It felt like guilt. The door was open. She tapped lightly on the glass.

"Come in Flood!"

She would have preferred "Caz."

"And I'm not sure, sir, but I think maybe a change would help. I was wondering about Child Protection, if there's a place."

It was all Caz could do not to shake uncontrollably. She was letting him down, she knew it, failing him after all. He stood up and walked past her. He looked outside, both ways, then closed the door. As he came back he touched her shoulder then he went to the door which led to the DCS's office. He opened it, looked in, closed it.

"So, Caz," he put his finger to his lips. "What is it do you think? Do you think Lanzarote has caught up with you, is it this case? The DCS and myself, we did say ye shouldnee ha gone inta that room."

Caz looked at the cream wall above the DI. She thought briefly, incredibly vividly, about the man she had killed on the island. "No, sir. It's not Lanzarote."

"This case?"

"I don't know, sir. I just seem to have spent a year surrounded by death. I thought I could handle it, but now I'm not so sure."

"What's changed, Caz?"

"A question from a friend, Tom?"

He nodded.

"It's affecting me and Val. I don't think I can let that happen."

MacInnes seemed genuinely surprised. "Ah knowed y'was keen on the lad, Caz, but, no' that keen."

"I'm afraid so."

MacInnes shook his head. Momentarily, Caz was horrified, then she realised he was smiling. His eyes twinkled and then he reached down to the bottom drawer of his desk and pulled out a small bottle. He poured a capful and swigged it back after swilling it round his mouth for three seconds. Then he put the bottle away and took some extra-strong mints from another drawer. After popping one he offered the packet to Caz.

"I'd rather a wee drop o' that whisky," Caz said, her accent better than the DI's.

"Nae chance," MacInnes said, but he was grinning. She took a mint and sat back.

"I've been getting dreams, sir, and flashes, you know."

"Oh, ah know, Caz, ah know."

"I was worried. I thought that if I went sick, got counselling, it might affect me in the long-term. I wouldn't want that, especially if things between me and Val – especially if they don't work out."

"There's nowt wrong with counselling, Caz. Y'must know that by now. Hillsborough, Kings Cross, Bradford, Clapham, some o' the worst killing – we know all about Post Traumatic Stress, girl."

"I know that, Tom, but I'm not convinced getting treatment for it doesn't mark your card."

"It shouldnae."

"But it might. If I don't have to take the risk, I'd rather not."

"And what if I say I need you t'stay on the team?"

"I'll give you a week and then go sick, sir."

"It's that serious?"

"Me and Val, it's that serious, yes."

He reached back down to the bottom drawer, then slammed it shut again.

"Jesus, Caz, ah thought it was amazing enough when Vaunda and I got together, but I never thought ah'd see the day."

Caz shrugged, trying to be matter-of-fact, but she felt heavy.

"Neither did I, Tom. It all came together Saturday night. I just came to a crossroads. I've got to give me and Val a chance."

"OK," Tom said. "So what do y'want me t'do?"

"I wondered about Child Protection. Jack Sweet is in there and he'd rather be out with the big-hitters. Me, I need a rest. I thought maybe he and I could swap places."

The DI softened a little more. His eyes were still grey-blue, but Caz thought they had more shine than she remembered. This could only be Vaunda's doing.

"D'you know, Caz. Ah thought it was you that was to take over from me." Caz went to protest. "No, not as DI. Ah mean, the place needs one person where the job allus comes fust. Doesn't pay to mix work and pleasure, y'know?"

"I know *exactly*, Tom. That's why I want to step off the train."

"Even if there's a risk?"

"Even if there's a risk, yes."

He smiled. It was a peculiar smile. Love, loss, bewilderment.

"Ah'll see what I can do," he said. "Yu'll be OK for the rest of this week, if needs be?"

Fifty-One

17:00

At close of biz in the War Room they posted up the few pathetic bits and pieces they had on Bourne's behaviour. Caz had made up a fancy A2 white-board taking most of the afternoon and had helped out with getting the information into HOLMES. No-one said a word. No other door-to-doors had scored at all and there was not a sniff anywhere of John Rayner, fancy jackets or Japanese bikes.

Maybe the going-nowhere tag was a self-fulfilling prophecy, maybe it was the coldness, the sordid feel about it all, but there was just this *atmosphere*, and Caz, for the first time ever, didn't really mind if she missed being in on what was supposed to be a big one. She just couldn't feel for the victim, and this was new.

"A quick bit of info for you all," Moore said. "We're losing Flood for a coupla weeks – special project – and we're getting DS Sweet back. His must be the shortest-ever post to CP."

Caz remained impassive. Good old Tom!

"Right, I want nothing outstanding when y'go home tonight and tomorrow, here half-seven for eight."

The slowness of the guys rising, the variety of the "anything-but" chat, yep, Caz decided, it'll be good to be off this one. As Moore left she wondered about a quick drink with Tom before he sloped off to whisper sweet nothings to Vaunda. She was staring at the wall, the list of people

Bourne had spoken to, the people who appeared to know him a little, the ones that didn't know him at all . . .

She was walking around idly, waiting for the room to empty, wishing that she *felt* more, could get more involved with this one. It was strange to feel so little empathy and strange too that Bourne had made friends with some people and not even broken the ice with others. Then she heard Billy Tingle's voice. She turned round.

"What?"

Billy was smiling. Good sign. "Just off home. Saying goodnight."

Caz was distracted. "Oh, goodnight, Billy."

She turned back to the picture wall. Behind her she heard Billy mumble something and then the doors flap shut as he left. She was alone with John Bourne. Alone. Not alone. She had that War Room feeling, the buzz of the sudden silence, the ghosts, the sensations, the peculiar lack of noise that was louder than filtered-out banter.

She grabbed a chair, spun it and sat on it the wrong way round, leaning against its back, tilting it forward and hovering, balanced, then rocking like an autistic child, systematically looking up and down, left-to-right, trying to see something in the whole thing, coming back time and again to John Bourne's face.

"*I'm glad you're dead, You fucker!*"

It was a thought, sudden, but it was an actual voice, something like her own but not her own.

Jesus!

"You fucker! I'm glad you're dead."

Caz heard it again. She looked at Bourne. Was it the eyes, the mouth, the shape of the face, the ears? Was it that the smile didn't include the eyes? Why couldn't she feel bad about this? Then she heard herself speak.

"Yeah, me too, Bourne. Some like you, some don't take to you at all. You're a creep, aren't you? That it? That why you were killed?"

Then she heard the doors open and someone cough.

"Angel!"

"Billy said I might find you here."

"Yeah, too tired to go home. How's tricks?"

"Getting by. You fancy a drink?"
Caz looked at her watch. "Could do, I suppose."
She turned to look, almost wistfully, at the wall again.
"Something bugging you, Caz?"
Her voice was distant, echoey. "Yeah, yeah. But I can't put my finger on it." She unwound from the chair and shrugged upright. "Ah, who gives a fuck!" she said much more brightly, "Let's go get pissed."

They went to The Grapes. Angel was a pints man and he got Caz her usual whisky and ginger, a couple of packets of peanuts that he threw into the middle of the table. "The beer down here is *piss*," he said as an opener.
"That's why I drink Bells and Dry," Caz said. She raised her glass.
"Did you hear Bob Saint had to have a nail off?" Angel said. "Fucking splinter was way down under. He's on penicillin jabs in the arse."
"That's what you get for putting your hands in the wrong places."
Angel frowned and his head moved back an inch. He was definitely pausing. Then, as if a switch had clicked in his head, he said, "Oh, right!" and clicked on a wide, fuck-another-copper grin.
Caz smiled, "And Greavsie's madly in love with the woman from number twenty-three."
"The one with the two boys, three and four."
"Yer, on the ball."
"I'm a DS, Flood."
"On the ball, even for a DS. Anyone would think you were keen."
"On *Janice*? You're joking, right? She's way too young for me—"
"I meant on the job. As in keen to make DI. Jill Bartholomew said you were working all hours."
"Not really. I just don't go home. There's not a lot to rush back for."
"I guess." She sipped her drink. "You been divorced long, Jack?"
"Nine months. I lost her nine months ago. It's why I

transferred down here – that and the guns and drugs, the kids on mountain bikes delivering smack."

"We've got plenty of drugs down here."

"Not like Manchester, Caz. That's a different world. It's Dodge City now, Moss Side. It's not that I couldn't hack it – it's more what it makes you like. You fight fire with fire and it changes you. You drive around armed all the time, most the time, your attitude changes, suddenly it's a war. It's not right."

"What's not right?"

"Well, wanting the confrontations. Hoping a few guys will take each other out or that they'll pop off something at a patrol car, so we can give them a big slap and show the law still has a bite. It's like they've got gangs and we're one. I didn't like it that much."

"So you got out, came down here?"

"I nearly went to the Met, but I was worried I'd end up in the same situation. I don't want to be a village bobby, but I don't want to be carrying, either."

"So you ended up here."

"So I ended up here."

Caz smiled. "So Angel, you eat Italian?"

"Does a bear shit in the woods?"

"Drink up," Caz said.

Fifty-Two

They walked down to Armando's. Caz hadn't bothered to ring Val who always worked late anyway. She figured she could just walk up to his flat later, after the *zabaglione.* If Val decided they should go out, she'd grin and bear it, watch him eat whatever, and chew some breadsticks. The thought pleased her.

It was a cool September evening, the school holidays gone and Brighton just about getting ready to settle down for the winter. They both wore jackets which made the cool feel pleasant. It was one of those edged-off, wind-down sunny evenings where the world smelled good and it still felt like hope was just around the corner.

"It makes me wonder . . ." Angel said.

"What does?"

"A night like this. You can smell the sea; there's something good and right in the world and everyone should be happy, but there's so much shit out there, like sewage in the channel; people being ripped off, killed, women attacked, little kids . . ."

"Isn't that why we're coppers?"

"Oh, sure, but I wonder sometimes. We're like those special guys at Disney, following the elephant parade and tidying the shit away. No one stops it happening. You know how many kids get killed every year by their parents, Caz? I don't mean kids get killed by cars, by drunks, I don't mean kids killed in stupid accidents. I don't mean stranger murders, just killed by their parents."

"You mean like Maria Colwell?"

"Yeah. Maria, Sadie Hart, James Ribb."

"I'd guess at one or two a year, five maybe."

"Try one a week."

"Are you serious?"

"Of course I'm serious! In 1990 there were fifty-four deliberately caused deaths of children in the UK. One a fucking week! These are the proved cases. Never mind the unproved ones or the kids who are badly injured but survive. Never mind the sexual abuse, emotional abuse. Caz, I'm just talking one thing, parents murdering their kids. Fifty-four a year."

"I had no idea."

They stopped to cross a road. A couple of seagulls left a rooftop, screamed and swooped away.

Angel watched them then turned his head to speak. "I had *some* idea, but not the scale. We're a pretty shitty animal, Caz."

"We know this."

"Yeah we know this. Most crime we can understand. Burglary, shop-lifting, the betting-shop robberies last week, a lot of murders, rape. But there are some things that I can't understand, can't even think of explaining away."

"Like our hacked-up man? Like Bourne?"

"No," Angel said.

"No?"

"No. My instinct there is that he might have deserved it."

"What? No-one could deserve that! All his bits . . ."

"Well, a lot of that was done post-mortem wasn't it? Looks more to me like he was a drugs dealer or something and he was tortured for some information."

"And that's deserve?"

"Maybe deserve is the wrong word. I just have this feeling that we'll find out our Mister Bourne wasn't lily-white, that he got what was coming."

"Jesus!" Caz said. "Maybe you did work Moss Side a bit too long."

"Maybe I did."

They were outside the restaurant. Caz touched Angel's arm.

"Hokay. We change the subject, right? Talk about something else? I can tell you about my running or show you my holiday snaps. You must have a hobby."

Angel stopped. The switch again. Cerlunk.

"OK," he said.

Caz pushed him in through the door. She was laughing at something he had just said.

But she was thinking. "*I'm glad you're dead, you fucker!*"

Fifty-Three

In the ultra-violet light of the restaurant's foyer, Angel looked even more angelic. His white shirt bright, the whites of his eyes shining, and his golden curls made him look more like the Pear's kid Bubbles than a hard-nosed fifteen-years-in-the-job copper. Caz was grinning as she looked past for Gabriele, her very favourite waiter.

"What's so funny?" the DS said in an awkward, half-embarrassed way, almost as if he guessed he was the object of the laughter.

Caz saw Gabriele speaking to some other customers. He raised one finger. *Uno momento.*

"I don't think you want to know, Jack."

"Know what?"

"That I think I just guessed your other nickname."

"I doubt it, but try me."

"I thought you didn't like it?"

"I don't want it used, true, but I don't want to sit opposite you for the next hour or so and watch you break out into a stupid grin every couple of minutes."

"We won't fall out?"

"We will if you keep this up."

"The Pears' advert? The naff little kid looking up at some floating bubbles? Am I right? Oh look our table's ready."

"Fuck!" Angel said.

Caz was yards away.

"They do Il Grigio here, a *Chianti Classico Riserva*, absolutely *magnifico*! I recommend."

"I don't drink wine."

"Hey don't sulk, everyone drinks wine."

"Not me. I'll have a beer."

"But that means I'll have to drink a bottle by myself and I'm supposed to be in—"

"Cazee, *mia bella*! Il Grigio?"

Fuck it.

"Yes, please, Gabriele. This is Jack Sweet, a colleague."

Gabriele extended a ham-fat hand. He had the strongest fingers Caz had ever seen and his party trick was snapping corks. He shook with Angel and then nodded through some sort of *mano-a-mano* exchange. He seemed to approve.

"And a beer for me," Angel said.

Gabriele grinned with the whole of his huge body. "*Si, senor*. For a minute I think David Gower. I am sorry. Lager OK? Carlsberg?"

"Carlsberg's fine," Angel said. Gabriele left, chuckling.

"How the fuck did you know, Flood?"

"What about, the Il Grigio?"

"Bubbles!"

She was grinning ear to ear. "Dunno, Sarge. I just saw you in a certain light and—"

"Fuck you!"

She feigned seriousness. "I won't say a word. I promise."

"Thanks."

"But it's not that bad, is it? It's not that much worse than being called Angel, surely?" She looked at him, ten years older.

"Bad enough," he said heavily. "But it's a very long story." They had Dracula-drool garlic bread, Caz taking it steady with the Chianti, Sweet doing the opposite with one, two, three quick lagers. Caz wasn't sure why she was making a pretence. Fast or slow, she was going to drink all the wine, and Sergeant Jack, well, for a gun-toting Little Lord Fauntleroy, he was OK, good company, and she was already trying to think who she could set him up with for a blind or a half-blind date.

"So, you getting out much, Angel? Since the divorce I mean."

"Too much to do. Things. No." The sharp edge was off his voice.

"D'you ever hear from—"

He cut her short. "No. That's dead. Talk about something else."

"Like what? Sex, politics, religion? The job?"

"How about your running? I heard you were pretty good, good enough to run for England."

Caz tilted her almost empty glass. "I was. But the job, and a little bit of this, it's hard. My fellah wants me to go on the wagon for a year or so and see what I can get my times down to. I'm tempted, but I think the bastard's just trying to trick me into going teetotal."

"That so bad?"

"It is as long as we keep getting bodies, like John Bourne. You think I went home after seeing that and had a cup of Bournvita?"

"I guess not. Seeing some guy with a piece of cooked dick in his mouth – not exactly easy to deal with."

"It wasn't. Billy Tingle was worse than me, but then he was there with it for a long time."

"So you have a drink?"

"Yup. But tonight I've got no excuse – except I'm out with a mate and I fancy a few glasses."

"Seems pretty normal to me."

"Me too. But Val won't approve."

"Val?"

"The fellah, we're engaged. He works at American Express. We walked past his house on the way here."

Angel asked what Valerie did at Amex, but Caz's mind was racing. Two things. She spoke again.

"Hey, are you looking to buy a place or rent? Only if your bed-sit is as bad as you say it is – well, between me and Val, we've got a spare place. I'm in Inkerman Terrace, Val's flat is two streets away from here, very handy for the nick. You interested?"

She could see Gabriele coming with the dinners. Fresh Turbot.

"I could be," Angel said.

Fifty-Four

Tuesday

Very early, still dark, you wake from a nightmare. You and Jack Sweet are standing over someone and he's saying, "Go on, the shit deserves it!" Your eyes click open. You're at Valerie's. Last night you had a terrible fight. You came back from Armando's quite late, badly drunk and Valerie wasn't amused. He wanted to know where the fuck you'd been, you could have called. You said, "On a case!" and he said you were a piss-head.

You and Jack, somehow or other you had more than just the bottle and you let a few secrets go. Jack was asking about what happened on the island and you said how glad you were, glad you'd killed a guy. He was sympathetic. Sometimes that's the way justice is, he said, something like that. You were having your second royale coffee and the brandy and sugar and cream were so good. *Jack said that there had been times when he wished he'd not held back and you thought, "He's bullshitting me, he's been there already."*

But you remembered when you were both leaving, about the flat and you thought, when you got in, how you'd be extra romantic and say to Val, "Hey, let's sell one of the flats!" and once he had agreed you'd tell him about Jack and then with a bit of luck, on the lounge floor, to that French group, Bronx.

But somehow, and there was the fight and oh shit and now you feel awful. You want to stroke his back but you know that anything you do right now will be wrong. You get out of bed.

And you pee, wash your face, then walk through to the lounge. You've got no clothes on and it's a little cold. You walk on eggs back to the bedroom, grab the nearest thing, Val's dirty shirt. It smells of him. You put it on. You walk back into his lounge and you sit in a chair and you wonder why you can't just be ordinary. It makes you want to cry but you've forgotten how.

Last night Jack told you about paedophiles and you drank.

"They plan, Caz. We are talking long, long term. We are talking pure, committed, spread-over-years, long-term evil. You know the lonely-hearts columns? Lots of guys, right? Lots of young mothers too. You wanna know what these bastards do?

"You want to fuck eight-, nine-year old boys? You're a sick shit who buggers tiny children? Go get the lonely hearts. Pick out the mums with two, three lads all coming up to eight. No, you love *kids, you tell her on the phone, you absolutely* love *them. A month down the line you've moved in and you're working on the oldest, just waiting for his younger brothers to mature.*

"I had the misfortune to interview one of these shits, Caz. Know what he said? 'I just give her one now and again, to keep her quiet.' They plan, Caz. But get near them, they can switch it off. One of the reasons they're so hard to catch."

Angel is on his fifth or six pint, maybe it's his seventh. He's very controlled but his eyes are dark and there's hate and disgust there but you feel exactly the same. You don't know how this came about but it was after you said about the island.

"And babies, Caz, I mean infants, I mean they don't walk yet. You know why?"

You shake your head.

"The suck reflex, Caz. Put anything in a baby's mouth, it sucks."

And you're not so much disgusted as angry. Angry, angry, angry. Now you know that there are at least a thousand incidents for every conviction. There are sex tourists, fathers who rape their daughters, sometimes with help from the wife. And there are gangs, networks who pass information by phone, by the Internet. And there are kids go missing, kids drugged, gang-banged at "parties" then lost, they must be dead.

And Angel tells you how he's seen the pictures of the things men can do to children, things so awful he won't tell you, you'll have to read the books yourself. He tells you there are nearly fifty thousand kids on child protection registers and only a quarter actually in care. He says do you realise that means there are at least thirty-five thousand children known to be in danger and still with the people most likely to hurt them.

"Poisoning," he says, "Pinching, Punching, Slapping, Lashing, Raping, Scalding, Burning, Starving, Cutting, Buggering. Choose your evil, they're all on record, photographed, documented, filed away."

You can see he wants to cry, this hurts so much. But there's something else, some wild instinct and you want to leave now with Angel and find one of these bastards and kick him shitless.

"You want to know," he says coldly, "why Child Protection is as big as CID?" He looks straight at you. "Because the kids can't fight back. Some of them can't even talk. It's a sickness, and it's everywhere, and someone's got to try to help, try to help."

And he looks at you, and you feel him making a decision. And he takes a breath and shakes his head, and he looks at you again, and he shakes his head again.

"Go home to your bloke," he says.

Fifty-Five

Now it's cool-cold early morning grey. Maybe you'll make some coffee, as quietly as you can. But you're wondering already, is Child Protection going to be a rest? Angel has told you it'll break your heart, so many, so many get away with it. If the child is under five he can't testify, that's if he ever told the mother, that's if the mother believed him, that's if there was enough for the police to even approach the molester.

And as the kettle rumbles and you have your hand on the handle to quiet it, you remember when you stopped believing in God and you think why is the world so wretched, and you think, you think, Oh, Valerie, Valerie, you have no idea; the little bit of pain you've seen, you have absolutely no idea.

And now, you're back in the big cream chair and your legs are tucked under you and your finger-tips are cold and you wrap the cup and you decide you'll let Valerie be your husband and you'll try, you'll try, but you know, you, your dad, Tom MacInnes, Angel, there aren't that many left and you can't give up fighting.

And you uncurl, you find some paper. You write on it carefully.

You write on it, Valerie, I love you, I don't want to wait. We'll sell a flat, both the flats, do the I do and give it a try. I love you chicken-shit, and if you love me, remember I mean it. And remember I'm a bobby. It's what I do.

Then you go to the bedroom, look at him a while, then you pick up your clothes, get dressed and leave.

Fifty-Six

07:00

It wasn't much after five-thirty when you got home; you'd jogged there from Val's, through yellow-lit streets, below the faint buzz of misted neon, past dark reflected windows, chemists, travel agents, wool-pattern shops, smiling faces, perfect teeth, families of four.

It was about two miles and you felt uncomfortable in jeans, Tee and top, but you ran all the way, steady eightish, and when you got to the prom the wind was in your face, the sea was high and spray was lifting, stinging. And you knew, as soon as you got in you'd be changing and you'd be going back out, in shorts and vest, looking for the cold.

You stretched quickly, your head still hurting from last night, and then you slipped out, your house key strapped to your shoe and ran back towards Valerie but only as far as the Palace Pier. You loved the sheen of morning damp, sea-damp, thick enough to glisten, thin enough to tread. And you ran fast, faster, faster, faster.

The sea was green-grey, the cobbled beach brown-grey, and when you slapped down the steps and headed west, memories rushed in; of villains hopelessly escaping across the shingle, of once stepping into the littered dark beneath the disused pier-stub, of running cruel intervals in the shifting pebble-wet until you collapsed, cursed and washed away some other pain, some other time.

Caz came home, undressed, showered, then slipped into a

deep pink bath, impossibly hot. In the lounge, not too loud, Harry Chapin, a voice so achingly happy-sad she always wondered what kind of lover he would have been. He was dead, of course, and she knew that some people were meant to be memories, that gone they were more special, browner, warmer, more golden.

Tom MacInnes had promised her an answer asap on her going over to the Isle of Wight to see James Munro. He'd tried to get her to toss the rapist's interview back to Peter Mason and she'd had to explain that Trevor Jones had said . . .

"OK, Flood. I'll talk to the DCS, soonest."

She figured, today, maybe tomorrow, and she wondered, should she drift away from the case, was it right? Didn't she know as much as anyone, feel as much as most, didn't she have a responsibility?

She closed her eyes and thought back, re-played things, waited until she could see Bob Moore, the War Room, rippled with light.

She listened again.

"One: Victim rendered unconscious, strapped into chair.

"Two: The castration, while unconscious.

"Three: Wound cauterised with the iron found in the kitchen.

"Four: A time elapsed.

"Five: Some fingers removed while the victim is conscious: mouth was taped. Face showed signs of tape being applied, removed, and re-applied. May have been another time lapse. Most likely scenario is that then the victim fainted. Traces of ammonia in the nostrils suggest use of smelling salts.

"Six: The rest of the fingers, the thumbs, the toes, were removed after death, ditto the lips, nose, ears.

"Seven, some sort of large pruning shears, curved blade used for the fingers and toes, something like a Stanley knife used on the face and the belly. The belly looked liked a few swipes, like this . . ."

What was it? What was she forgetting, not hearing? Or was she remembering exactly what she had heard? Didn't she trust herself? She stroked, soaped idly between her legs, opening her eyes, closing them, running the scene by again.

"One: Victim rendered unconscious, strapped into chair.

"Two: The castration, while unconscious.

"Three: Wound cauterised with an iron.

"Four: Time elapsed.

"Five: Fingers removed while the victim conscious: mouth taped. Tape applied, removed, re-applied. Another time lapse. Victim fainted. Traces of ammonia in the nostrils. Smelling salts.

"Six: Fingers, thumbs, toes, remove. Lips, nose, ears.

"Seven, some sort of large pruning shears, curved blade used for the fingers and toes, something like a Stanley knife used on the face and the belly. The belly looked liked a few swipes, like this . . ."

She warmed the water up with some hot. The top surface reached the overflow and slurped away. She realised, "I'm hungry", started thinking about breakfast, started thinking about Valerie waking, his breakfast, remembering a breakfast once with Moira in a café in Southampton, 5:30 a.m., bacon butties and hot sweet tea.

She was thinking about something missing. A difference between DS Moore's presentation and what she knew. It wouldn't come. She relaxed, wallowed deeper, waited, but no. Bastard!

Now here she was, parked up underneath John Street already, 07:21 and bright as a bunny, walking through the nick's back corridors, sniffing at the morning, in before everyone except maybe Blackside and MacInnes, raring – for some God-forsaken reason – to go.

She started in the canteen; two coffees, one with a lid, one with extra milk, then went up the back stairs to check out her desk, then through to the War Room, the second coffee in her hand.

She sipped, listening, her shoulders slightly lifting every time she heard an outside noise. She looked at Bourne, the ripped up face, the rebuild photo, the best-guess artist's try, and then Ernie King's sketch. The more she looked, the more she saw *interpretation*, the more she saw an opinion. Ernie King didn't like Bourne.

"Sammy was off school, and this Mr Bourne, he took quite a shine to 'im. He seemed like a real nice bloke."

"Well, I didn't take to 'im. 'E was a bit smarmy for me."

"But you can't blame a bloke for being well-spoken."

"He called himself Brown. John Brown. He didn't, like, say, 'My name is Brown, John Brown', like in the films, but when he spoke to us, he said his name was Brown and then, when he was talking to Sammy, he said his name was John."

"Well, it was just he came back a few times, that first day and the next few days. He was quite keen on the house and we gave him Ray Patel's number."

She looked at the picture again. It was there, a vague distaste, the eyes slightly hooded maybe, the smile incomplete? It wasn't Mona Lisa but the enigma was there. There was *something*. If there wasn't, she needed another holiday.

She heard the first few blokes coming in, filling the corridor, the usual banter, one or two words, maybe as many as five not ending "uck" or "it", and a sprinkling of "wankers!" to show linguistic range.

Bang-Slap!! and the door opened, Ken Mitchell, Frank Lloyd, Ray Carver, Joey Jones.

"Hey, it's Cinderella!"

"Fuck off, Ken. Morning Ray, morning Joey, morning Frank."

"You in or out, Flood?" Ray asked. "I thought you was off on some dildo project."

"You know how it is, Raymond. I woke up early and thought, what should I do, wash my hair, wash my smalls or come in to the nick early and tidy everything up for the boys?"

"And?"

"My knickers were in the laundry and my hair was fine."

Mitchell grunted. "And the boys got lucky!"

"You still here, Ken? I thought you had an appointment at the VD clinic this morning?"

Ken grinned. "Ain't love grand?"

"Sure," Caz said.

Then she made them an offer they couldn't refuse. She'd get the coffees in – *if* if they'd just tell her what happened to John Bourne.

"Trick question, right?"

"Go and get the fucking coffees, Flood!"

No movement.

"OK. Guy got zapped, his bits cut off, his dick fried, the face stuff, fingers and toes, stomach."

"Thanks, Ken. Ray?"

"Yeah."

"Can you actually tell me? Say the words?"

"Ken just said."

"No, he didn't."

"Go and get the drinks in, Flood."

She stared.

"OK. John Bourne, known-as, approx age fifty, IC1 male. Own home, rented; overcome by assailant, tortured, castrated, penis found in kitchen, partially cooked. Some injuries before, some after death due to heart failure. Masking tape across the mouth had been ripped off a few times. Someone after information—"

"Joey?"

"You getting off on this, Flood?"

Caz blanked him. After a second he responded.

"Ditto what Ray said. Fingers, toes, mouth, ears, nose. Ha, a poet! Some of it hurt, some didn't matter. Frying pan job, that didn't matter either, yer man was well dead. Coffee?"

"And you, Frank?"

Frank turned round, feigning stupidity which was double-bluff.

"Well this bloke, white, fat, bollock-naked only he didn't have any – bollocks, that is. All his problems had been ironed out though. Late night cookery course, courtesy of his guest, but he was already out of it, dead to the world, you know?"

"I'll be back in five minutes!" Caz said.

She rushed out, down the corridor, ten yards.

"Oi, Flood!" Mitchell shouted after her, head between

the War Room doors. “And four Kit-Kats; and an Eccles cake!”

Above her head she showed the finger.

She hurried on down to the canteen.

Fifty-Seven

"Caz, it's really nice to see you. *Confusing*, but nice. Take a seat and park yer bot."

Jill Bartholomew was smiling her large, made-up face beaming from somewhere in there, between the left and right hand shock of dyed barmaid-blonde.

"You probably know, but I'll tell you anyway. You won't be able to do any interviews until you've attended the course on techniques. We do 'joints', always, with the social services and the big thing is, with these kids, is trying not to disturb them, and more-so, not leading them. We have to be so careful."

"I'm not exactly sure what I'm doing here, Jill, It was a kind of instinct thing, not an impulse but—"

"Hey, Caz, don't bother to explain. You've got a good reputation and we're pleased to have you."

"You said confusing?"

Jill smiled again, the corner of her eyes crinkling. "I did, didn't I? I was thinking about Jack Sweet coming in, saying something about you then he's out and you're here. Just funny."

"Angel was talking about me?"

"Asking questions, mostly. There were those rumours about what happened to you in Lanzarote. He was curious. Then he said he thought you were a ruddy good copper and you'd be good in CP."

"Oh?" Caz said. "And what did you say to that?"

"I laughed. I said you thought this was duffer-land."

Caz took a long, slow breath.

"We had meal last night, Armando's. Angel told me some things. Whatever, I know the job's important now."

That smile again. Kids must love her.

"Good! Good! Let's get some coffee!"

The DI had said, "Isle of Wight, OK, tomorrow." It was cleared with the DCS but DS Mason from Southampton would have to go along. MacInnes shook his head when she tried to argue. "No buts, Flood, that's the way it is. Jones can't be your snout and James Munro is from off their patch too. It's that or nuthin'. Make do as best y'can."

She had asked about intelligence, mentioned the Bitterne burning over in Southampton. Not the same MO, but worth looking at, did the DI think? It was all in hand, McInnes said.

"Nick Evans passed a note through on it. Ah've spoke already to your DS Mason and his DI, Denham. We've been comparing notes, but the only similars are the lack of any ID. They're following up a lead. Seems their man may have owed someone a lot of money."

"No problem, sir. That's why I didn't mention it yesterday. Nick doesn't miss much and I knew Mason was aware of both ends. Just a thought was all."

"No problem. You're meeting DC Bartholomew later?"

"Half-nine, sir."

"She's good, Caz. Don't jump to any conclusions."

"Conclusions?"

"Y'know what I mean, Flood."

10.45

Caz and Jill Bartholemew walked along another typically John Street scruffy corridor towards the child interview suite. Jill was explaining how they tried to make it as much like a home as they could. The kids, often traumatised, had to be made comfortable.

They turned and suddenly the walls were wallpapered, and the flat green doors were wooden, dark and with brass handles.

"Here," Jill said. Caz stepped in.

No venetian blinds, but curtains, more wallpaper, heroes in bright colours, reds, blues, greens; Superman, Power Rangers, Batman & Robin, Captain Kirk. Instead of a flourescent strip-light, a lampshade shaped like a hot-air balloon and slung underneath, a mini-basket with a tiny teddy looking out, down, waving.

The furniture – a corner suite, not too expensive, chain-store brown and fawn, rib-striped, a few scattered navy-blue cushions. On the floor, a fitted carpet, pale blue and unnoticeable; elsewhere, a blackboard, a whiteboard, paper, crayons, dolls, toys, Lego, an old wooden train, a television up on a raised bracket. On one wall, a felt stick-em-on board, a large mirror.

"Two-way?" Caz asked.

"We film all interviews. But we tell the kidlets everything about it. We show them the control room, and the cameras, let them see how everything works and we ask them if it's OK. They always say yes. They get to be on TV! You can watch from through there, Caz. This is Jimmy Bright's sixth time. He's just about starting to come out with what happened."

"And what did happen?"

"Just watch, love. Keep an open mind."

Fifty-Eight

Just watch, love, keep an open mind.

Caz sat in a small studio-style room, about twelve by six feet with a few electronic bits and pieces, a small dashboard of lights and a large Fergusson colour television. Somewhere a videotape rolled slowly and sound quietly recorded. She watched an empty room.

Caz could hear a faint buzz of electricity and already she felt drowsy. Then the sitting-room door opened and a little boy walked in, pretty and blonde, he could have been Val's. He looked no older than four, tops. He ran to the box of Lego. Jill followed through the door, and then a woman in her late thirties, full without being fat, page-boy hair and squeezed into designer jeans and top. She nodded to Jill and walked to a corner to pretend to potter. Jill sat down on a sofa and grabbed a cushion to hold to her stomach.

The boy ignored them and played more or less normally. Once he looked up at the camera, at Caz, and her stomach lurched. She saw something missing or something added to the "boy" of his face, but she couldn't be sure. She whispered to herself, "Open mind, Caz, open mind."

Then, cheekily, Jill said, "Well, I dunno, Marje. You'd think after all me trouble I could get a car made've Lego, wouldn't yer?"

Jimmy glanced back at Jill as the social worker turned round.

"I mean, I made an aeroplane, diddun I? You'd think, you know, you would, that maybe a little car . . ."

Jimmy Bright had put together something out of camera-shot and was whizzing it back and forward, making vrrrum noises.

"But there again," Jill was laughing just a bit, the cushion pulled into her tummy, "maybe no-one we know knows how to make a car."

Marje came in on cue. She was kneeling down now.

"Well, *I* know how to make a car, Jill."

"Well, I do too," Jill said. "It was just . . ."

The boy pushed something across the floor, then looked away. Jill leaned forward to pick it up.

"Oh, wow!" she said and slid quickly off the sofa. "Look at my car, Marje!"

Marjorie came forward on her knees and caught the whizzed over model. "Hey!" she said, "Cool!"

The boy looked quickly over, quickly away again. Jill looked up at Caz and gave a hidden thumbs-up and a sign for one-two minutes.

Then Jimmy said, "I'm good at cars."

Fifty-Nine

Caz was wrong, there was still something that could make her cry.

When it was over, when these two sweet women knew for sure and yet again that the little boy was still stuck at the point where the fear stopped his breathing, when the memory, the way the man had said "It's a secret, Jimmy!" and had talked of monsters, dead parents, children being eaten, children being locked away, sent away, kept in the dark – when all this, so quiet, so obvious, so inadmissable had happened for the third time and Caz could see the pain in Jill Bartholemew's eyes, feel it in herself, feel the impotent anger, she let go. And when the interview room emptied, she slipped out quickly, mumbled something at the three of them and went quickly past to the toilets. There she kicked a few things, clenched a fist, wished foul murder on the low-life who had done this, locked herself away, came out, blew her nose, washed, and went back to work.

She went first to see the DI and or Bob Moore. Tom was out, but Bob was playing with a chart.

"Sarge, just clarifying what we are sitting on, ref John Bourne."

He told her.

"That's what we're keeping from the press?" she asked.

"Yes."

"And the lads?"

"We're not keeping anything from the lads, Flood."

"You sure, Sarge?"

"What do you mean, am I sure, detective? Do I look feeble?"

"Your formal run-through, Sarge, you never mentioned that the guy's dick had been cooked. I'm sure you didn't."

"So what? Billy might have said something. Maybe the doc leaked it or S-O-C. No secrets in the nick, Flood, you know that."

"Yes, there are, Sarge. We're keeping it from the rank and file at other nicks, keeping it from the press. You said you knew everyone knew about the fry-up. You said if it got out you'd go looking for whoever mouthed off and he'd be in deep, deep shit."

"Fer fuck's sake, Flood, are you my answering machine or my conscience? Get to the bloody point!"

"Sarge, what, *exactly*, mustn't we tell the press?"

"You're taking the piss now, Flood . . ."

"Please, Sarge."

"I don't know what you're on, Flood, but the DI said you were going into Child Protection. Sounds like a good idea."

"Sarge, will you tell me? Just tell me?"

"*Jesus!*"

"OK. I'll go to Blackside."

Moore's face reddened. "Don't threaten me, Flood."

Caz came back calmly. "Sergeant, it's important. I simply want you to say what it is that me and the guys have to keep a lid on, that's all. No threat, but I've got to know. *Exactly.*"

Moore stood up and slammed open a filing-cabinet drawer so violently that the cabinet moved. He came out with the file and scrabbled through paperwork. He read angrily from his notes. "No mention, directly, indirectly, or via any joke, aside or innuendo, shall be made to the specific sexual injury to the deceased; nor shall any mention, directly, indirectly, or via joke, aside or innuendo, be made of the fact that the victim's penis was partially cooked."

"That's it? You're sure?"

"Get out of here, Flood."

"Nothing more?"

"Get *out* of here, Flood. As in piss off."

Caz felt cold. "Yes, Sarge."

She walked back to CP, rounding one corner as Jill Bartholomew came the other way. Jill mis-read the look on Caz's face.

"You OK, Caz?"

"I think so, Jill. That poor kid."

"It's a pig of a case, Caz. The way things are going, we won't be able to do anything. We know something happened to the kid, we know where, and we can narrow it down to one of three guys – but needless to say, none of them have a record. We can't *prove* anything, and they co-operate fully, of course."

"Isn't that what people are supposed to do?"

"Caz, if someone accused your chap of molesting a little boy or girl, do you think he'd be shocked, very angry, defensive, hostile?"

"Yes."

"We went to see the main suspect. He was sweetness and light, couldn't have been more helpful. He smarmed all over us with a twinkle in his eye."

"So maybe he's not the molester."

"And he's not *angry*, he's not shocked? He doesn't feel insulted? They have to *remember* to be insulted, Caz. They spend their lives learning to act out their rôle; that extra special neighbour, one of the few people you'd trust with your kid. The call-on-me-at-any-time baby-sitter. We turn up and they're not angry *enough*."

"Not exactly evidence, is it?"

"Let's go to lunch," Jill said.

Sixty

It was barely twelve-thirty as they stepped out past the front-desk, and into bright sun; out from yellow-green corridors, a dull front foyer, and from not so long ago, a bright, rainbow-toyed room. Late fat summer. So why did the world look wrong?

"There's a little place I know, Caz. My treat, OK?"

Warmer than last night, brighter and sunnier than yesterday, golden and gleaming; and acute sadness.

"Sure," Caz said.

Down the far end of the long-sloped street, cars passing at ninety-degrees, beyond those, white fencing, beyond that what would be the drop from the sea wall, beyond the sea. – people drown in the sea – and beyond that France, so they said.

"You're thinking about Jimmy," Jill said.

"Yes," Caz said.

The café was in a small side street, Greens posters on one wall, a quaint CND badge on another, and on another wall a bald old man staring across a centre-page at an equally bald baby; in the background an orange and black mushroom cloud and scribbled across the bottom of the picture, *Could we have done more?*

The owner wore dungarees, her hair turbanned out of sight like a war-working factory girl. Her smile for Jill was huge and real.

"The usual?" she said.

"And a menu for my friend," Jill said.

They sat down by a laced window. Caz thought she could smell a long-dead smell of spliff. Jill nodded and smiled.

"Janet, twice a day, every day, ten-thirty and three-thirty, just the one, while the shop door is locked. Sometimes I come over late on Saturday and we share a couple, plot the demise of John Major. We all have our dreams."

Caz showed her surprise. "Jill, I just never would've . . ."

Jill shrugged but smiled too. "You don't know that much, do you, sweetheart? Best look at the menu." She leaned across and tapped the top. "I have the special, it's cottage cheese with lots and lots of fresh fruit, a couple of Ryvita's."

Caz looked up.

"About some things. Important things," Jill said.

For some reason Caz didn't want to argue. "Sounds good, what's it called?"

Jill was making a complex series of gestures towards the kitchen. "I dunno, Caz. Janet calls it, 'Can I have some more fresh fruit to cover up the taste of this shitty cottage cheese, please'. And coffee?"

"Please."

"Real coffee, or something that's good for you?"

"Dangerous, please."

Jill made a few more gestures, then satisfied, she dropped her eyes slightly and her smile changed. Caz waited.

"That this morning. It got to you, right?"

"Yes."

"You're going to find things tough, Caz."

"I know."

"Get it right, you can save some of these kids."

"I know."

"Wrong, you can hurt them, hurt some others, too."

"I know that too, Jill."

"Well, it's a start, I suppose." She leaned back as the coffees were delivered, then forward again as Janet moved away. "OK," she said, very softly, "let me tell you exactly what happened to little Jimmy."

Sixty-One

"It's nothing like as neat as this, understand that. It comes out in dribs and drabs, bits and pieces, lots of confusion, doubt, little things that don't make sense, things that worry the mum, the dad. It can take ages to get to the truth, often we never get there. There are times we can look in the face of a child molester and know there's nothing we can do. It's hard, Caz."

The tropical salad, cheese, came, two more coffees. Outside the street went by.

"Mummy got the first whisper, the smallest thing. Little Jimmy was playing and saying he had two daddies, that was all.

"The first time she left it, but the next day Jimmy was unusually quiet, and then he started talking with a slightly different voice. He had a daddy at home and a daddy with a motor-bike.

"Jimmy's mum told Jimmy's dad. She still thought nothing of it, but she imagined her old man might think she had a boyfriend."

Jill paused. "Eat yer stuff, Caz."

"Dad got involved, his name is Tom. He's an English teacher and he'd done some counselling. He showed some sense and was easy on the kid. He laughed around it, very gently. He had an instinct he said; he just *knew* something was different. Of course, as soon as they *thought* something was different, they kept seeing things. But he wanted to be sure it was real. He wrote down all the odd things

Jimmy said, looked at the tiny clues, tried to work out what was going on with his kiddie."

Jill paused again and when she stared, Caz ate a mouthful of the cottage cheese with a slice of banana.

"Try to appreciate, Caz, the first thing you think of isn't that someone is molesting your baby. If you're a nice human being it's hard for a thought like that to come close. It's one of the things that the men who do this bet on.

"But there were other things. Jimmy started to wake up screaming, and be inconsolable. Then he started to fill his pants in the evenings after a year of being dry and clean. Then he started being violent, and then he started being so sexual with his parents, particularly the father, that they became uncomfortable."

Sixty-Two

"Sarah . . ."

"Sarah?" Tom laughs and slaps his own head. "That's a funny name for a daddy!"

"Sarah."

"Is Sarah a boy or a girl?"

"A man!"

"Have you got any man-teachers? Who looks after you?"

"Vicky and Josey and Sharon and the other Sharon."

"Which Sharon do you like best?"

"My Sharon. Big Sharon looks after the tweenies, and my Sharon helps me with cutting-out, Play-Doh and when we do dressing up."

"And Sarah's one of the lady teacher—"

"No, Sarah's a man! I said."

"But I thought Sarah was a girl's name. Do you know any girls called Sarah?"

"Sarah McCauley."

"So is this Sarah, Sarah McCauley?"

Jimmy shakes his head. "No, silly! My daddy-Sarah isn't a girl. My daddy-Sarah is a man."

"Who is your daddy?"

"You're being silly!"

"Am I?"

"You're my daddy and you married mummy!"

"But you told mummy you had another daddy, one called Sarah."

"No."

And now little Jimmy won't look at you, your chest is full of something you can only sense, you feel unbelievably angry but lost and bewildered too. Can you phone someone? Who? Who do you ask for and what do you say?

Carol brings you a drink, a strong one and you sip it, half-seeing some kid's show on the telly. You thought it was Jimmy's favourite, but he doesn't seem interested, he just plays with his car, backwards and forwards, backwards and forwards, backwards, forwards . . .

"Sarah's a man like mummy's daddy's a man."

You were drifting. You say what?

"Like grand-dad?" you ask.

"You're being silly," Jimmy says.

"Like me? Jimmy do you mean like me?"

"Yes, you and mummy are mummy's daddy."

"I'm your daddy. Mummy is my wife and I'm her husband."

"Sarah is my motor-bike daddy."

"Oh, a make-up daddy, like Tinky is a make up?"

"No, silly. Sarah's a daddy and you're a daddy and mummy's a mummy and your mummy's daddy."

Oh, hope! "Is Sarah someone's daddy. Do you mean someone who comes to get one of the children from the nursery? Sarah's daddy?"

"Oh, silly! Of course not. Sarah lives in the nursery, in the top, up the upstairs-upstairs, in the roof."

You call Carol. Your drink is empty. You tell her you could do with another and then you tell her little Jimmy is making things up.

"He says there's an upstairs-upstairs and this Sarah lives up there. And he insists that this Sarah is a man and not a parent and he's got a motorbike and Jimmy sits on it or something."

Carol looks faint. "There's a flat above the nursery. The owner uses it in the week and his brother sometimes over-nights there. Both of them have motorbikes."

Carol goes to Jimmy and when she tries to hold him he acts as if he doesn't know her, then he turns and kisses her on the lips, not a child's peck but a full, weird, long kiss. Carol flushes and looks close to tears. You're desperate for a drink.

You make the mistake of being direct.

"Tell you what, Jimmy, you tell mummy and daddy all about motor-bike Sarah and then you and me we'll go down to Toys R Us and get a new Lego model."

"Uh-uh!" shakes his head, "Seeeeee-cret!"

Sixty-Three

"Tom put it together so slowly. What he and Carol thought might be happening they also thought just couldn't be happening. They were being told by their boy that he was being molested, at his nursery. Think on that, Caz, you pay to send your child to school, you place him within reach of some animal. You can't believe it's possible, you can't believe it's happening, but worse, you realise that you sent your baby to this man.

"Jimmy had been disturbed for a while but they had put it down to an age thing where he was growing, feeling more independent, trying to stamp his personality on things. It was a coming together of things that was the key; the bad behaviour, the nightmares, the weeing and soiling, the odd sexual references to his father and his mother and sister."

"Were they still sending him to the school?"

"Yes, and they are trying to come to terms with that. If they had realised what was happening, they would have stopped straight away, but they didn't. Tom had more or less decided to pull the two kids out. He took his brother with him to the nursery, picked the kids up, took them out to the car and left them with him while he went back in to speak to one of the staff, the young woman, Sharon. Tom thought she was strangely evasive and he knew then, for certain, that something bad was occurring. He kept the kids away next day, rang Child Protection and the Social Services. It's sad now, but he apologised for bothering us."

Sixty-Four

"Oh, hi, Sharon. You got a minute? I was just wondering?"

"What is it?"

"Could we talk in private; just a minute?"

She leads you into one of the kiddie play-rooms. Your head buzzes, and your neck crawls. You are desperate for some other explanation and maybe Sharon can give you it, because last night . . .

You're surrounded by toy bricks, jig-saw puzzles. Innocence.

You must be very, very cool.

You laugh.

"Sharon, this'll sound a bit funny, but who is Sarah?"

Instantly you see shock run straight through her. Fuck!

"Sarah? You mean Sarah McCauley?"

"No, I mean a grown-up Sarah. An adult. Jimmy keeps going on about someone called Sarah."

She looks perplexed but it's not a real perplexed.

"Sarah? No. We don't have a Sarah on the books. None of the full-timers or part-timers. I'd know. Jimmy must be confused."

"He's adamant," you tell her. "He says there's a Sarah here. And if I'm not mistaken it's a man, someone with a motor bike. Could he be getting a name confused, perhaps?"

Look at her fucking face. If she threw up now you'd expect it.

"Well, the owner has a motor-bike, so does his brother and he sometimes parks it here. And the gardener has a little

Honda. But no one is called Sarah, or anything like it. Jimmy must be mixed-up."

Mixed up, sure. He's just a kid. Like last night he grabbed your dick and you were shocked. And then about three a.m. he started screaming in his sleep and you couldn't, you couldn't, couldn't wake him and the sobbing was awful and you just knew, something . . .

Watch yourself now, a big smile.

"I told Carol that. Must be a girl in Power Rangers or something. He always had an amazing imagination, did Jimmy."

"He's a very clever boy, very advanced."

"Yes," you say. You don't know exactly why but you want to smash this fucking woman's head against the wall. In your throat is hot and cold and you might throw up.

"Was he OK today?" you ask.

"He was fine."

"Only last night he was a little bit hot. Carol thinks he might be sickening for something."

She smiles, patronisingly. "He was fine, today."

Jesus fuck, you could, you could smash her face in . . .

"What a relief! I thought maybe he was getting another one of those chest infections."

"No," she says, "he was fine all day."

You leave.

Sixty-Five

"We can talk about it some more this afternoon, Caz. We've pretty much pieced it all together. We've got an unusually articulate three-year-old, but we're up against proving it."

"We are?"

"Yeah. Jimmy's dad made a bit of a hash of things; he lost it on the Monday, went to the nursery school and confronted the owner. It's understandable, but they had warning. We could have raided the place or stuck someone in maybe. We could have put a discreet observation on the building and the playground."

"I thought you said he was in control?"

"He was. They took Jimmy and Maria out of the school on the Thursday, played with the kiddie to find out more, talked through it themselves all through Friday and eventually they rang the Social Services late that evening. They got the duty officer who put things in hand. We spoke briefly on the Saturday night, and again on the Sunday, and we put together a team ready for the Tuesday.

"But Tom felt guilty, and from what I understand, little Jimmy said something or did something which pushed Tom over the top. He went up there with his brother to confront the owner and try to get a reaction. He was blanked, lots of sympathy and spoken to in such a way that he could say or do nothing. I've said before, Caz, they are practised at smooth-talk. It's their stock in trade and poor dumb Tom, he walked right into it. He gave them time to cover their tracks." She looked at her watch. "Hey, we'd better get back."

They walked slowly back up the hill.

"There are four brothers in their forties and early fifties but the holding company is still run by the father. There's this nursery in Brighton, one in Reading, one in Bournemouth and one in Cardiff. They've other business interests in road transport. We haven't been able to look at the other nurseries but this one has the flat above and an office where the brother Julian works."

"So how common is it to have male owners of child nurseries?"

"Depends what you mean, Caz. On paper, not that uncommon. Men sometimes help their wives set something up, sometimes they become one of the minimum two directors. But actually on-site, involved, running the business, that's much rarer; in fact, apart from the Acorn & Tree-Top chain, I don't know of any. It's not a man's thing really."

"Unless you want access to a steady stream of children."

Jill paused to look down a side-street.

"Exactly," she said.

Sixty-Six

It was twenty-five past one and chances were that Tom MacInnes was out having a quiet sandwich somewhere, or sipping something medicinal in the quiet lounge bar of The Grapes of Wrath. Caz excused herself anyway and said she'd nip through to his office on the off chance of catching him. Jill smiled and said there'd be plenty of paper stuff when she returned.

Jill walked away, towards the ladies' and just for a moment Caz felt indefinably peculiar, almost sisterly towards her. Briefly, she felt the oddest sensation, as if she wanted to stop, turn round and call after the older woman. Jill would turn round. Then Caz would say something supportive, something deep. She shook her head.

But Jill was all right, Caz knew it, more than all right, special even, and, and, Caz searched for the word, she was *strong*, like Caz didn't know anyone who was so strong. Not hard, maybe, not maybe one-on-one gutsy, not so get-in-there-and-do-it brave, but *strong*, moral, certain. Caz envied her.

She knocked the glass of the DI's door.

"It's open, lass!" he said, only just loud enough and not directed towards the knock. She guessed he was opening his bottom drawer, and when she stepped into the room, sure enough, he was ducked out of sight. She grinned and said, "Afternoon, sir!" then added, "Caz", by way of explanation. Then she heard him loose a satisfied "Ah!" before he rolled back from behind the desk and up into sight.

"Caz!" he said, "Have a mint, hen."

She didn't know how to put this.

"Sir – Tom . . . I was wondering. There was something – I wanted to ask you about it."

"This the something you were pestering Bob about this morning? He said you were a right pain in the arse."

"I was, sir, but there's something niggling me and . . ."

"Ah know."

"You do?"

"Bob said you wuz worried y'mighta said the wrong thing t'some reporter or something."

"He said that? No, sir, that wasn't it at all. I was wondering, sir, if I could ask you a couple of questions about John Bourne's death?"

"Yer a mite mysterious, lass. That why the DS was a bit peeved?"

"Would you bear with me, sir?"

He paused and took a breath. For a second Caz thought he was going to open the bottom drawer again. Then he seemed to give in.

"OK, lass, what is it?"

"You may think I'm as daft as a brush, sir, but would you tell me what was done to John Bourne? Would you tell me just as if I didn't know anything about the case?"

He stared. Yes, daft as a brush.

"Please?"

And the DI told her, just like the lads had told her. How Bourne, in his strangely sterile room had been overcome, had been stripped of clothing, strapped down, his mouth taped. How he had been systematically tortured and at some point castrated, his penis then cooked. And later, *post mortem*, the further cutting, the horrible mutilation of the face, the bizarre image on the wall, the pieces stuck there. And like the others, one thing missing.

"Sir, would you walk down to the War Room with me?"

"This is goin' t'be worth it?"

"I don't know, sir."

He stood up.

As they opened the door to the War Room they thought the place empty, but then, as they stepped in there was someone there, his feet up on a desk, Greavsie, talking on the phone. From his sudden embarrassment and his quick change of tone, Caz guessed he was talking to Janice James. It was lasting better than she'd expected.

"I'll call you back," he said.

"Ah, Jim!" MacInnes said. "Me and Caz here, a desperate thirst."

"Coffee, sir?"

"Aye, lad. What a grand idea! Thanks f'r offering."

Greavsie moved to leave.

"Ay wan shooger." MacInnes said.

They ignored the DC only aware he was gone when they heard the flap-flap-flap of the double doors. Caz had moved toward the picture wall and was staring, nodding, wondering.

"OK, hen. Explain yersel'."

"What do you see, sir?"

"Y'know what ah see, Flood. Sem as you. Bourne cut up, nae dick, and his guts spilled."

"And no lips, they're cut away."

"Get on, lass."

"The teeth are closed."

"Aye."

Caz turned, still unsure. She stepped towards another picture, a blow-up of the Polaroid that had landed on Robert Foster's mat but meant for his temporary lodger.

"This is the photograph John Rayner received, sir. Bourne still had lips then but he'd been knocked about a bit." She stepped again. "And this is the scene 've crimes stuff, no lips. In both cases, though the teeth are together."

"Aye lass, ah'm no blind."

"OK, sir. You went through and listed John Bourne's injuries, same as Bob Moore did. I even asked Bob to read out the official warning about leaks to the press. Well, sir . . ."

She had stopped again, wondering where this was going.

"Well, sir. Billy has never said anything, nothing official was ever said, and there's nothing on the photographs and nothing on the list of injuries, but I feel sure you told me that Bourne's murderer had tried to make him eat his own penis after it had been cooked. It was a bad night, sir. Have I remembered you right?"

"Jeez, lass is that all this is? Why did'yee no just ask?"

"Because if I ask it, you remember. If I don't, you don't."

"Well the answer's easy enough, lass. The night I telt yer not that yon man Bourne might ha'bin forced t'eat the stuff but that the *doc* thought he *mebbee* had. The doc musta changed his mind, cos there was nowt about it on the PM report."

"Are you sure, Tom?"

"There w'z nothing. I'da remembered."

"I did, sir. I remembered. But I was beginning to think I'd made it up. I've been getting dreams."

"Ay all the silly jokes about eatin' hot sausage," The DI said.

"Yes," she said. "That'll be what it is."

Sixty-Seven

Caz began to read. At her desk, Jill Bartholomew answered phone calls, scribbled notes, stood up once to open a filing cabinet.

Smothering is violent; a young child who cannot breathe struggles and tries to get air. The smothering needs considerable force, even when the child is young: the child has to be laid down on his back or against something firm for the mother to press hard on his face.

And she looked at pictures, read references, she saw the poisoned, the deliberately scalded, the raped and the buggered. Sometimes she would realise she wasn't breathing and she would gasp, look up and see Jill. Jill was never looking Caz's way.

After two hours, Caz stopped. After the beatings, the burnings, the starvings, the broken bones, after severe vaginal tearing and anal fizzuring, after sexually transmitted diseases, in babies, in boys of four and five, of tiny girls, she stopped. She stopped reading the *ABCs of Child Abuse*, *The Journals of Paediatrics*, Abstracts of symposia, conference notes, learned argument.

Caz got up, left the room, went out through the corridors, through the front office, through the main doors, into the late afternoon sun, and walked.

She walked downhill, then left and up, then right, and down past Valerie's apartment, downhill still, past Armando's, past sidestreets with Green cafés, past pubs, past a shop selling Brighton rock and one with pink plastic rubber rings, inflatable ducks, giant bananas, and Chinese buckets and Chinese spades.

Then she was down on the shingle beach, seaward, deathward, below the deck-chaired families, the staring blue-rinses, the old fat ladies in light colours who never showed sweat. And she stared too, but the sea was steep and grey, utterly ambivalent, and she heard birds, the rock of the waves, the occasional squeal of a kid or the bark of some dog called Spot.

And she crouched then, and she looked into the water, squatting like a peasant about to shit, and she looked deep and she wondered: could she ever be Jill-calm and Jill-strong or would she always want to kill?

And what she saw and what she merely looked at, what she heard and what she listened to, all that; what she knew and what she thought she knew, what she speculated on, what she could follow up, she wondered did any of it matter, did Valerie, or did Moira, did Billy once, lying in a hospital bed, her fault, or dead men on holiday islands, her fault and not her fault, or the women she'd watched be saved, the young woman she had saved, the man she once pushed off a bridge, did all that, any of that matter if we couldn't even save the children?

And suddenly, at last she understood why she would never, never, be happy – but that was all right – why she would never, never be content – but that was all right, too – and why people like Vaunda were like Vaunda, – how else could they be? – people like MacInnes drank drawered Bells and sucked mints, of course; and she would always be Flood, and guys like Angel, and guys like Angel would . . .

And she stared at the sea and she thought very hard and she thought, if I can think this, think this, and if I'm right, I'll have to ring the police doctor, Ernie King in Manchester, speak to DS Puzo, speak to DS Mason, speak to Billy. If I can think this . . .

Sixty-Eight

John Street, 16:44

Caz came back in, smiled at the PC behind the front desk, smiled at the two civilian workers, smiled at her reflection in the glass of the poster cabinets. In the corridor she saw Greavsie, smiled at him too and asked him if he fancied a drink at knock-off.

He said yes.

Then she went down to the canteen for coffees, back upstairs to the CP offices, back to the files, picked up the stuff she had avoided reading, bawled something silly to Jill and stuck the three spare coffees on the edge of her desk.

The next folder was, *Paedophile Methods – an Analysis.*

She picked up the phone, tapped a number and spoke to the duty sergeant. Yes, Billy came off at six. There was no overtime on the cards, unless something blew up in the next hour. She rang Moira.

"Mother! How is things?"

"You know, Caz. Neighbours, Knots Landing, Breakfast TV, a tough life . . ."

"You getting out yet?"

"You offering?"

"Sort of."

"When?"

"Tonight? Fancy an Indian. Can yer Mum baby-sit?"

"*Can* she? This is sarcasm, right? Course she can."

"So we'll pick you up about half-seven?"

"How about we pick *you* up, Caz? I'm not drinking."

"Neither am I," Caz said.
"Since when?"
"Almost since a coupla days ago, actually since lunch-time today."
"You're serious?"
"Deadly."
"Great then, Let's just hope Billy doesn't have to work overs."
"He won't," Caz said.

"Valerie Thomas."
"Er, this is the Genito-Urinary Infection Unit, Bonk Street . . ."
"Hi, Caz."
"Night out tonight, OK? Moira and Billy? For an Indian?"
"I gotta pile of work on, Caz."
"Please? I'm on the wagon."
"And I never played with myself when I were a lad either."
"I'm serious, Val. I need to be faster, slimmer, stronger, right?"
"You are? You're serious?
"Deadly."
"OK. I'll be home, my place, at seven."
"Ditto," Caz said. "Home Val's house. Seven o'clock."

"DS Mason."
"Peter, just confirming tomorrow. We on OK?"
"Everything's in hand, Flood. As far as Parkhurst is concerned, we're following up on other rapes. The fast ferry goes on the half-hour from Town Key to East Cowes. We're booked to go at half-eight."
"No problem," Caz said.

Sixty-Nine

"Doctor Kelman?"

"This is he."

"Good afternoon, sir. I'm not certain we've ever spoken, but we've met. I'm WDC Kathryn Flood from John Street."

"Slight, blonde, pony-tail?"

"Yes, sir."

"Then I know you. I think, once or twice, I've seen you with Detective Inspector MacInnes."

"That's correct, sir but this is an off-the-record enquiry. I'm after a tiny bit of information but it's sort of personal, I'd rather not make it official just yet."

"Is?"

"I'm on the team investigating the murder in Hornby Terrace, sir. You attended there as I did."

"Yes."

"It's a tiny thing, sir. I'm working, entering data on HOLMES and I wanted to check I have something right. I was there that night, sir, though we didn't speak and DI MacInnes mentioned you thought that maybe the victim had been made to eat a portion of his—"

"His penis, when it was cooked."

"Er, yes, sir."

"And there is no mention in the autopsy report. You're a little confused?"

"Yes, sir."

"I understand. If you speak to your DI, he should be able to clarify everything. It was a guess on my part, at the scene, a small amount of matter not in the victim but on the wall."

"Where the face had been stuck on?"
"Yes."
"So we don't think the victim had to eat anything?"
"He had eaten a large meal that evening and I believe your normal enquiries will have been looking at Chinese restaurants in the area. But no human flesh was in the stomach, at least, none that was easily visible. We would need to do a very detailed investigation to be certain, DNA analysis et cetera."
"But the cost is not justified?"
"Absolutely."
Caz paused. "Could I ask you one more thing, sir. What made you think the victim had ingested, the err, part?"
"I'm not sure now, but it was . . . it was, a certain residue on the teeth which appeared to have the same characteristics as the cooked remains and juices discovered in the kitchen, in the frying-pan. I am more inclined now to think that perhaps the murderer tried to make the victim eat part and failed. It's even possible that the victim pretended to bite off a chunk."
"But the penis was presented to the mouth?"
"Yes."
"But not ingested?"
"I think not."
"I apologise for this question, sir. I know Mr MacInnes knew on the night, that maybe, Bourne had – but did you discuss this with anyone else?"
"What do *you* think, detective?"

Seventy

The dark was lifting, the morning cool when Caz stirred, and she woke untense, cat-soft. Oh, last night! Last night had been so sweet, so slowly giving, so . . . damn the cliché, nice, and she felt so *different*. In Cosmo they called something like this love. And, hey, it was OK.

When she slipped out of bed, she did so very carefully, padded like talcum into the bathroom, padded out of there afterwards, padded into Valerie's lounge where her running clothes were ready, hushly dressed and carried her shoes out of the door, and, with the lock turned, closed it like an airtight safe sloughing wordlessly shut.

On the ground floor, still in darkness, she pulled on her shoes, laced them up, the key tight against the tongue, then she stretched, still quiet, and slipped into the street.

There was no mist and the morning was rising pleasantly enough, the sea a lit lightless green as she aimed at it, the last night-tired streetlights waiting to go out. Life actually seemed to be dropping into a new order and she took a huge sea-breath.

Billy had seemed so much better. Moira had sat in the front of the Daimler, bright and brown-eyed, talking to Val, and Billy had sat in the back, with Caz but sideways, his hand gently touching Moira's neck, gently, gently, stroking her black, black hair.

And the baby was cooooo-wull. They both said so. And Caz was driving them all back. Childhood was indeed miraculous.

She turned east above the sea. She could smell the salt.

It was better to be direct and Caz had caught Billy by the arm, just as Val and Moira laughed through the door of the restaurant.

"Listen," she said quickly, "One question about the night, one."

"Flood . . ."

"I gotta know one thing. I heard a whisper that Bourne had been made to eat his own thingee. You heard that?"

"No."

"Not at all?"

"No."

"Right!" Caz said. Her eyes were flashing with silver.

They went in and went for a spread for four. Billy laughed all night. And he never failed to be touching Moira except when the girls went to the loos. The one and only time he really looked at Caz he shook his head. When he did, Caz leaned to Val and put her tongue in his ear, said something filthy. Even without any lager, it was a really, *really* good night.

Along the top road, Caz opened up, running a mile at just sub-six. The sun was the colour of custard and just as useful.

She had failed to get hold of DS Puzo and no-one would give out his home number – but she knew the number of Ernie King's digs and she managed to ring him on the way back from the toilets. She had sent Moira back to go hold Billy's hand. It had been five minutes and he was looking distraught.

She waited on a landing up one flight of stairs, her mobile ringing out in some distant B&B, a coin-phone at the bottom of another flight of builder-trod stairs. Eventually, eventually, an answer.

"'Oo? Oh aye, I'll see if he's in."

She waited. She had another two minutes before guilt would pink her cheeks. Then somebody answered, "'Ello?"

"Ernie King?"

"This is his oppo, Sam. Ernie's 'avin' a shower. 'Oo's that?"

"Oh, hi, Sam. I'm the woman copper who came to see

you – Caz Flood. I need to speak to Ernie, but you'll do for a minute. I want to ask you both about the bloke you met at Hornby Terrace."

"The dead one, Mr lah-dee-dah?"

Who else? "Yes. Ernie did that fantastic drawing for me."

"Made him look too nice, if y'ask me. Guy gave me the creeps. Too bloody nice f'my liking. Dunno why zactly, but I just din't like 'im."

"Really? You can't think why?"

"No, I can't. My little Sammy loved 'im – but not me. And the weird thing is I couldn't tell you why t'save me life. 'E din't do anything wrong, it was just a—"

"Instinct?"

"Yeah, that's the word, in-stint. I just couldn't take to the bloke."

"Sam, do you have a pen?"

"Course I does. Every chippy's got a stub be'ind 'is ear."

"Take this number down then, would you? Get Ernie to ring me when he comes out of the shower?"

As Caz passed below Roedean school and saw Rottingdean village sweeping ahead, she slowed to a steadier 7:15 mile. The sun was not much better but the cool helped her run hard. She turned at the outskirts and kicked a flat out half mile, feeling good.

Val had hardly been miffed at all when her mobile rang. If it had been five minutes later they'd have been in the car but they were drinking their free liqueurs. Caz had a Baileys. It was free and she didn't consider it drinking. As it touched her lips she felt hopelessly randy and Val smelled it. Maybe that was why he excused the call.

"Caz Flood."

"Hello? This is Ernie. Can you ring me back when the pips go? Just, I only 'ad the one ten pee."

She rang him back and the phone was engaged.

"I was just thinking, Val, about the last time I drank Baileys . . ."

"So was I. Let's pay the bill and get home."

"Hello? Ernie? Detective Constable Flood . . ."

She cruised back down into Brighton with a seven, a seven and a half and then a gentle eight-ten mile.

"Ernie, your picture was great! It worked a treat. You've got a memory for faces, right? An eye for a character."

"They say I do."

"Ernie, your Sam didn't like the man, did he? But his little lad did. You seem take-it-or-leave-it and I was looking at your picture. It's OK, like the man next door almost, but, I don't know how to say this, but, just from his *picture*, I don't like the guy."

Ernie King coughed. "I know what you mean. I was never sure about the bloke. I couldn't find fault, but then when my Cheryl came round one day, she seemed t'like 'im. It's funny, isn't it but if your daughter and yer grandson like somebody . . ."

"So he was helpful, funny, what?"

"Helpful, yeah. Sort of, at least with Sam and Sammy. Me, I don't know. He was a nice enough bloke but he hung around a bit too much I think, but then little Sammy liked him and kids are always right aren't they?"

She jogged to the bottom of the street before Val's, the feeling growing. If only last night she could have spoken to Mario PZ.

Seventy-One

She met Peter Mason in a neat little French-Style café on Town Quay and they sat on frilled, dark-green metal chairs, sipping espresso. Around them the cheap-first-lease shops were boarded up and lost people wandered slowly by on the boards, echoing above the grey water.

"So how's the Bitterne blowtorch case, Peter?"

"Slow."

"Nowhere with the bad debt thing?"

"Naff street talk. People figuring there has to be just cause and making up their own minds. You know how it is, Caz, '*Maybe* he owed someone money . . . Hey that right he owed someone money? . . . I 'eard he owed a whack've cash . . . Some heavies were into 'im fer a load of dosh . . .' Five or six whispers, it's accepted fact and that's what we get on the door-to-door. It goes nowhere."

"Nice range of voices, Sarge."

"Used t'be an act-er don't y'know?"

"Yeah." Caz said. "And I used to be in the Royal Ballet."

The trip over was on the Red Funnel Hydrofoil, broad in the beam with immense power and, once out of the Solent traffic, fast and dark across the water. At Cowes, rich men's yachts, lots, furled white sails, pregnant white hulls, summer leisure wrapped, lifting and falling on another swell, rigs and ropes clicking.

Caz and Peter weren't rich. They caught a bus to Newport.

It was a Number 2 omnibus, yellow-green. Caz rushed upstairs, Peter grunted something, turned to the driver paid for two single fares, then followed. He found her at the front, perched forward on her seat going brrmm-brrmm and pretending to be the driver.

He told her to grow up.

"Yer joking!" Caz said, her eyes wide. "When was the last time you went on a bus, Peter? Blimey, this is like being a kid again!"

The bus phuddered and moved, climbing out of Cowes, impossibly squeezing through too-narrow streets, round unnegotiable bends and out above the tight town; then out into humdrum country, past the occasional cuddy cow. Caz was light in her seat, fascinated. She had never been on to the island before and this felt like a holiday.

She had left the Mazda in the ferry company carpark and she could picture it now, hot, red, and sexy, the sun on it's bonnet, it's rounded rear. She had left Brighton and Val before seven, driving over after kissing him goodbye, cruising in the up-glowing morning sun, Simon and Garfunkel on the stereo, detached, in a dream, rampping past Portsmouth, just beating the commuting Sierras, the Fiestas, the Cavaliers. She had thought about Angel Sweet most of the way and she had wondered when she would call Manchester.

She felt Peter's arm. "Psst!" he said.

She looked up as the DS spoke, and the twin-sprawled prisons of Albany and Parkhurst loomed in the distance: wooden buildings, cottages of stone, porta-cabins on brick bases, shrubbery, flowerbeds, a living village outside the castle walls, but in the middle of it all, the colour-dead fatness of high, high, ungrippable blub-topped walls and behind them Caz's secret fear, bars, the narrow-ranked windows, the stink of shit and piss, confinement.

"Jesus!" she said.

Seventy-Two

James Munro, convicted rapist, was not at all like Caz expected but then he was everything she knew he would be. It was only later she wondered about her preconceptions and thought about what prison life might have done to him.

They had signed in and been led through an echoing building and into a small temporary office, away from the normal interview rooms. They waited maybe two minutes before the door opened and Munro was nudged in. He saw the DS and stopped.

"But Trevor told me . . ."

"Trevor was wrong," Mason said. "Come and sit down."

Munro stayed where he was and looked at Caz. He was about six feet: skinny, dark, swarthy, head shaved.

"You Flood?"

Caz said yes, wondering where he had got the curved scar on his forehead. It looked new . . .

"I ast Trevor, I said . . ."

Caz took over. "It's all right, Jimmy. I'll be doing the interview, but DS Mason here has to observe. You're from off his patch."

Munro looked warily at Peter, decided, then came to sit down. Caz thought his scar was changing colour but then decided she was imagining things. Mason tossed a pack of cigarettes across.

"No hard feelings, Jimmy?"

Munro pocketed the fags without lighting one. Maybe he didn't smoke. Caz smiled, another cliché blown away.

"Flood here will chat to you, I just have to be here. Besides, you know, you're in here for . . ."

Munro was not impressed, suddenly he showed steel.

"Look, you, whatever! I'm banged up in here because some bird decided she didn't want her boyfriend to know she'd slept the night with me and liked it, right? I doan av to talk to you. I *want* to, cos someone's got to know." He leaned forward and spoke low. "Think what you like, *Sergeant*, but I'm as straight as you, maybe more so."

"Everyone in here is innocent."

"This one is!"

Mason shrugged, "Sure."

Caz cut in quickly. "OK, Peter, let me do this, yes?" Then, as an afterthought she added a loaded, "Please?"

Munro was nodding. Caz looked from Mason to him and saw a red mark and a little depression in his skull. Fresh again . . .

"Jimmy, I've got another sixty Silk Cut for you for after, OK? If you're not dicking us about, they're yours, no matter what."

He smiled.

"OK," Caz said. "So what's so important?"

Jimmy Munro sat forward, then as suddenly sat back again, then he looked towards the door.

"I don't want anyone to hear," he said. "I don't want to get killed."

Mason went to say something cutting but Caz got there first.

"The DS will check there's no-one near enough, OK?" She turned her head slightly, "Peter?" She leaned forward, toward the prisoner. "Try talking quiet, Jimmy, while the sergeant takes a look."

Munro leaned forward too. Caz didn't sense "rapist".

"Look," he said, "this gets out I might easy get dead." Closer still. "Someone, someone. I think they are killing little kids."

IV

Seventy-Three

"I was sent down for six years, from Winchester Crown Court. I was going to appeal, but my brief said there was no grounds. He told me being innocent didn't count.

"I got sent to Wandsworth first. They assessed me, medical shit, psychological stuff. Then they sent me to the Island. You know what they call the sex offenders in Albany? Bacons. You know why? Because they're pigs, shitty and dirty. Well, I'm not a sex offender. I got offered Rule Forty-Three, but I didn't want to go in with a load of perverts; so I didn't take it. They put me on A wing. That's where I got this. And this."

He was touching the scar, the dent in his skull.

"So I applied. I got my solitary and then I got my transfer. I was hoping maybe I'd get lucky and get bunked with an ex-copper or a grass, but I didn't. I got stuck in a cell with a fucking animal.

"And I *mean* a fucking animal. I didn't know that shit could be piled that high.

"His name is Richard Clay and he's been telling me things; fucking terrible things, things I didn't know anyone in the world could do, to little boys, little kids.

"You've got to know. The bastard has been boasting about killing kids after him and his gang has had a party. A fucking party; that's what he calls it. They kidnap a kid, drug him up and one after the other, they rape him; for a weekend they just rape this poor little kid, over and over and over."

Jimmy was shaking, his voice breaking. Caz put her hand out.

"Have a ciggie, Jim."

He looked up. His eyes were wet. "I don't smoke, remember?"

"Sorry," she said.

Jimmy sniffed. "Clay fucking *boasts*, you know? He boasts. Every fucking night he tells me something new. He talks about his 'circle of acquaintances', the rest of his gang. One's over the way in Parkhurst, the rest are up north or they're out already. Clay, they think he was the ring-leader, but he wasn't. He got eighteen years but some of the others got as little as five years. What's more, he says, the police missed a few, some guys with money and a couple of other scum-bags, one's a teacher."

He took a long breath and Caz was shocked to see his face.

"Take your time," she said.

He laughed. "Time I got!"

"Yeah, OK," Caz said.

Fairgrounds are good, lots of movement, lots of lights, distractions. The dodgem cars are good for prospecting; there are always kids on their own, or in twos. It's not hard to split a pair of kids up. At a push you can grab both of them – just means you have to be a bit more careful. No one ever looks. Even if the kid screams, it's rare a head will turn. Use the rag, they go limp in a few seconds. Then pick him up, just another eight year-old asleep, too excited. He's on your shoulder, hiding one side of your face. Just be relaxed, a dad out for the evening. No-one will see. I tell you, it's so easy. Get him to wherever you've set up and then ring your acquaintances. These mobile phones are incredibly good, don't you think?

"The thing is. I thought it was just chops. People do that in here. They hope they can make a reputation that'll keep them safe. It was only gradually that I began to think it was for real. I thought all sorts. I even thought of doing the fucker myself, in the showers, but when it came down to it, I wouldn't have been able. I just don't think like that."

His voice changed, deeper.

"Then I thought about the bastards still out there. I'm divorced, but I got a kid, a little girl eight years old. Lucie lives with her mother over in Chichester. The idea that—"

Caz waited. She watched the tension in Munro's forearms come and go, come and go.

"Look," he said. "I want to find a way to get them. I don't know how exactly, which is why I contacted Trevor. He told me you were hard, but straight. He said you could help."

"Help how, exactly?"

"I don't know. Maybe I could wear a microphone or something, and you could listen in. I could get Clay to talk and—"

"Not in here, Jimmy."

"Well, what then?"

"I don't know," Caz said.

Seventy-Four

Caz and Peter walked free from Albany into clouded almost-October dullness. Directly ahead of them was Parkhurst.

"That place," Mason said, nodding, "is so bloody ancient it used to house the poor bastards due for transportation."

"To Australia?"

"Yup."

"Jesus," Caz said. She felt cold and grey.

They found a stop and waited for the bus back to Cowes. If this had been afternoon, there would have been a long queue of women, a few with kids, all slightly flattened, but with a commonality which came from us and them. Caz suddenly thought of Val locked up and tried to imagine herself visiting him. The thought didn't come easy.

The bus came. They got on. Caz paid and they sat downstairs.

"*Clay is not lying, he's not making it up. Him and these blokes, they really have been grabbing kids, and the kids, that's it, they never go home. I think they've done at least four but sometimes, the way Clay talks, there could be more. Once he told me the next one would be number ten. You've got to realise, these animals, they've got a proper system – they don't leave things to chance and they work carefully. Sometimes it's vague, but every now and then I get a checkable fact. We've got to find a way of putting it all together and burying the fuckers. They're evil. No way should they ever get out.*"

Caz was miles away, listening to echoes. Then she heard Mason.

"Let me guess," he said.

Caz came to. "Right first time."

The DS sounded resigned. "It's going to be hard to set up. One iffy visit is one thing, but if we want to see Munro and interview him often, we are going to have to talk to the governor and security. If we screw that up, they'll find Munro in the showers."

"But we're talking *evil* here, Peter. Surely—"

"Grassing is grassing, Caz. The code's simple."

"He's got guts, then."

"Yeah, sure," Mason said, his lip curling. "The kind of guts it takes to rape an eighteen-year-old girl and ruin her life."

"Ruin her *life*? You've read the case notes, have you?"

"No, but I know one of the guys who arrested him and now I've met the rapist myself. That's enough for me."

"Good to see you've kept a sense of proportion, Peter. So you don't believe him when he says she changed her mind after the event?"

Mason laughed. "Oh, sure! Happens all the time, dunnit?"

Caz loathed rapists and when she spoke, she thought she was someone else. "It happens, *sometimes*, Peter." Then she remembered an unopened package. "That envelope you left for me Friday. I'd guess and say there's forty-five quid in there. About right?"

His face changed. "What's that supposed to mean?"

"You and Moira. You're not sure about the baby. There was that one night way back, you and her, and remember, we were talking rape there for a while—"

"But I didn't—"

"That's just what Munro said."

"You're classing me with some shite banged up in Albany?"

"Peter, I'm not putting anyone with anyone. I'm just saying that James Munro is risking his life. He refused Rule Forty-three and went in with the mains, so convinced was he that he wasn't a rapist and they'd know. Now he's talking to us. We're not going to find out the truth about his conviction but let's give the guy a little bit of credit."

For a minute Mason was quiet and Caz thought back a little over nine months; a foursome, a Thai meal and Peter and Moira leaving the flat, already pissed. The countryside flacked by as she stared.

"If you haven't opened it, how'd you know how much is in there?"

"An educated guess. Fifty was the limit and you do have a bit of a soul. And there's a letter in with the money, telling me to put it towards a present but don't say anything to Moira. The odd amount makes it look like it's casual, like a whip-round."

"You've got a sick mind, Flood."

Caz pulled her handbag round to the front and snapped the clasp. "I'm a copper," she said. She came out with Peter's envelope. "You want me to open it? You want me to tell you what the letter says without looking?" She stopped, this wasn't the best time. "Look Peter, we understand each other. Neither of us is thinking 'you and rape', OK? But this should go back in your wallet. I don't want to put a secret between me and Moira just to help you deal with your sense of guilt. Mo and Billy are happy now, and they've got a pretty daughter, let's leave it at that."

She handed him the once-folded envelope and he slipped it away.

"You're not going to check it?" she said.

"No."

She smiled and tried to lighten things. "OK," she said, "seeing as you're forty-something quid better off, how about lunch?

Seventy-Five

Over pizzas, Caz and Peter talked ideas. Maybe Caz could become a regular visitor – no, they wouldn't be able to talk properly. Smuggled mail? – too risky. The phone? – no privacy. Via the governor? – too easily sussed by the inmates. They came down to something behind closed doors, a repeatable medical condition, dental treatment, maybe something set up via the prison chaplin.

Caz had said no to the wine and asked for a Perrier with a splash of lime. Mason was drinking a lager. He seemed concerned.

"I'm not convinced the Crown Prosecution Service will go with it. Everything is down to cost now. The main evidence will be from a convicted felon, and they've already got the gang banged up."

Caz corrected him. "*Some* of the gang. And they're all due out in the next couple of years. If there are bodies, how can they not act?"

The DS laughed. "You need to ask?"

Caz drove back slowly along the M27, so low the stereo was off, the top up and the car was just a car. This wasn't like her but she wanted to go home, go to bed and be cuddled down. She tried to think of Val, but kept picturing Vincent, her pot-bellied pink pig. She wondered was melancholia a side-effect of going dry?

Near Chichester she stopped in the car park of a Little Chef, took out her mobile and dialled Manchester. Detective

Sergeant Puzo was on a day's leave. She needed to contact him, she said. Could they pass on her number?

When she got back to John Street, Caz briefly showed her face in CP and then nipped through to speak to DI MacInnes. He looked brighter and he stayed away from the bottom drawer.

"Update you on the prison visit, sir, maybe you've got some ideas? And there were a couple of things, later, about the Hornby Terrace murder—"

"Fire away, lass."

She told him about Munro, the difficulties, Mason's doubts about the CPS.

"This'll be run from Southampton? DS Mason?"

"Yes, sir."

"OK. I get any ideas, I'll speak to him."

She went to protest but MacInnes raised his hand.

"Let it go, lass. Yer cannae do everything. Mason's a good enough copper; leave it to him. What else was there?"

All these vague ideas, and impossible, improbable conclusions.

"Sir, I was wondering, the house in Hornby Terrace. A peculiar set-up but we searched the place, found nothing of any interest. We checked for hideaways, even lifted the floors and peeked under. Apart from bits of rubbish, there was nothing."

"Yes?"

"I was wondering, sir, if you'd let me look at the rubbish?"

"*What*? Now, why should I do that, Flood? Yer off the case and working in Child Protection. You told me yerself y'needed a rest, and now you want to take on extra work? No."

"We've kept it, sir? Basically it's rubbish but it's bagged and held, yes?"

"Yes."

"Well could we at least make certain it's not lost, sir?"

"What's not lost?"

"The bits and pieces sir, the stuff we found under the floor of the front room."

"Flood!"

"I'm off the wall again, sir. You'll lock me up if I say."

"Ah'm not amused, Caz."

"I'm sorry, sir. Another idea, sir. These men. I mean Bourne and the guy in Southampton. They were tortured, we're saying, and we've not yet said they're connected. But two men, loners, nobody knows who they are, both appeared at the same time and both were mutilated so bad we couldn't ID them."

"We've identified Bourne."

"We've got the name he used, sir, nothing else."

"Yer saying?"

"I'm wondering if these guys are connected, sir, never mind the different MO's. First one guy gets tortured for information, then a second one gets killed. Maybe the information the killer wanted was the address of the second guy!"

"We've found no connections. We *have* looked, Flood."

"OK, sir. But the other thing about the mutilations is that both of them meant we had no finger-prints. In one case the fingers were gone, and in the Bitterne killing the hands had been systematically burned. Now why would someone worry about fingerprints?"

"Because they knew the victims had form!"

"Yes, sir. And from the bits and pieces we've picked up on the door-to-door, I'd say the form is for paedophile offences. Bourne appears to have been befriending young mothers, one grandmother who looked after her daughter's kiddies. And there were a few tidbits in the house that would fit."

"So what are we thinking?"

"Child-sex offenders linked in some way, released about the same time last year. We know when Bourne appeared on the scene, it's in the same time-frame as the guy killed in Bitterne. Maybe they upset someone in prison or something?"

"And the rubbish?"

"There was a page of a porn mag, sir. I just wondered what sort of porn; gynae stuff or, just maybe, children."

"You didn't look at it?"

"No, sir, DS Sweet picked it up and bagged it with the rest of the junk. That was the only room that had anything. Everywhere else was clean."

"It wasnae kiddies. Same magazine as thaise on the book-case, not even hard-core."

"*Fiesta*?"

"Aye."

"What month?" Caz said.

Seventy-Six

Back in Child Protection, just the last hour and a half of a long, long strange day and you read and you read and you read. And wherever you turn you see pain, the theft of innocence, families torn apart from inside, from outside. The physical abuse is terrible but this is almost always within family and you learn that sexual abuse is sometimes, like rape is, an abuse of power.

At some point a cup of fresh coffee appears on your desk and you hear Jill Bartholomew ask you something and you say "That'll be fine, Jill" and later she says something else and you say, "Of course, thanks, yes, five minutes."

But you read of strangers, neighbours, baby-sitters, molesting. You read of the men who PLAN to use, to abuse, who treat tiny lives like meat, who see what others see as vessels of hope, joy and dreams incarnate, as orifices. And you read still, you read formally what Angel had told you, how paedophiles can wait, how they will spend years getting friendly with a family until, so ultimately trusted, they can baby-sit, even bathe, little boys and girls.

And you read of one man, a "magician" who had twelve separate wands to be earned by his little girls and how the ultimate wand came from recruiting a friend into the circle and how the children progressed from wand to wand from service to service and how this man was LOVED, loved by everyone, until the twelfth, the twelfth girl, finally told someone, when twelve, twelve children all had his mark, not until the twelfth was anything said.

And you think about things that Angel has told you, and

things that Richard Clay has done and you think of all the children lost, murdered, prostituted, with AIDS, Hepatitis B, STDs and despair.

And you read about this compulsion and you find that they can CONTROL it when under suspicion, how they can lose the photographs, the contacts, the need to touch and suck and be touched and be sucked, for more than a year lest they be caught. And you think then this is an evil, this is a choice, these people are aware.

And then you read about conviction rates and sentences and in your throat and in your belly there is a ball of rage so hot you think you might not breathe and you know with utter certainty how you would deal with one of these disgusting animals if you caught one, how you would treat it with more respect than it treated its victims but you would make so sure, so very damn sure, it would never, never, offend again.

And now you hear a voice and you ignore it but you see the clock and it's a quarter to eight and the voice says your name again and you look up and it's Angel and he looks at you and you look at him. You look down at the paperwork then into his eyes again and he nods and you come back far enough to realise you're stiff from sitting and he asks you for a drink. And you say yes.

Seventy-Seven

Caz and Angel walked to the Grapes of Wrath, the evening cool. Inside, the bar was noisy with plain-clothes and uniforms, and rich with cigarette smoke and beer. Even at an extra fifty pence a pint the atmosphere was worth it; one big step up from the formica-clad deadness of the police social club. Angel went to find a quiet corner and Caz went to the bar. Angel was drinking bitter, Caz Diet Coke.

She found him, sat down. Quiet was comparative

"So Angel," she said, a hint of fun. "Why the CP offices and why so late at night? Nowhere better to go?"

"I was just passing. Saw you and thought, maybe a drink."

"You really haven't anywhere to go?"

"The bed-sit, the pub, or a meal out somewhere on my tod. I might as well work. I don't see me sitting alone in the third row of the pictures."

"No, I guess not," Caz said helpfully. She looked up at him as she said, "Did I tell you, by the way? I went to Manchester for a coupla days on the Hornby Terrace murder? It rained most of the time I was there."

"Manchester? What the hell has Manchester got to do with the case?"

"We go where the leads take us, Angel. And one took us there. It's where we got the drawing of John Bourne."

"Oh," Angel said.

"Leads are coming thick and fast now. MacInnes is looking at the possibility that this case is linked to a death in Southampton."

"Am I missing something, Flood?"

"I don't think so, Angel. The DI is looking at the possibility that the dead men are linked and that they've got form. They appeared on the scene at the same time and got bumped off a few days apart. From the door-to-door, the set-up in the house and a few bits and bobs they are beginning to come round to the idea that maybe both of them were child-molesters, maybe in a paedophile ring and killed by someone else in the ring. It's possible, wouldn't you think?"

"It's possible."

"You don't seem convinced."

"No, I'm not. Where does the big jump come from? Why do you think nonces in the first place?"

"Oh, Angel, come on. Two men, single, both keep themselves to themselves but friendly with the local mothers, fathers, anywhere where kids are involved. The house, a man's house, it had sweets, plastic ducks and stuff. And then of course there were the murders themselves, both involving genital damage, and the cooking . . ."

"This is hardly scientific policing, is it?"

"Too right, I'm notorious for it. The old female intuition. I guessed first when I saw Bourne's picture and when I talked to the builders up in Manchester. Y'see Bourne looks all right and not all right and that just kind of got me thinking. Then there were the other tid-bits and the way his dick had been cut off and fried and everything. And why would a bank blagger or a drugs villain want to make friends with lots of families? I checked, the animal in Southampton was the same, very friendly very distant, takes some doing, that."

"So what are you saying?"

"Well, I figure by late tomorrow we'll know if there were any connected pairs released from prison at the right time, either two guys from the same prison, or guys who went down for the same group offence but were separated. Twenty-four to thirty-six hours and I think we'll know who they were. Then we'll be a lot closer to finding the killer. Of course . . ." Caz stopped to run her finger round her dry glass. She could see the faintest tremor in Angel's face. "Of course, if someone *is* knocking off paedophiles, we don't want to rush to catch him . . ."

Seventy-Eight

Playing the game like this, you feel a fraction safer. It is such a big jump to come out with it, so why take the risk? Everyone thinks you're odd anyway, Flood, so just keep talking.

Tell Angel about the guy you went off a bridge with, how it was the right thing to do and you didn't care if it was murder or suicide or both; you did what was right. There was something more precious than you to save so you didn't have to think. Now tell him, if you could have you'd just have pushed him; you wouldn't have called it murder.

"But the way it was, he was a man and trained up. I just did it. You know they say that the moment of *seppuku* is supposed to be very peaceful. The certainty is the thing. The real decision is the moment, not the act."

"How do they know?" Angel said.

"I know," Caz said.

And how much are you going to tell Angel about the man you killed on Lanzarote? Sure he deserved *to die, but you killed him and you didn't have to. Don't say? Just hint?*

"This bastard, he'd killed three people for certain, almost killed another one. He was a toe-rag, nothing. There was a fight, he tried to kill me, and he ended up dead. It was sweet, truly sweet. I went back and had a pizza and a bottle of wine."

"You got away with it?"

"Well, obviously I did! I'm here and still a working copper, not stuck in some Spanish jail."

"You never had sleepless nights?"

"No. None. At least, not over that. The sleepless nights come from seeing people get away with things, rapists, murderers, the scum who hurt kids."

"You know the figures now?"

"Yes. They are sick, but it's freedom and liberty and all that shit isn't it? Like three year old kids make a habit of imagining the next-door neighbour fondles them, don't they?"

"Innocent until proven guilty, Flood."

"Sure. I've no quarrel with that, but this civil liberty shit doesn't even allow us to record suspicion, or to pass information on to other forces. How can that be right? How can it be right that a paedophile can move in next to Moira and Billy and they don't even know?"

"Because he's cured? Don't they have rights?"

"Cured? Are you serious? Paedophiles aren't cured, ever. You've read the books, they're sociopaths, the lot of them. They learn to conform, learn to present an image, share their techniques, talk on the internet, swap their prospects. Where's Moira's rights, Billy's rights? What about the rights of children, Titiana?"

This is how you feel, but don't push it, Caz, wait and see, wait and see if Angel comes with you, wait and see. So far you're just a little bit right wing, most coppers are. Doesn't someone have to balance the loony left, the liberals?

"It's the kids that are the key," Angel says. "Whatever the rights and wrongs, the kids should come first, shouldn't they? One fainting Robin, back in his nest, right? Who gives a shit if some vulture doesn't get full process? I don't."

Angel had stood up then: his turn for the drinks. Caz almost asked for White & MacKay, but then something clicked and she said same again. While Angel was away she calculated. When he came back she waited until she could catch his eye and then she asked him. "Jack, you never did tell me about your wife. Want to now?"

Angel was stone-faced.

"No. What makes you think I would?"

Shit!

"Nothing. I'm sorry. It was just a feeling that maybe you

might want to talk. I was trying to say, you know, I'm on your side."

"You think so?"

"Yes."

"You haven't got a bloody clue, Caz. Drop it, OK?"

Her heart raced. "OK," she said.

Seventy-Nine

Child Protection Unit, John Street, Friday 09:00

Caz had been in early, half-an-hour early, still working her way through the statistics known and the statistics estimated. She was still shocked at the size of the problem and the near-impossibility of convictions. For offences against under-fives it was estimated there were at least a thousand cases of abuse for every conviction. Some sources thought this was way too optimistic.

"You ready, Caz?"

She looked up, "What?"

"We're off to see little Jimmy and his family, remember?"

"We are?"

"Caz, we talked about it last night! I told you and you said, 'Yes, that'll be fine, Jill.' So get your skates on, ay luv? We're due there in twenty minooten so we have to tootle along."

Caz stood up, embarrassed, but Jill smiled like a Mum.

"Don't worry about it," she said. "When I started, I was deaf, dumb and blind for a fortnight. Now you know why we are as big as CID."

Caz grabbed her coat.

Jimmy and his Mum and Dad lived in an ordinary three-bedroomed Barratt house north of Brighton, just off the A23. The garden was neat lawn surrounded by white-painted rocks and a gorgeous tiny-flowered purple. The windows were Georgian, freshly painted. Jimmy's dad was scraping paint from the glass, using a razor-blade. He stepped down from a stool as their car pulled up, then came to meet them as they walked up the drive. Tom shook Jill's hand and they went in through the open front door.

Inside, again conventional, middle-England, middle-class, middle of the road. They went though a hall and into a long lounge-diner with a leather three-piece suite, a coffee table, a TV and video and two stuffed book-cases, evidence of job and hobby. Caz saw a shelf-and-a-half of gardening books, and novels – Forster, Greene, Golding, Austen, an Open University book on the nineteenth century novel. What looked like Carol Bright's bookcase was full of female authors: Alice Munro, Alice Walker, Maya Angelou, more Austen, some Doris Lessing. Caz guessed; both teachers, but Carol had given up work when Jimmy came along? And then he had reached three, time to try out a nursery . . .

Little Jimmy was there, fumbling over a jigsaw puzzle – Captain Hook duelling with Peter Pan, the mouth-ready crocodile, waiting for the loser. Jimmy seemed fine but separate, somehow slightly removed, as if the jig-saw was more interesting than these people. Caz and Jill sat down to tea while they waited for the social worker to arrive trying to make small talk, trying to be normal, when they all knew that the boy who now pottered round the coffee table made normality seem like a distant dream.

They were saying something about book prices when Tom Bright said "Ah! Here she is!" and little Jimmy pushed his jig-saw away and started crying, not like a small boy cries, but wracked, like an animal torn from its young. It was a horrible sound that cut through Caz and churned her gut. For the first time here Jimmy looked at her and the depth in his eyes made Caz feel ashamed. He blinked and Carol Bright picked him up, hushing him in whispered circles round the room until he calmed. When she stopped he was asleep.

Eighty

Marjorie Schnell had one of those large box-briefcases, black, which clacked in the silence as the room waited. She fussed a moment, her head down, before emerging with a fat folder and a clipboard. Her face showed concern and Caz thought it real without being deep.

"Mister Bright," she began.

The Tuesday before, I remember now, little Jimmy was fractious and I took him to the nursery. He started off upstairs in the main room. They always did that until all the kids were in and then they split into their groups. I was coming up the stairs with him when this chap crossed the landing. He saw us but very quickly looked away and went into the nappy room. I did notice, but what I noticed was the rudeness; they weren't like that as a rule. It was only later I thought it odd. He'd come out of the flat, but why go into the nappy room? His name is Lester Treece, Julian's Treece's brother.

"And though we are certain that something happened to Jimmy, we cannot find sufficient evidence to proceed against any individual, or indeed against the nursery. Mrs Bartholemew has already explained to you the requirements in law. From the many interviews with Jimmy, from your records of things he has said, there are far too many key points of sexual knowledge for us to doubt that incidents did occur, but these points are circumstantial and Jimmy is too young to testify in court."

"No Sarah's a man because he has a willy."

"A willy?" You try to laugh. "You don't know that, Mister Mixup!"

"It's like this," his hands are spread, "and it's grey-colour and hairy like you, like my plane, like all grey-silver, the colour is different. Different, not like another willy in the bath."

"In the bath?"

"In the bath. You've got a floppy willy but the hairy is brown. Sarah's willy is silver and it's a bit floppy and a bit not floppy and his hairy is different. I haven't got hairy."

"Jimmy, where do you see willies?"

"In the bath of course!"

"Whose willies?"

"Your willy and my willy."

"But not Sarah's willy?"

"NO-OH. That's in the upstairs-upstairs when we played Power Rangers and I had to take off my shirt."

"Your shirt?"

"David had his shirt off, he likes *being a Power Ranger and Sarah said kiss David and he had a camra."*

"A camera? Who had a camera?"

"Sarah and you could see his willy, out his front."

"And what was this willy like. Like yours? Like Daddy's?"

"Grey sort of and flobby but not like."

"Not like?"

"Different. They pinched me."

"Jimmy, who pinched you?"

"Sarah pinched me if I didn't kiss David."

"Did you cry?"

"I said only my Mummy and Daddy does pictures."

"We have spoken to David's mother but she insists nothing of the kind could have occurred. The child is a few months younger than Jimmy and far less articulate and the mother refuses to allow any home-suite interviews or doll-play.

"We believe that at the very least the children were being forced to strip and assume sexual positions, and kiss and touch each other. But despite four interviews with Mr Julian

Treece and interviews with Mr Lester Treece we have no further avenues to exploit."

"*Daddy, willies squirt.*"

"But you can do *something*, surely? You know they've got other kids there, other kids to abuse. They're even talking about opening more nurseries. Can't you stop them, close them down?"

Marjorie Schnell was uncomfortable. "Mr Bright – Tom – we are as devastated as you, believe me, but our legal department has told us that without further evidence we would be sued by Acorn & Tree-Top and lose millions. We need more. We will not give up, but we must have more. All we can do for now is keep an eye on the place and make spot-checks. I'm sure Mrs Bartholomew has explained that any parties concerned will be squeaky-clean now and will know they will be under considerable supervision for a considerable time."

"You're telling me they are going to get away with it?"

"No, Tom. They will be watched."

"They're going to get away with it. Jesus fucking Christ, they are going to walk away!."

"Our hands are tied, Tom. We can ensure better standards, we can keep a stricter eye, but without something more we cannot proceed. But that doesn't mean they will get away with it. We know of them now. It's just a matter of time but we will get them, Jill will get them."

Eighty-One

At some point Carol Bright suggested another drink. When Jill said yes, it was a tiny mew. Caz nodded. Marjorie nodded.

"Is there anything else?" Tom Bright asked.

Marjorie mentioned counselling for Jimmy; the pros and cons.

"Sort it out with Carol," Tom said.

"It's a balance between—"

Tom rose, to leave, his face dark with frustration. "I said, sort it out with Carol! I've got windows to finish."

Carol Bright brought in another tray, a few delicate biscuits on a gold-rimmed plate. Outside her husband was wedging the razor-blade back and forward in small, half-inch scrapes. "Counselling?"

"Carol, you have to choose. Counselling may help Jimmy, but it will open up the trauma first. If Jimmy was older we wouldn't hesitate to recommend it, but at this age, he will probably forget."

Carol was staring out at Tom.

"So I should or I shouldn't let—"

"We think he may not need it."

"Not need it. OK."

She was still looking out. Caz turned and saw the blood. Then she saw Tom tuck his slashed hand under his arm and continue working with the other. Red spread from his armpit into his front.

Caz said, "Let me go! Carol do you have anything?"

She rushed out quickly.

Eighty-Two

Caz went out through the front door. Tom Bright ignored her. There were smears of blood on two rectangles of glass and on the crucifix between the panes.

"The silent one," Bright said, an unpleasant look on his face.

"Can I look?" she asked.

"It's nothing, go and drink your tea."

"Let me look and I'll go away."

"I said it's nothing."

Caz went close and spoke quietly, firmly. "I can help you, Tom. I mean, I can *help* you. Do you want me to help you?"

"What?"

She was holding a handkerchief. "Let me see it."

Bright pulled out his hand. Fresh red blood flowed freely from a long, nasty razor-slash. Caz turned and held his arm under hers and pressed the folded cloth into the palm.

"Something like this should have happened to Treece, not you," she said, speaking away from Bright. "Now squeeze on that. I think you're going to need stitches." She folded his fingers over the pad.

"And arm up here. Hold it at the elbow."

Bright obeyed.

"OK," Caz said, "we're going to have to get you to casualty, toot-sweet, I think, get some stitches in this. Let's sort something out.

"Are you with me, now?"

"I think so," Bright said.

Eighty-Three

Marjorie stayed with Carol while the detectives took Tom Bright to Accident & Emergency. Mid-Friday morning was a pretty good time to cut an inch out of your hand and they only had to wait fifteen minutes. By twelve o'clock they were away from the hospital and they were back at the little Barratt house for quarter-past. Caz was the silent one again – she had said her piece, but Jill had been asking Tom not to give up because they hadn't. But now they had to go. They still had some policing to do. On the way, questions and answers.

"No, we can't just ring up the CP Units in other forces and warn them. No, they can't look up the Jimmy Bright incident on some central database. And there really isn't anything the council can do to shut down Acorn & Tree-Tops."

"So you do nothing?" Caz said.

"No, we ring up the other nicks on the Q-T and ask their advice. We at least let them know that the Nursery chain might be iffy. But writing it down is against the law, so if the detective concerned moves on . . ."

"It stinks, doesn't it?"

"Stinks is too nice a word, Caz. At least Michael Howard is *talking* about a central paedophile database. It might happen yet. I'll be dead, you'll be a DI, but it might happen."

"Duck your head!" Caz shouted.

"What for?" Jill said.

They were pulling in behind John Street. "Low-flying pigs."

Friday 12:42

Even as they pulled into the car park, Caz knew straight away; it was a major shit-and-fan moment, either a G-28 sudden death or the betting-shop blaggers on premises somewhere and alarms going. It was blues 'n' twos time, flashing lights and two-tone horns wooing as squad cars left burning rubber, people running, adrenaline.

She shouted a question to a uniform she half-knew.

"Major-Major, Flood. Down under the Palace Pier. Some poor sod strapped to the rigging like he's on a cross or something. Pretty neat, between high and low tide."

"Oh, right!" Caz said and turned away. She didn't need to rush.

It would be John Rayner.

V

Eighty-Four

12:49

The familiar smell! Blood pumping behind the eyes and in the ears! Serious action and how the hormones flew! Caz walked more briskly now, lifted by the bodies bustling down narrow corridors, the raised voices, someone with an armful of computer, a door slamming, and way off, above the rush and rattle, the distant boom of Blackside's voice. She was heading to see if she could catch MacInnes when she heard her name, half-heard her name. The second time the shout was different, much louder. *"Detective Flood!"*

Oh, Jesus!

She stopped but didn't turn round. Her neck prickled. Jesus, shit and fuck, this was no longer her case!

"Caz! Where the hell do you think you are going?"

Now she turned round. She had re-arranged her face into a sheepish grin.

"My mistake, Jill. Adrenaline rush – you know how it is."

"Yes," Jill said. "I do, but you're needed elsewhere."

"OK," Caz said. At the next right she took a left, turned into CP and sat down at her desk. Her hands were shaking. When Jill came in, seconds behind her, Caz looked up and asked what was next?

"More reading," Jill said. Then she smiled and said she'd get some coffees in. Caz returned the smile, holding it, like an adulterer, waiting hot-breathed for her chance to use the phone. When Jill left she had to force herself to wait ten seconds.

12:55

"Tom?"

"You took your time, Flood. One minute."

She heard movement and then a door closing.

"Where are you, Flood?"

"Round in Child Protection, sir, swotting. I've just heard all the ruckus. Can I guess? The man on the pier, this is John Rayner?"

"Fits the description, but he's not easy to get to. The Coastguard is there on the water, but it's difficult with the swell. They're setting something up to drop the doc over the side of the pier. He's on his way there now and from all I hear he's not very impressed with the idea of abseiling into the channel."

"It'll be Rayner," Caz said.

"If that's his name."

"Yes, if that's his name. How come you're not down there, sir?"

"DI Laing is handling it. If it's Rayner and it's connected, Dick and another ten lads will come on board the Bourne enquiry; if it's not, then he'll be running this new one on his own."

"It'll be Rayner, Tom."

"Ah think so."

She paused and her voice altered. "I need to get some sandwiches in for lunch. I thought . . . that nice place just down the hill, about ten minutes . . ."

"Ah c'd do wi' some sarnies," MacInnes said.

"You want me to get some for you, sir?"

"Nay, lass, Ah think ah'll tek a wee stroll before summer's done in completely."

"Good idea, sir. Bit of sun, do you the world of good."

"Ah was thinkin' more on the lines've prawns in mayonaise."

"Aye," Caz said. She put down the phone, got up and walked around. Three minutes later, Jill returned with the drinks and a simple, friendly face.

"Sandwiches?" Caz said.

"How's the DI?" Jill said.

Eighty-Five

Caz slurped her coffee, took Jill's order and left. In the corridors the activity was settling into "tense" and she buzzed, sensing the force.

She went out the front way, into an OK afternoon and down the hill, looking at people. Behind her was murder-rush and this other world, perhaps fifty, a hundred yards away from it, sauntered. Here the world trickled, drifted, the big decision for the afternoon being whether to risk the sun staying out or go to the cinema.

It was surreal and she expected what she saw at any moment to cut to slow-motion film and spangly drawn-out background music, the whites and pinks and fawns floating, the bald heads, the corsets, the nodding shops, even the puttering cars, aliens, alien, creased out-of-the-case jackets over the men's open-necked shirts, cardigans on top of flowered dresses and . . .

At least she knew why she was a copper.

Tom was already there and a plastic bottle of freshly-squeezed orange juice was on the counter with the prawn sandwiches. He was just paying. In front of Caz was an office junior who looked like she was going to pick up a big order. Caz wondered if it was one for American Express and Val was on the list somewhere. She'd bet on chicken-salad if he wasn't ordering two BLT's.

Tom turned round and nodded, then went out into the un-madded crowd. The junior picked up a box the size of a small car, Amex for sure. Caz grinned and blew a secret kiss to Val's lunch. Then she got her gear and went outside to speak to the DI.

"Like to walk, Caz?" He was fighting the pack.

"Sure," Caz said, "It's a nice enough day."

"Open this f'me would you?" he said.

They walked slowly through the thickening crowds, down towards the Old Steine, the view of the Brighton Pavillion to their right, and to the left the squad-car cordoned Palace Pier. They resisted the temptation to walk that way and instead took two rights, walking back uphill to the nick on a parallel road.

"That idea y'had, prison releases – there's a lot, but wuv narrowed it down awriddy, three or four pairs to be checked out. Wuv got local forces treating it as urgent right now."

"Sex offenders?"

"Aye some of 'em. There's a lot these days. Y'should know that, if y've bin to Albany."

"Point taken. So are any of these pairs paedophiles?"

"The one, and the descriptions match, two guys from a ring, one was in Strangeways, one was in Cardiff. Came out within a week of each other, but neither of em wuz paroled to the South Coast."

"I presume we tried the other way, sir, parolees and releases down our end?"

MacInnes just looked and Caz made a face.

"You did. Sorry, sir, just thinking out loud."

"There's some and Southampton has been on the phone to the probation service or on the street checking out names an' addresses. So far everyone is living where he's supposed to be. They walked in on one with a room full of video cameras – been out two weeks."

"But no murder victims?"

"Not yet. It's early days."

An area car was drifting down the hill and the faces were familiar. The front-seat passenger raised his hand and Caz waved back. "So do we know anything abut this G-28, Tom? We know if it's been mutilated, like Bourne?"

"Only the coastguard have been that close. The best view

otherwise is off the shingle with binoculars. It looks likely not."

"Different MO."

"Different murderer, mebbes, Flood. Don't be so quick to jump."

"Not that quick, sir. I'll be happy to eat crow if it's not J Rayner, but I'll bet it is. I've been expecting this one for a few days, same as you. I wonder where the purple jacket is, and who's riding the Kawasaki."

"So why no mutilation?"

"No need is my guess, Tom. Not any more. I think our killer was working his way through a list of names but didn't have any addresses – except the first. The fingers and the burnings were just to slow us down a little."

They were close to Williams Street, the back of the nick. Clouds had passed over again and from cool rushed cooler. MacInnes puffed. "Yer saying?"

"Our man is committed, and he knows exactly what he has to do. He just wanted time. John Rayner wasn't living alone; the other two were, so different plan. He left the Bourne photograph on the hall carpet to be found. He would have to know that Rayner would run; he knew he was warning him. He was banking on that, hoping that Rayner would lead him to somewhere or someone. The question is who, and where, and why. I think we've still got at least one more body to come. I hope I'm right."

MacInnes stopped. "Pardon?"

"I said I hope I'm right, Tom. I can see no reason to rush this case. If we're too quick our killer might not have finished."

Caz couldn't quite read his face. Maybe MacInnes wasn't sure what he was thinking either. But then the DI pointed to the station. "Don't ever say that inside there, Flood. I couldnae ignore it."

Caz nodded.

"We'd best go in. Jesus, lass."

Caz was defiant. "He suffered the little children, didn't He, sir?"

"Aye, he did that, Flood and they crucified him."

He turned to walk on and Caz called after him. She saw him stiffen before he turned.

"One other thing, sir – , the magazine, did you check?"

"Aye, lass, it were *Fiesta*, like y'said; March this yee-ah. Missing fr'm yer collection is it?"

"Very funny, sir."

"Now go back to CP and finish yer lunch."

"I'll just wait here a minute, sir." She held out Jill's sandwiches. "I wonder – y'couldn't . . .?"

MacInnes looked up at a quickly fouler day.

"Y'sunning yersel'?"

"Thinking, sir. I'd appreciate . . ."

He took the package and walked off, shaking his head. If he was anyone else, she was anyone else, this wouldn't have happened. Caz still loved him.

She crouched against a wall and thought murder.

It really *was* gloomy now.

Eighty-Six

How would you do it? What kind of man would you be? Would you have to be an animal too? You acted like one. Or could you divorce yourself from the acts, because these were necessary, for the children, the innocents, the nested fledglings who deserved the chance to leave their trees and fly.

So how did it begin? You needed to know where one lived, but was it chance, or did you scour the country? Did you know that parolees had to have an address, even if it was only a hostel? Did you guess that Bourne was not where he should be? Did you know that if he was a convicted felon his finger-prints and other identifying marks would be on file?

And you burned the man in Bitterne, no fingerprints, no tattoos, no face either – was this to win some time too? Where did people get the idea he owed money? From you? Were you there before? No, this was chance, this was gossip, this was your second man, you couldn't leave it long, you knew you had to strike quickly before he wondered where Bourne was, why he hadn't rung.

And why did he let you in? Did he think you were a friend? Were the things done to him the actions of a friend? You weren't part of his group were you? He didn't let you in because you were an associate; you weren't a friend, a co-conspirator. He must have feared you or respected you, or bowed to your authority.

But he let you in friend, didn't he? And then you did what had to be done. You have done a saintly thing but are you saint or devil?

Eighty-Seven

13:56

Jill Bartholomew was talking to a couple of uniforms when Caz slipped back in. Jill appeared engrossed but raised a finger to show she had seen the other detective. Caz slumped into her chair behind a small pile of case notes and yesterday's reference books. She felt guilty. There was a post-it note on the top of the pile: ring Moira, ring DS Mason at Southampton. She rang Mason first.

"Update you on the mad rapist, Flood. My DI isn't sure, my DS doesn't fancy it, and the first word back from the CPS is, no chance."

"What? Are you *serious*? If Jimmy M is right we have one to ten unsolved murders we can clear up."

"I know that, you know that. But the way they see it is how tough it'll be to prove. Our man is a weak witness. If he ever stands in court the defence will have a field day. Can you imagine – a convicted rapist, who wants anonymity and the jury have got to believe him?"

"Christ, Peter. Have they said no, already?"

"No, they've said they're not at all keen. I knew they would. I tried to persuade my DI to keep shtum for at least a week to see how far we got. I figured if we had some leads to the whereabouts of some bodies, they'd have to do something. But you know Denham, he's by the book. He wouldn't say yes to the time without an OK from upstairs, and our upstairs rang their upstairs."

"So, is it dead?"

"No. I've got to go and see them for a chat on Monday. Correction: *we've* got to go."

"Oh, Christ! Where, exactly?"

"Winchester. Hants HQ."

"Just to be told they're going to kill it?"

"If it was definite, they'd've killed it already."

Caz sighed; she knew better. "Peter, they've *decided*. They chat to us and give us three hours of bullshit to cover their arses. The minutes of the meeting will show how much they *wanted* to but the plan was unworkable."

"Yeah, well."

"Yeah, well, *what*, Peter? These people kill *children*. There are mothers and fathers out there who still don't know what happened to their kid. Is he missing because he ran away to London, or did some bastard low-life smother him? Or was he gang-raped before being strangled and dumped?"

"Steady up, friend."

"I don't want to steady up, *Sergeant*, if it's all right with you. I just want to start getting some of these people off the streets."

He waited. She could feel him letting her calm down.

"You any cooler?"

"Not much."

"Flood, I got a kid, remember, a little girl. Clare is seven and she's the best thing that ever happened to me. Don't you think I care too? But it's not always as cut and dried as you'd like it. We spend three months on a case, it falls apart, what about the bastards elsewhere we could have been catching? Yeah, the CPS are a bunch of idiots. Doesn't mean they're always wrong. Keep yer cool, OK?"

"Sure," Caz said. "No other option, is there?"

Eight-Eight

14:07

There was too much, too much abuse, too much in Caz's head, too much to decide on, too much responsibility . . . There was too much noise, too much quiet, not enough light or dark. Whether Caz looked or not she saw the pictures, Hassleblad professional, tiny vulvas, bruised and torn, dilated anal sphincters, barely formed hymens ripped and stretched by a savage penis, a sick finger, a crayon, the arm of a doll. She knew this was forensic, had-to-be-done stuff, but Jesus wept, it was too much, too much, too much.

She felt the tightness in her chest, not gore rising but anxiety as some animal fighting up out of her, horrid, dark, uncontrollable. Her face burned and she needed an outlet. This wasn't her, not the cool, gentle, methodical, Jill, not the stoic, not the patient Job, she was an action-woman, a shark, doomed to die if she was still. What was she doing here? This job would kill her in three months.

The CPS, wasn't nicknamed the Criminal Protection Service for nothing. How could they put *a cost* to catching these vermin, put numbers into machines and play percentages? Had they seen the pictures? They talked of probabilities and allocated resources. Did they have kids? Could Caz ever have a child and expose her to shits like John Bourne? Jesus! She closed the books, pushed away the files. She knew for sure now, that this way wasn't her way.

She picked up the phone and pecked out a number. When the answer came she said, "It's me. Do you still want that help?"

Eighty-Nine

War Room, 17:01

Caz had spoken to the DI, got his temporary OK, then slipped into the War Room early and sat two thirds of the way back. With the addition of DI Laing's ten extra men, the Hornby Terrace murder squad was over thirty-strong now and by five-to-five it was packed. Caz was head-counting but she couldn't see Angel anywhere, in the seats, or among the half a dozen guys who were having to stand up at the sides of the room. But it was full because this was special and she could smell it. Yes! Flood was back in harness, feeling the buzz.

Then, at five o'clock exactly, the room instinctively hushed. Thirty seconds later, the rubbered doors flapped open and DCS Blackside, DI MacInnes, DI Laing, and DS Moore came in. The room reeked of tension as the DCS took the stand.

"Gentlemen . . ." he said. Caz could feel her heartbeat in her throat. "We have three bodies, three names, one connection. Blinds, please!"

One of Laing's lads pulled a couple of strings and the outside was shut away. Blackside nodded and the Kinderman clacked, a split second before the lights went off. Up on the wall, a mug-shot, a classic new-prisoner front-and-two-sides. John Bourne.

"Anthony James Sago. 49. Was an estate agent. Paedophile."

Click. Sc-lack!!

"Derek Edwin Paul. 35. Accountant. Paedophile."

He nodded. Sc-lack!!

"Ray James, AKA John Rayner. Salesman. Paedophile.

"And gentlemen, they are all very dead. Shed no tears."

Caz was wondering what Tom MacInnes was thinking, and now she had checked, she was wondering where the hell Angel was . . . The DCS was now doing a run-through of Operation Iris.

" . . . by West Midlands, Staffordshire, Greater Manchester and Cheshire. Nine months, eighty-seven men and more than a million pounds . . ."

Caz was itching, thinking, hoping.

" . . . Anthony James Sago, eight years; Paul, six years; and James, six years. Sago and Paul are still officially resident at their parole addresses and no parole violations. James last seen at his hostel two months ago, left in an agitated state . . ."

Only two months of fear? Not enough.

" . . . A paedophile ring believed to contain a hard-core of up to six men, plus an outer ring, more casual, of perhaps another seven or eight. Despite extensive enquiries, only five men ever faced charges; these three men, one Christopher Loft, and John Andrew Bull. Loft was sent down to Parkhurst for eighteen years but suffered a fatal accident not long after his arrival there. Bull is now detained at HM's pleasure in Broadmoor."

Four out of five. It's a start.

"Gentlemen. When the ring was first uncovered, there was a rumour that its leader was someone in high places. The press even tried to suggest there was police involvement. That is *crap!*"

He waited briefly for effect, then continued.

"We are following up the possibility that one of the gang is trying to cover his tracks. This makes sense. The Parkhurst death was nonce-justice; a double-lifer name of Booker confessed to the murder soon afterwards. Apart from an extra prison move, it didn't affect him. He was in for the duration anyway."

17:44

As the room cleared, Caz stayed where she was and let the bodies melt away. Up on the walls now, things were changing. There were more photographs, real names and now red lines and arrows everywhere. A big case.

She heard Greavsie laugh and saw Billy turn momentarily. She raised her hand, half good-bye wave, half acknowledgement. She wasn't sure Billy had meant an exchange but he made the sign for drink and she nodded. The DCS was gone. On the stage MacInnes was running through something with Bob Moore.

Yeah, she looked a twat, she looked a prat, switching in and out of sections; but she had only asked for a short break from the murder squad. Sure, she'd let Jill Bartholomew down, but better to face the facts now than be a screaming rectangular peg in a way-too-tight round hole. One day she'd buy Jill a drink and let her know she was on her side. She just had her own way of doing things, that was all.

"I'm not like you, Jill."

"I know, luv. I was just hoping some of your case-luck might rub off on us."

And she had left, gone to see MacInnes and said she was rested enough. She felt guilty. He wasn't surprised.

Ninety

The Grapes of Wrath was thank-fuck-it's-Friday full and there was a lot of tension being let out. Someone had started a float, fiver-a-head, and there was plenty of beer being spilled. Laing's newbies were being particularly noisy and a DC had just said the wrong thing to Bob Saint about his war wound. Bob stood up. He looked like he was joking but Caz knew different.

"Hey, Lick-Penis, unless you want this thumb pressing on your prostate, I suggest you take the piss out of someone else, all right?"

The other guy did a quickly-camped, "Oooooh, promises!" but then his eyes lowered to his drink. It was OK. Someone had slopped a lager in front of Caz. She thought about it but decided saying she was TT would not be a good move right this minute. She drank up.

Billy was a few seats away, still not really himself. Caz suddenly realised she hadn't rung Moira. Presumably it was just to set up another night out.

"Hey, Billy, Moira rang me!"

She saw his face change. When he lifted his glass to acknowledge, it hid his face.

"Oh, *fuck*!" someone said to the right, and three chairs shot back. Beer rushed along the table. When she looked up, Billy was pouring his lager down, big hurry. She got up and cornered him before he could slip away.

"You promised me a drink," she said.

"I need to get back."

"This won't take long," Caz said. He wasn't going anywhere. "I'll have a tonic. Anyone asks, it's got three gins in it."

Billy's shoulders dropped but he dutifully went to the bar. While he was there Caz leaned in behind Greavsie.

"Don't piss off 'ome without speaking to me, Jim, OK? I need a quick word. If you're very good, I won't tell the lads about your new girlfriend."

Jim nodded.

"Good boy," Caz said, and tapped his shoulder.

As Caz turned round, Billy swung away from the bar with a half pint for him and the tonic for her. He nodded towards the other bar. Caz walked ahead. "So how's things?" he said as they sat down.

"OK," she said. "You?"

He stiffened. Not much, but it was there. He managed a smiley-shrug, but Caz knew him too well.

"Trouble, Billy?"

He looked down at his drink, up. "I dunno. What did Moira say?"

"I didn't speak to her. I was supposed to ring her this afternoon, but I was on the phone to Southampton trying to stop the CPS fucking up yet another case."

"You haven't spoken?"

"No."

"Oh," he said, and took another sip of his lager. He was doing a fairly good job of avoiding eye-contact.

"I've got my mobile, Billy. I could ring her from here."

"Don't do that," he said.

"So – trouble?"

"No," he said. "I stopped myself."

"And you don't call that trouble?"

"I love Mo, you know that, Caz. And little Tee. It's this case . . ."

Caz flipped open her Micro-Tac.

"OK," Billy said. "Moira – I nearly hit her."

Ninety-One

"Flood!"

They both looked up as Greavsie's red face sought them out. He saw them and came over.

"Flood, look, you wanted a quick word." He gestured over his head towards the bar. "Only I gotta go pretty soon. I'm driving, and me and Janice, we're out tonight, got a baby-sitter."

Caz looked at Billy. He relaxed back into his seat.

She turned back to Greavsie. "I didn't see Angel today."

"You got the hots for him or summat, all that pretty hair?"

"Fuck off."

"He called in sick, food-poisoning or something."

"Shit!"

"Woss the prob? You leave yer knickers in his car?"

"You're not funny, Jim. No, he borrowed some cash of me, a fifty, and I was hoping to get it rather than go to a hole in the wall."

"I got some spare. How much you want?"

"I need fifty."

"Oh," Jim said.

"You've dropped him off after shift a few times, haven't you? Where's he live? I'll go down there with a bottle of Lucozade and empty his wallet."

"Camelford Street, off Marine Parade. Don't know the number though. House has just been done up, blue and white. He's on the first floor. You sure you two ain't got something going?"

Caz fluttered. "Jim, why would I when there's you?"
"Get in the queue," he said.
Then he was gone and Caz turned back to Billy.

Ninety-Two

Caz went home, went to Val's flat, it was the thing women in love did. Val was there: paperwork again, his Toshiba laptop open with a spreadsheet showing. In the background Barbra Streisand. She kissed him on the cheek and said she'd make some coffee. "What's for dinner?" she asked, shouting it over the sound of running water. When he said, "Nothing," she leaned through and asked where they were going. The nearest Italian to Tom's flat was Donatello's; the nearest one to them was Armando's.

She smiled, "You fancy a four out with Tom and Vaunda?"

If they didn't talk shop, he said.

When she dialled the DI's, it rang five or six times – rare for him in the old days, before Von turned up from his secret past. She was ready to put the phone down and rethink when he answered.

"MacInnes."

"Tom, it's Caz. I was wondering . . ."

He was tired, just in, Vaunda was in the shower.

"I'd appreciate it, Tom, and Valerie has never really sat down with Von; it's about time . . ."

"Ring you back in two minutes," he said.

"Half past eight!" she said to Valerie. "Don't know where, but Tom says he'll book and ring us back. It's about time you got to know Von, wouldn't you say?"

Val was tapping keys. "Flood, I just do what I'm told."

"Do my back then? Five minutes?" His computer beeped.

She left him his drink and took her mug into the bedroom.

She hadn't run that much this week but she felt light. It was either the adrenaline of the case or the cut-back on the booze. Either way she felt alive. She stripped.

Caz was musty from the day and could smell cigarette smoke from the pub. She needed the shower. As she stepped in and under, used now to it's industrial cleaner pressure, for some perverse reason she was thinking about Batman & Robin. She shook her head and thought *"Bruce Wayne, millionaire philanthropist"* and clear as these tiles she saw the interview suite at John Street and little Jimmy Bright looking up at her through the glass.

She shampooed with some lemon Wash 'n' Go, not as carefully as she should, and thought double identities, Superman, Clark Kent, Raffles, Dr Jekyll and Mr Hyde, Frankenstein – no, Frankenstein wasn't a two-identity job was he? – Spiderman – who was his alter-ego? – good question to stump someone at a party – and who else? The Incredible Hulk, Mr you-won't-like-me-if-you-make-me-angry, the guy who went green and burst out of his clothes, well his shirt anyway. Oh, and Vaunda Goddard of course, so good at being lots of different people that it drove her slightly bonkers. Maybe she could teach Caz some tricks.

She was wondering some more about Jack Sweet, when Valerie coughed his way past. She'd been soaping herself down and this identity suddenly became very specific.

She shouted, "Thomas!"

He shouted from the bedroom. "What?"

"My back, you said, Thomas! Five minutes you said, Thomas! But you better take all your clothes off. It's *suh-lippery* in here!"

Then she saw him, very pink, the other side of the glass.

Ninety-Three

Armando's was small and dark and stank of garlic. Donatello's on the other hand was more open, much larger. And stank of garlic. If anyone ever invented a garlic aftershave, Caz was in *big* trouble.

She sat next to Vaunda (who tonight was being Vaunda) and opposite Tom. Valerie had taken charge and got Tom a large Bell's, Vaunda a G&T, himself a Southern Comfort and Coke.

Big test, huh?

"No," he said, with a wink. "I've just ordered a bottle of *Beaujolais Village*, your Friday night treat."

Beaujolais?

"Experiment a little," he said.

When the garlic bread came, Caz mentioned Angel Sweet being off sick. MacInnes said he knew, but figured he was taking a break from another mindless day of door-to-door. When the fish course came and MacInnes was sipping at his third whisky she joked about Angel not being sick. Tom had had a glass of wine too.

He laughed. "He couldn't have known Ray James was going to turn up strapped to the pier, could he? I think that might have cured a bit of gippy tummy."

"He needs a wife, I reckon. Someone to get him to eat his greens."

MacInnes glanced quickly at Valerie who had just laughed at one of Von's voices. "I presume you're not offering, Flood? You know he's divorced?"

"Yes. He told me. January, wasn't it?"

"January '89."

Caz looked puzzled. "He said he'd lost her nine months ago."

"He did. She died."

"*Died*?"

"Aye, he . . ." MacInnes said, but then he slowed as he realised he was out of school. Caz sensed shutters being lowered.

"Sorry, sir, didn't mean to pry. And I don't want to compromise you either, I shouldn't have asked."

She waved at a waiter and pointed to Tom's drink. For the second time that day she had a flash of guilt but she rode it easily. This Caz was slick.

"Did the doc have fun dangling off the pier?" she said lightly.

"White as a sheet, so Dick Laing telt me. Allus wanted t'see the cocky bugger in some kinda trouble. But I didnae know that he wuz baith scared o' heights *and* cannit swim!"

"D'you hear that, Val? About the doctor at the Palace Pier?"

Valerie was leaning towards Vaunda. He waved a hand. Then he laughed and looked at Caz. "What did you say, luv?"

"Oh, nothing," Caz said. "We were talking about little penises and I thought of you."

Ninety-Four

Saturday morning, telephone bedlam, the classic cop-show scene: twelve desks, twenty coppers on the phone, twenty fingers in ears, twenty detectives repeating, "I'm sorry, I didn't catch that, could you say that again? – I'm sorry – *can someone give me a* break *here?*"

Probation services, hostels, known associates, prison assistant governors, Head Kangas (roos-screws), other nicks, check out the whereabouts of, detain for questioning, confirm the residence of . . .

Hammer, hammer, hammer until by one o'clock if you have to say, "Good morning, my name is Detective Constable Kathy Flood, John Street, Central Brighton . . ." one more time, you will remove someone's face and fax it to the Chief Constable. You have drunk seven plastic cups of coffee and you are drumming like a vibrator.

Laing. "OK, lads. Let's call it a day. You've got 'omes to go to?"

Yes, sir. But The Grapes is on the way.

Last night you made love, you took ages, you ate each other, you sprinkled each other with talcum powder and rubbed it smooth and flat, it feels like oil. You teased, you giggled, you messed about. You were light-hearted like a starving man is elated and earlier when your boss and best friend was drunk you milked him, while his girlfriend did impersonations and told the story of when her cover was a specialist masseuse. That put an IRA gang away

You don't even think when someone passes you a lager.

You're back in the thick of things, one of the lads, and this time you're all knee-deep in a big, big, big, bloody case.

And you don't think that much when you pay for half a round and you add a whisky to the bill and you forget to think when your third lager arrives and suddenly, suddenly, all you've eaten is two packets of crisps – and Jesus, you feel pissed and it's three o'clock already and everybody else has a home to go to. And you can't even go home and bonk Val cos the bastard's gone off to a car auction and and and.

So you leave, thinking about Detective Sergeant Bubbles Sweet.

Bubbles. Now that is *funny!*

It's sunny, and you're outside, and you made friends with Billy before he left, after you talked to Moira, and you promised you'd be Tee's godmother and you were faintly slurred when you said, "Moira, if ever, ever if, Moira, if, Mo if anyone ever touches Titty-Anna I'll kill 'im. I'll kill 'im, if, Moira."

Now look, all these people. Fucking hell someone must've spiked one've those drinks – three lagers and a double whisky? Had more than that before without feeling like every-bloody-body in the world is walking the wrong way.

Hey and wow, Camelford Terrace! Well, whatyerknow? Blue and white house – take a bottla lemonade – lucozade *– sheet! Kiss Angel better and call him "Bubbles" ask the fucker why he said he'd only just got divorced when he got divorced YEARS ago and in January he didn't get* divorced. *He lost the Mrs cos she fucking killed herself! Get out of that, sunshine! Detective Constable Flood's on the case!*

So what do yer say to that, Bubbles*?"*

Ninety-Five

"If you call me that again, Flood, woman or no woman, I'll put your fucking lights out. Nobody, *nobody* calls me Bubbles."

You won't like me if you make me angry . . .

"Hey, I was joking, Sarge; been working hard 'n' had a few lunchtime drinks thassall. You're not the Incredible Hulk, y'know."

"I'm on the sick, Flood. What do you want?"

"I just come fr'achat. Yer not gonna let me in?"

"Come back when you're not pissed. I want to go back to bed."

"Oooh bed! Is that an offer? You offrin', Sarge?"

"Jesus, Flood, read my lips. *Go away.*"

"I feel sick. Can I have a bit've bread?"

"Jesus!"

But he opens the door and you're in. You're mad, being stupid, but that's because you're pissed. You just need something to eat. And you're not so drunk as you thought, just light-headed. You need something to up your blood-sugar, that's all.

"You got any chocolate, Angel? Or some biscuits?"

"I'll have a look."

You sit on the bed. "Don't move!" he says.

And you see the photograph, and you just know. *But you aren't as good at reading things as you thought. But there it is, Angel, a pretty woman, blonde, and a little boy, so cute he could be that kid bubbles, the one from the soap advert. Of course if you ask he'll say it's his sister and his nephew. But you're a super-spy now.*

Angel came back into the lounge, two thick slices of bread and butter spread with strawberry jam.

"So Jack, you got family, brothers, sister?"

"A sister in Canada. She teaches."

"I'm a one-off. She married?"

"Divorced."

"Same as you. Kids?"

"No."

Caz, remember once you were so pissed off with life, you went for a drink with Tom and then when he went back to work you wandered The Lanes and you ended up in Armando's? Gabriel made you some fish and you drank a bottle of wine with him then brandy coffee with him and then it was raining and someone stabbed you, you were too drunk to care, too drunk to put up a proper fight?

"So this is your wife, Angel? And this is your boy? His nickname was Bubbles wasn't it?"

Remember how it didn't really hurt? How it was peculiar, almost sexy, and red and black and the moment, the moment, when the world sort of shrunk in a circle and it wasn't bad at all and you knew that if it happens it happens but dying's not that big a deal, better than only being half alive? You remembered rain?

"Are you really so stupid, Flood? I've warned you already!"

If you're wrong it doesn't matter, he thinks you're pissed and he's on the sick and Monday everyone will have forgotten you were here.

"Look, Angel, your life's your own. I just want to know why you've been lying to me. I thought we were mates."

See, it's all something and nothing. Pissed or not you've still got your wits about you. Why should he think you mean more than you say? You could just mean, why the lie, couldn't you? You could just mean: you're an uptight bastard, Sergeant Sweet but why do you bullshit your friends?

"You're pushing it, Flood."

"I know. But I thought I was your friend. I've been trying to tell you I'm on your side. I understand."

Is this right? His eyes look slightly odd would you say? Remember, if it happens, it doesn't matter, win some, lose some, put up a fight maybe, try to win the big one, but you've been there, you remember drowning.

"Tell me what being on my side means, Flood."

Yes, the eyes are *different. Ah, well, ah, fucking fucked-up well. You put out your left hand, feeling for somewhere to push off from. It's under the pillow. Paper? You're not thinking, but you're screwing it up smaller while you think.*

"I mean you're involved somehow, Angel. Involved in this case. You're hiding evidence for some reason. You're in no hurry to see the killer caught and you've been bending things. And I haven't told anyone."

What would you call this then, Caz? Bravery? Sticking two fingers up to Big G and saying I can give you a run f'yer money you old bastard? Makes a helluva difference not being scareda dying dunnit?

"If that's all I've been doing, Flood, you talk to your DI and my career is fucked. But it's all bollocks, anyway. Where d'you get the idea?"

This is a good tactic, Caz, a way out for both sides. Give him a way out and you might not be on your way out . . .

"Where d'you want me to start? Gut feel? The way you frightened the living shit out of Greavsie without even raising your voice? You turning up just at the coincidental time and not minding a stint in Child Protection? You getting on great with kids when you said you never had one? The bubbles stuff – all that angst over a nickname?"

"And?"

"Oh, there's more, Angel. You were very conscientious when we turned over Hornby Terrace, lifting carpets, measuring walls, doing all the obvious stuff but you never said a word about the odd stuff, the sweets, the kids' things in the bathroom, the piece of kiddie porn you picked up under the lounge floor."

"What?"

"Oh, you swapped that, Jack. You slipped it away in the evidence bag but then you delivered it yourself didn't you? Not get some peon like me or Greavsie to take it in. Nah, you did it so you could swap some sick paedophile pictures for some tit and cunt. Trouble was I thought to check and the pages in the bag were from after the floorboards were nailed down."

"Bollocks!"

"Is it? How about the way you got Greavsie round the corner and were pretty cool about him taking time out? And then you stayed over that evening while we went home? That was when you lifted the floor in the hall. I never clicked when we did it the following day, but didn't those screws come out easy? You had us laughing and joking at the time but they just pissed out."

"So?"

"Well they would if someone had unscrewed them the night before to check for more evidence."

"Flood, if I was hiding evidence, don't you think all this crap is a bit hit and miss?"

"Oh, sure, Jack, but what else can you do? You've managed to swing it that you're on the house-search but you're surrounded by coppers, you just have to play it by ear. But you're good, you move us around and have us doing work where you expect nothing, you just make sure you're where it's going to count."

"You're dreaming now."

"Yeah, I know, Jack. Like you're sick the morning after the third killing . . ."

"Third?"

"Oh, pulleassse, Jack. You can't act. Our friend with the purple jacket. Strapped to the Palace Pier, four hundred yards from here. You and me, we'd been out the night before, and you were serious about what these bastards did to kids. It wasn't just anger, it wasn't just disgust, you hated the fuckers with a passion, just like me."

"Just like you?"

"Just like me, yeah."

"I don't think so."

"You don't? Well I was there that night, Jack, my angel. I saw what was done to Anthony Sago, I felt the emptiness of that room. I saw the display, that was what it was, the *display* of the hate. Sure I didn't know then exactly *what* hate, but I was close, I just hadn't said the words then. But you gave yourself away."

"When? And gave myself away over what, exactly?"

"When we ate together. I was drunk then, like now, although I'm getting rapidly sober. It was such a little thing but you said Sago had been forced to eat his own dick. I didn't think anything of it, because that was what *I'd* heard too. It was only a lot later I found out that it wasn't public knowledge. The doc withdrew the thought."

"He could have said something."

"I checked."

"MacInnes then. Blackside, Billy Tingle."

"I checked with them too."

Ninety-Six

Angel moved quickly, quick and deadly. Caz didn't even have time to move. He had stood and said, "I'll make us some coffee. Here, let me take that plate," and as he pushed Caz back against the bed she thought she heard him say, "Sorry."

But it was so quick and the other pillow was on her face, and his weight was on it, but she thought she could still breathe and then underneath, his hands crossed, holding the neck-band of her sweat-shirt and pulling, pulling, she had only just thought, "ah, carotid arteries, but . . ." when there was nothing.

VI

Ninety-Seven

Angel drove north, cutting across the Sussex Downs, then dropped his newly-bought second-hand car on to the M23 motorway, then the M25, the M1. He stopped at Leicester Forest services for petrol and then, at Junction 24, turned left and headed towards Derby via Shardlow. At the service station he had asked the attendant about the best exit for Loughborough and joked about a village called Bunny.

He took the ring-road round Derby until he hit the A38 and then drove down that until he hit the A5. At Brownhills he stopped at a transport café and drank a mug of tea and ate egg, bacon and chips.

He hadn't wanted to hurt Flood, she was a good kid, but there was nothing, nothing he could do, she would have known that. The carotid strangle was painless and very quick. Afterwards, he had arranged her body, packed his stuff, and left quietly.

He wasn't that worried about covering his tracks, but he didn't want to be spotted and picked up before he was finished. The crap at the services about the village near Nottingham, if they ever got on to his route, might gain him an hour or so or at least steer some of those looking for him that way. He had left clues suggesting Notts and Lincs all over, most of them well hidden but soon picked up by a good villain-taker like MacInnes. Angel was banking on him being good.

He drove at sixty-five on the motorways, sixty on dual

carriageways. That night he stopped in a small B&B and paid cash. He took the two guns inside, wrapped in sports gear, in a black *Nike* bag.

Ninety-Eight

Flood had woken up in the recovery position, on her side, her upper leg pulled up to waist level and dropped forward, her lower arm bent for extra stability, the other tucked under her tilted-back head.

She felt like total shit.

Angel had done a reasonable job. He had bet Caz's life on her not vomiting twice and had not come second. But it was her life and his bet. That, and the headache didn't make Caz feel a whole lot better.

This wasn't a James Bond film and she lay there sensing her bits, waiting to work everything out. There was the smell of vomit wiped away, the definitive whiff of Dettol and the sweet dark aroma of chloroform. If she was right, Angel had stuck the neck strangle on for just long enough – both carotids closed and the lights were out in seven seconds – and then waited with the doused rag until she regained consciousness. You came out of the minimal choke almost as fast as you went in, but it was a very good grip if you knew it. The chloroform lasted longer and Angel needed time.

If she could have got up and walked around, Caz might have felt woozy but when she started to move was when she realised Angel had hand-cuffed her to the radiator. Oh, fucking cheers, Sergeant!

It took her five minutes to spot the key, another five to work it over. Then she was free. When she thought to look at her watch it was ten to five. Time here, time there, and she guessed he had waited to see if she was likely to puke.

Angel killed child molesters, but basically he seemed a pretty decent bloke. If he had asked for a few hours' start, Caz would have given him it anyway.

She uncrumpled the piece of paper hoping it was something, then she went through to the bathroom and washed her face. When she came out she took half-a-dozen deep breaths and then started taking Angel's flat apart.

Ninety-Nine

At first there was not much to see but Caz knew that anything, everything, every apparent nothing thing might matter. Her neck felt sore, she had burn marks from her sweat shirt and she felt lousy, but she figured this had an edge on being dead.

In the toilet she found six or seven squares of torn paper; the rest, she presumed flushed away. Under the U-bend she found one more and it came out on her finger, smeared with shit and a few letters. She put them all, letters up, on the edge of the bath and then went to wash. Polythene gloves would have been nice . . .

In the kitchen, on the stove, a tiny dune of charred paper; this a rushed job. Scene of Crimes might have been able to get a word or two. She looked closely and found *Aber* . . . and . . . *th*, silver negative on the brown-black. Then, to be sure, she crushed the lot and flicked it to the floor.

She pressed re-dial on the phone. Somewhere a hand-set rang but there was no reply, and no answering-machine cut in. She tapped in the number of a local taxi firm and put it down after one ring.

Back in the kitchen she took the waste-bin and tipped the contents on to the draining board. Angel was a one-serving and tin man and she thanked the Lord she wasn't picking her way through rotting food debris. Stuffed inside a Sainsbury's low-cal lasagne she found a envelope addressed to Angel and posted Wednesday. It was old-fashioned handwriting, she guessed at his mother, led there by the Esq. after his name. The postmark was Chester.

She found the copy of *Fiesta* with the missing page shoved well down, in a black bin bag, the second of four, in the garden. There were brochures there too, a little bit too easily found, one for a hotel near Bunny, Notts, another one in Skegness, Lincs. Somehow she didn't think so and didn't even bother with the other bags. She went back up the fire-escape.

Back in the small flat she laid out what she had on the bed; the bed where Angel Sweet had put her lights out. For the first time she thought of the bet she had made with herself, that Angel was not a murderer; merely a destroyer of vermin.

From the toilet, ball-pen not felt-tip writing, a stroke of luck, she had *yswy*; three blanks, one with a diagonal line; *Hote* and *oyle.* On her last piece, (getting it, she thought had been below and beyond the call of duty), was the word: *Manx*! And what looked like the sharp end of an arrow.

But the crumpled sheet still waited. Caz wasn't certain why she had left it so long. Had she really bet so much on Sweet's skill? Was this a false lead like the brochures? Somehow, she didn't think so and she wouldn't think so. It had to have been worth it . . .

A mother to a son, crying for a grand-son.

One-Hundred

My Dear Jack,

I know how hard it must be to trust in the Lord, but trust in Him you must. It was He who decided I should lose my grand-son and you should lose our little Bubbles. I am so sad that all this hurt your marriage to Jeanette. I did love her so, like a daughter, I still do. I'm sad, but perhaps it's for the best. Now that you are divorced, perhaps you can both find a way to forget. Please come and see me soon. All this has made me feel very

Caz turned over the sheet. Older people often wrote on the back of writing paper – , but it was a poem, no author:

If I can stop one heart from breaking,
I shall not live in vain;
If I can ease one life the aching,
Or cool one pain,
Or help one fainting Robin
Unto his nest again,
I shall not live in vain.

And at the bottom, surrounded by thick black arrows; *Manx?*; and below this, *Aber?*

One-Hundred-and-One

It was early evening as Caz walked along the front towards her flat in Inkerman Terrace. The lights of the Palace Pier had just come on; and she could hear music, imagine foot-falls on the planking. She had to pass within fifty metres of Tom's flat and was aware of him there with Vaunda. She felt guilty.

Now she was stone-cold sober she wasn't just thinking of herself but of Valerie, of Moira and Billy, baby Tee, Jimmy Bright, Jill Bartholomew. Her choices might affect Tom MacInnes too and for the first time in her life she really didn't know the best thing to do.

In the flat Caz soaked in a bath of pink water, far too hot. She massaged her neck and agonised. She ached with indecision and tried to make an answer appear. It made no difference.

Officially, she had never been to Jack Sweet's bed-sit. Nothing had happened between them and she didn't know he'd left Brighton. Where he had gone and what he did now was nothing to do with her, none of her business, and more importantly, she was clear of involvement. And if Angel was to finish what he'd started – well, that was nothing to do with her either.

But he might end up under arrest and talk about what he had done to Flood. Shit Street. Or he might finish it all, and leave some note of confession. Shit again. She had thought she could leap in the MX5 and sail off to find the man; and then – then? She didn't know what then meant. But that didn't matter, she was over a barrel, and the decision was forced on her. She picked up the telephone.

"Tom?"

"Flood."

"I think I've got some heavy news, sir, official. Jack Sweet."

"A moment," he said.

She felt the hand go over the mouthpiece and, just, she heard her good friend shouting to his lover and her voice, even more faintly, shouting lightly back. It still seemed strange . . .

He lifted his hand. "Fire away, Flood. What's the problem?"

"Jack Sweet, sir. Involved in these murders, protecting someone at least, and tonight he attacked me, gave me a smack, sir, and then legged it."

"How long ago?"

"I'm not exactly sure, sir. I think I passed out. Then I came back here. I could do with you coming round, though. I feel a bit iffy."

"Where's yon fellah Valerie?"

"I'm at my place, sir."

"Ah'm a wee bit . . ."

"Could Vaunda not drive you, sir?"

"Ten minutes, Flood."

While she waited, Caz rang Valerie. He had told her he'd be back between seven and eight. When he answered she told him she was waiting for the DI and she'd ring him soonest. Her voice wavered.

"You OK, Caz?"

"Yeah," she said. "Just a hard day."

"I love you," he said.

"Me too," she said. Then she asked about the cars and he groaned.

"Shoulda stayed home and spent the afternoon in bed with you."

Caz suddenly saw Angel's face, the eyes that one split second . . . "It would've been nice," she said slowly. "But that's life."

One-Hundred-and-Two

"There've been lots of little things, sir and I kind of hinted, but there was no way I could say the word until I had something concrete."

"And you went round there?"

"Not to *tell* him, sir. Christ, do you think I'm that stupid? No, I had the afternoon spare and I went down there to see how he was, if he wanted any shopping done. He had a family photograph out, him, his wife and a little boy, and I said a few things about all the BS he'd been handing round. He said something else, I asked him about the kid and why he lied to his mates, and then he flipped."

"So he might."

"Might what?"

"Flip. The boy is missing. He disappeared five years ago, in the January."

"You never said."

"Of course not, Flood. It's Personal File."

"And the wife?"

"On the anniversary. It split them up and then it killed her. That was why Sweet applied for his transfer. He said he needed a fresh start, and the psychologist thought it was a good idea."

"And he chose the south coast."

"We'da thought to get as far away as possible, not this."

"Then we're thinking it's something more serious than covering someone's tracks?"

"Seems as like. Ah think we'd better ring the Chief Super."

One-Hundred-and-Three

Saturday 20:02

Norman Blackside had been due at a function and for the second time in as many weeks he turned up in an immaculate dinner-suit and patent shoes. Formally dressed, he looked even more of a giant. He gleamed, and the best word Caz could coin for what he looked like was "magnificent".

She had dried and dressed before Tom MacInnes had arrived at her flat and was "smart-casual", in fresh light-blue 501s, a Nike designer tennis-top and her fave white Asics. MacInnes was in soft, relaxed-at-home browns. The Three Musketeers they were not.

To "magnificent" and "gleaming", Caz was quickly forced to add "bewilderingly impressive", as the DCS barked orders. Just as slick, war-powered, were the team: a few DIs bundling in, then DS Moore, DS Reid, DS Lindsell and, slowly but surely, the lads. Greavsie was the most outstanding: dressed as a pirate, called out of a fancy dress in Shoreham.

Sergeant Jack Sweet was now officially the main man. There was a team down at his flat (DI Laing) with Scene of Crimes, and faxes and telexes were winging with details to all forces but prioritised to Norfolk, Suffolk, Lincolnshire, Leicestershire and Nottinghamshire. Yes, Caz had explained. A few times the East Coast had come up in conversation and he had relations there, she believed. And hadn't there been some sort of go-nowhere lead in Operation Iris that had suggested Lincolnshire? She found the lies effortless.

20:38

This one would be a major "all-forces", Blackside said in the first War Room assembly and they were going to have to use the television people and issue a "do-not-approach" warning. The attack on DC Flood was now officially attempted murder.

Caz, on cue, complained of feeling unwell.

The Police Surgeon was already on his way, anyway, and within ten minutes of his arrival Detective Constable Flood was out of there, severe migraine and sickness on the chit, post-traumatic shock the extra element. She had managed to look quite wobbly and white and they had insisted she rang Valerie to check he was home. Then they insisted she let Julie Jones walk her over there.

Caz needed the car but it was too awkward to swing.

She managed to get rid of Julie on the front steps to the block and was inside with her back to the door by the time Valerie had got as far as the first landing. She called up to say she was fine. Her mind was whirling and the branch she was now stepping out on was the thinnest ever.

Jack would never know but Caz reckoned he'd got an extra twelve hours, maybe more. It was the hair that worried her most. If he still looked like David Gower he was spottable at four hundred yards. She would have dyed it and gelled it flat.

"Hey, baby!" she said as she came up the stairs, "I doan feel so good. You feeling motherly?"

Valerie looked concerned in the hall's half-light. She smiled at him, a neat, I-can-take-it-I-'m-a-hero smile. "It's just a headache," she said. "Nothing a toddy, three aspirins and a cuddle can't fix."

"Oh, babe," he said. "Why couldn't you have been an accountant?"

One-Hundred-and-Four

Jack Sweet had booked in as Charles Rivers and it was only later he thought that though the name had seemed to pop out of nowhere it wasn't that far away from "Flood". He was stopping just outside Knutsford in a something and nothing place, convenient for the motorway and that was about it. In the morning he was going to drive to Chester using A roads.

It was the hair that had worried him most. He had figured it made him immediately identifiable from four hundred yards. With this dark brown slick-shiny wave he felt a little foolish but no-one so far had even batted an eye-lid. Flood had still been unconscious when he'd used the wash-in, wash-out dye. If the situation hadn't been what it was, he well might have laughed when he first looked in the mirror.

He had cleaned it all up very well, then cleaned the sink again, dried his hair roughly and then slicked it down with some hair-crap. As he had driven north, periodically he had to turn his rear-view mirror to remind himself what he looked like. He had stuffed the gel, the dye and the towels in a polythene bag and taken it all with him.

He made himself eat and he drank a few whiskies in his room. Then he cleaned the guns. All he could think about was saying goodbye to Mammy Sweet and then going to find Doyle.

When he tried to sleep he kept dreaming of Flood. She was naked, lowering herself on to him and nodding, "It's OK, Jack. It's OK."

One-Hundred-and-Five

At ten o'clock, Caz rang Tom's flat; Vaunda answered. No, he wasn't home yet.

"Are you OK, Caz?"

"I'm fine, Von. Got a bit of shock, I reckon."

"You take care."

She rang the nick and they put her through.

"MacInnes."

"Tom. Any chance of an update?"

"In two hours, Flood? There's nowt. Anyway, you're sick."

"I know, sir. That's why I rang. I really think I need to force a break. My sick note's good for a week. I was going to go to my Gran in Hereford but I thought I'd mention it. Any problem?"

"No, Flood. Say I said. If yer mebbee can ring me now and again, in case?"

"Will do, sir. I'll see if I can persuade Val to take some leave."

"Good idea, lass. Gay tek a few days."

She put down the phone. When Valerie came through from the kitchen with the hot drinks she told him she was going away.

"You want me to see if I can get time off?"

"No," she said. "I just thought I'd shoot down to my Gran's, stop over the one night and then come back. If you could get Tuesday or Wednesday off, that'd be nice."

"You sure?" he said.

She grinned. "*Very.* And tonight's not over yet."

One-Hundred-and-Six

Sunday 04:57

Caz had been awake at least an hour, staring at black nothing, the darkness so complete she felt numb. Alongside her Valerie, the man she would marry, she knew it now, the man she would keep secrets from for the rest of her life, or until they parted. She could sense the sting-smell of semen. Last night Val had taken her from behind, but only after she had persuaded him, his hand round her, cupping her sex, allowing him to push deeper as she slowly climbed . . .

About a hundred years ago, after another brush with being dead she had needed the same; this, the most basic animal recognition, and then too it had been from the rear, then because anything else would have been too painful . . .

Now she wanted him again, like last night, the sense of him lost in her, and when he had gone closer . . .

And closer and closer, fighting it, and then she'd squeezed and he had cried out and then actually cried after he had come and she had twisted off him, pulled him to her and wiped his face and asked him why and Valerie had said he didn't know but please, please . . .

04:59

She rolled out of bed, stood beside it and looked down at him. He was no more than a shape and a sensation. She tried to imagine having his child.

05:11

Caz closed the front door, dropped down the steps, turned left and jogged down the hill towards the sea. The town, Sunday-morning mute, was so sleep-quiet she could hear the buzz-crackle of neon signs, and then, after fifty yards, the restless sound and smell of the sea after a cold night. She was dressed in Lycra, more night black but with scattered reflective stripes bouncing and the bobbing silver shine of Scotchlite patches on her heels. She wore white gloves too, sensing the first cold day of October and the morning's extra dark.

She went west, towards then past the grey-white, sighing Palace Pier, where the sea hiss-slapped its skirts and the shingle rattled, then fast along the Parade, past the Brighton Centre, The Grand, The Metropole, the pavements slick and black beneath her, the salt cold burning her flaring face.

And she ran *hard*, she ran short and hard and fast and hard and wind-borne and fast and hard; until she felt the sex-burn of control, and the sparkle come back to her heart and the power, the power, of being an animal, of having choice, of knowing what she was.

Then she turned, and hammered a mile, lamppost after lamppost, glorying in the pain, then she slowed to an easy lope, back past her own home, back past the hotels, the pier, back past where yesterday she'd sat on a murderer's bed, and back up the shallow hills to Val.

05:47

And then, complete, shower water cascading over suds, herself again, she thought of Jimmy Bright, of Carol and Tom Bright, of Moira and Billy and baby Tee and of Trevor Jones and the kid she hadn't yet seen, and she thought Trevor, Trevor, yes! One favour, and one possible answer. And then she thought, is it fair to ask?

06:01

Dried, the towel as rough and as quick as possible, talced, as soft as she knew how, Caz emerged and went back to Val.

There was light now but he was still foetally asleep. But she came close and he turned to her smell and, as she knelt over him, astride him, he slowly rose to being awake. He mumbled her name and she took his cock and slipped onto him. He gasped.

Caz squeezed the once and said, "Good morning!"

Val managed, "Wha?"

"Going-away present," she said softly. "I want to beat the traffic." Then she leant, kissed him, whispered for him to be still and then, slowly, delicately, rock and clock, up-down, round-and-round she drove him stupid. He lasted no time at all.

After, she said, "I want to get away early, sweetheart. You want something to eat?"

"In bed?" he said.

"If you mean toast," she said.

06:46

Caz walked into the John Street front entrance, brought the staff to life, then, once cleared, went downstairs, through to the car park and rescued her Mazda. As she went out from the car park she pressed a button and the Blues Brothers whacked out of the windows, twenty points above the legal limit.

She left town quickly, to "Soul Finger," then "Who's Making Love," "Do You Love Me," and "Guilty."

Guilty? Hah! Not at all.

Like Jake and Elwood, she was on a mission.

07:10

The MX5, bright red, passed Old Shoreham, then swept across the Adur Bridge; Caz knew precisely how long it took to fall from there into the soft shallows of the river. To her left the small airfield; up to her right the huge privileges of Lancing College and its Church air. She'd been there too.

Seconds ago, she'd put the Stones on the stereo, one hand lightly on the steering wheel at six o'clock. Now Jagger was raunching out "Jer-umpin' Jack Flash it's a gas-gas-gas." She was so high she was dangerous and she drove fast. The sun had finally agreed to come up and the road beckoned.

08:29

Caz knocked a door in Dover Street, Inner Avenue, Southampton. Jenny Wilkinson answered, wearing a throw-away plastic pinafore. Nappy time! She was surprised, happy, then switched to worried, all in the space of a second. As quickly as she could Caz said there was nothing wrong.

"Blimey, Flood, it's Sunday morning!"

"Yeah, I know and not nine o'clock. Sorry Jenny, but . . . Gonna be away for a few days, and I needed to square things up with Trevor."

"The Isle of Wight thing?"

Caz smiled. "Any chance of a cuppa?"

"Of course," Jenny said. "You haven't seen Trix yet, have you?"

Trix?

"Beatrix, as in Potter," Jenny said. "It's—"

There was movement and a laugh behind them. Jenny turned.

"It's cos ahr Jenn 'ere goes like a rabbit!" Trevor Jones said from the doorway. "Hello, Caz."

One-Hundred-and-Seven

Trix looked like a baby, small, droppable, with large eyes, a slightly pointy head, various colours and smells, and a slight rash. Trevor had her in his arms and Caz knew he'd kill for her.

"You don't take sugar?" Jenny said.

"No."

"Except when chasing *murderers!*" Trevor said, lots of emphasis.

"Long time ago," Caz said. "And you were a *suspect*, that's all."

Trevor stepped over. "Didn't stop you legging after me, did it, ay? And you were the first copper ever caught up!"

Caz took the offered child, very, very cautiously. He'd gone off way too fast, she told him, but wasn't he glad he'd been caught?

Trevor looked at his baby and across at Jenny. "Yeah, all right," he said. He softened, sat down and picked up his tea. "So what can we do for you?"

"Nothing, maybe," Caz said.

"You two need a few minutes?" Jenny said. "Only, the way Trix is chewing, I think she wants some milk."

Caz lied. "It's not really private."

Jenny smiled and took the baby anyway.

"No matter. I'll feed her now, get her off." She stood, took Caz's bundle and cuddled it close. "I'll be twenty minutes," she said.

Trevor stood up and touched the shawl, looking in. "Bebsie wan' some booby?"

The baby quite rightly ignored him. Jenny left.

"So?" Jones said as the door closed.

"We're off the record, Trevor."

"OK."

Caz sat forward. "Are you clean now, Trevor? Completely clean?"

"As a whistle. I see windows open and easy pickings, but I'm not interested. Those two upstairs mean too much for me to go inside again. I won't even buy cheap gear in the pub, just in case."

"That's what I thought."

"So what's up? This not about Jimmy on the island?"

"Not directly, Trev, but maybe it is, indirectly. There's things you should know."

"Like?"

And Caz told him. She told him about the scum who preyed on kids, on babies, on tiny, precious things like Trix. Then Caz told him about the man who had abused Jimmy Bright, what he owned what he controlled, how the chain of nurseries were expanding. She told him about Acorn & Tree Tops. She told him they could prove nothing; that after a quiet time, the brothers would start up again.

"Yer kidding," Trevor said. He stood up and grabbed a pile of local papers.

"What is it?" Caz said.

Jones was shuffling, flicking pages quickly. "Shit, I was right! They're due to open one in Southampton!"

"That's why I wanted to talk to you, Trevor."

"I'm all ears," he said.

One-Hundred-and-Eight

Trevor is brilliant, you watch and you listen and you think this man will go far. He rings a number, he laughs, then he says, "Frank, this is deadly serious, we need a meet." He nods, he looks across at you and raises a thumb. "Ten o'clock's fine," he says. "Trust me," he says.

Trevor is smaller than MacInnes but he wheels, deals, commands like Blackside. You saw him as a nobody thief once upon a time and he had some form for laddish violence. What you hoped for, what you dreamed of, you can't remember, but a Godfather you did not expect. You are quiet, admiring as troops are marshalled, dates and places set. At one point he says to you, "For expenses I could get you a hit, Caz," and just as quickly he shakes his head in a comic, exaggerated way. He coughs and then, into the phone, he says, "Nah, Leggsy, not a great idea. I did tell you this was filth."

Eventually he says, "Brighton's sorted, Bournemouth's sorted. My mate Leggsy says he can do Reading. But I got no one for Cardiff."

You hear yourself telling Trevor that's not a problem and then you start listening to "21 Tips for the Novice Burglar". You tell Trevor you think he should write a book. He says he's really thinking about it, you can't be too careful these days.

You explain everything again and ask his advice. You, hot-shot cop, you ask Trevor Jones, burglar, pub-fighter, shop-assistant, for advice. He tells you some neat things. He smiles and tells you two years from now he'll be manager of Dixons.

His speciality is stopping shoplifters. Then he says, Caz he says, this is a right done thing.

You feel like someone else, but no, you really don't feel bad. You're on a mission. You stand and you buzz while you wait for Trevor and when he comes back he says, it's OK. He says Jenny's not happy but he told her it was for Trix, and that they both owed Caz.

Now you're ready to go and Jenny comes down the stairs.

"She's asleep," she says.

You smile. "It'll be OK," you tell her. "I promise."

You know you'll come clean, anyone is caught. You know you'll say you coerced them, threatened them with a frame. And you know too, that a court case would be fantastic because it would make everything more public. Trevor thinks you're a plonker. He tells you, him, his mates, none of them ever got caught doing *a job. They went down because they were caught with stuff at home or some fence rolled them over to keep himself on the outside.*

You're driving, Trevor beside you. He's animated, talking quickly, he wants to do this for you, the others, but you can see he's excited too, he needs some extra in his life. "Towards Winchester," he says, then "Left, left" and you're heading for Farley Mount Country Park. You know the place, it's got a fucking huge hill you have to do twice in Hampshire Cross-Country League races and in the forest, on the trails, it's inches deep with thick, thick mud. You miss it.

"Left again," Trevor says, then "Right!" then, "Here, this is the place!" Then he says, "Now we wait. Shouldn't be long."

And you slew the car on gravel, the trees drip. You remember once, you were at your fittest; you almost caught Lordshill's Sue Dilnot over the last four hundred yards, but she had just too much for you.

You're not quite with it but you tell Trevor, "This better be worth it, Jones."

He says, "Trust me, Flood. Trust me."

One-Hundred-and-Nine

Sunday 09:56

The tap came on the roof above Trevor. The shotgun barrel came through Caz's window. Caz had seen shotgun damage. She sat very still.

"Window down some more!" the voice said.

From where Caz sat she could only see a wax-jacketed, green-jumpered waist, dark brown cords and the top of some blue-grey wellies. She had a sudden awful thought, some memory that a sicko had been haunting the park, attacking couples and raping the girl. If it wasn't so frightening, it would have been funny.

"My name is Flood," Caz said. "I'm a policewoman. I'm going to open my jacket and take out my warrant card."

She moved slowly. Then she produced it, opened it. The gun slid backwards, dropped to the right, then cracked open.

"Well, you'd better come out then, Flood."

The man was as big as Blackside, with a handsome, sunburned white-toothed smile and accentless, as if any background he might once have revealed had been coached away.

He apologised for the gun and said yes it was licensed and then he said, "Trevor calls me Frank. I buy and sell things."

"Hiyah Frank," Trevor said.

Frank nodded. "So a policewoman needs help, is that correct? A police officer is prepared to talk to professional criminals?"

"I'm talking to husbands and fathers," Caz said. "We're in the same army and I think we're in a war."

"Trevor said. Straight villains loathe nonces. You should know that. That's why they have Rule Forty-Three. There's a nutter roaming these parts, did you know?"

"I'd heard."

"You heard correctly. With any luck he'll fall over and shoot himself with his own gun."

Caz grunted. "Save some time, at least."

"Maybe I'll get lucky," Frank said. "Anyway."

"Anyway?"

"Anyway, I think you'd better come to my place, meet the wife and kids, have some decent coffee. It's about five miles. That OK with you? You can follow me."

He waved at a Range-Rover tucked under some trees. One of the stickers in the back said "I support Neighbourhood Watch!"

He probably did.

On the way Trevor told Caz just how good a bloke Frank was.

"What's he do, Trevor?"

Trevor smiled.

"He buys and sells things."

One-Hundred-and-Ten

11:22

Caz drove north, up the A33 toward Newbury, then joined the M4 motorway towards South Wales. The first sign she saw mentioning Cardiff said it was ninety-something miles away. She drove at a steady seventy-five miles an hour, not too slow to attract attention, not fast enough to be pulled over.

She felt faintly love-sick and stopped at Membury for a coffee and to ring Val on her mobile. It was Sunday and it would be nice to hear him talk. When he answered she laughed and said she had just wanted to make sure he was out of bed. He told her she was full of shit; love for sure.

She stopped again at Aust and sat in a concrete café and looked out on to the mud-flats of the Severn. On the far side was Beachley. Down in the shadows of the suspension bridge there was a ferryman's cottage, now deserted, guaranteed to stink of shit and piss. These places always did. She guessed the ferrymen never ever imagined change until one day a tower of concrete cut them from the light.

The mask was slipping again. Gradually, as Valerie and home seemed farther away and Cardiff came closer, the excitement had begun to fade and nervousness, then a mild depression, had taken its place. She fancied a drink, but she'd sworn off it, at least until this was over. She wasn't being good, she was re-sharpening her edge but sharp or not, she still felt low. Maybe it was Angel.

He must be so lonely.

One-Hundred-and-Eleven

11:24 Sunday

Charles Waters, Detective Sergeant Jack Sweet, arrived near the Roodeye, Chester racecourse after a slow, timed and planned trip via Northwich, Middlewich and then Nantwich, Cheshire.

In Northwich, not far from the ICI factory, he had found where he'd grown up, the tight-terraced house now brash with plastic windows, fresh pebble-dash and an Amstrad satellite dish below the eaves. He had sat in his car and stared at the front door, then driven slowly away, past the canals he once played along, past a rash of houses, once pits and fields, and to a churchyard where his father was buried. He stopped for five minutes.

In Middlewich and in Nantwich there were remembered things, should have been remembered things – his first real girlfriend was from Middlewich, the first time he'd had sex was after a Nantwich dance – but roads had moved, shops closed down, whole streets replaced by supermarkets and car parks. He felt lonely, dead, as if he were in darkness and looking in on a world distorted.

And here was the Roodeye, not far away the City walls, the tight pretty streets of Old Chester. He was still functioning and about to take the only real risk in all this, *maybe* take the risk. He owed his mother that, but if he had guessed wrong, or MacInnes and his team were ahead of themselves, they might, just might, have thought to trace family members. He could be stopped and that would be a crime. But he really wanted, just once more to see his Mum.

One-Hundred-and-Twelve

14:18

About a hundred years ago, on a case, Caz had briefly needed to work with a slimeball sales rep called P.P. Tomlinson. They'd gone out together as salesman and assistant and she had called herself Kathy Waters for the evening. It was as K Waters that she booked into The St Mellon's Country Club Hotel, six miles from Cardiff on the old A48. She paid cash up-front for her room and said she might be leaving early. No, just a holiday she said, she was born near here and was going to wander round old haunts.

She went to her room, stripped, did twenty minutes of stretching and push-ups, showered, then lay on the bed and rang Valerie to talk dirty. He was out. She cursed, and dug out the *Yellow Pages* instead. At three-thirty she was ready to leave.

"You may as well wear dark clothing, Caz and make it ordinary, unreportable. People don't look very hard, but light clothes get seen easier than dark ones."

"So no mask, striped sweat-shirt and a bag marked swag?"

"No," Frank said. "Trevor was a good burglar in his time. What's more, he knocked off rich, insured places. And they were always cased so there was no one home. Professionals don't like the scum who hit their neighbours' houses or knock over the homes of OAPs for their life-savings. Rolling one of those in, usually drug addicts, that counts as a public service."

"So let's not be silly, Caz. You understand about alarms?

We doubt these places will be wired up, but they may be. They are not going to have secret alarms and it's not likely they'll have any at all. They don't want an over-zealous beat bobby answering a false call-out or a real one and making the wrong sort of discovery."

"So look for the box on the wall?"

"Right. Some are just dummy boxes but presume they're the real thing. If you go in, check round quickly. Check the windows for sensors, the corners just under the ceiling for infra-red, and look in the hall or under the stairs for the central control unit."

"Right."

"Unless you hear the beeps."

"The beeps?"

"Come on, Flood, you're the policewoman. Most alarms will give you about thirty seconds to tap in the code. The alarm counts down and after the thirty seconds all hell is let loose. Well noise, anyway. On average, it takes another ten minutes for someone to ring the police, two to twenty for a car to turn up."

Caz gave a nervous laugh. "And I run like hell!"

"No," Frank said. "You go jogging, and look ordinary." He paused. "But we don't want alarms anyway. We want to hope you can get in and out, use the stuff we've put together, and no-one knows you were there."

"I'd quite like not to get caught," Caz said. "Being a copper, I like."

Trevor spoke. "Caz, you know I don't mind doing it."

"Oh, I know, Trev," Caz answered, "But this is more than enough. And Jenny would kill me, anyway."

"You'll be OK," Frank said. "And wear the gloves."

Caz had put down the *Yellow Pages* and written the address on a piece of paper. She left, dressed in dark clothes and with a pair of light cotton running gloves in her pocket. A mile down the road she bought an A-Z of Cardiff and back in the car, she flicked pages. She found the place easily, just off the road to Caerphilly.

16:05

There was no car in the courtyard, no motorbike parked at the side of the building, and no-one there to answer the door-bell, the one for the downstairs, the one for the upstairs or for the upstairs-upstairs. One thing that chilled Caz was how similar this building was to the set-up in Brighton. Inside there would be access to the nursery area from the flat, and, just like Brighton, she would bet there would be access to the children's sleep-rooms via the fire-escape. She was shaking. It had been nerves, but now it was unrequited anger.

"Be positive. Walk briskly. Just look like you live there or you're canvassing. Pretend you're a policewoman, just don't slink, *don't be furtive. If you act normally, just as you are, people won't register you. Creep about and they'll get interested.*

"Try the door, just go up bold as brass and knock, or ring the bell. If there's someone in you're just another young mother wanting to place her kids. Chances are there'll be no-one there.

"If you get stopped, you've always got your warrant card as a last resort, but bobbies aren't expecting pretty blonde burglars. You're not likely to be arrested on suss or asked to come down to the station unless you're actually caught in the act. And that won't happen, Caz. Put this down your back inside your trousers, the rest of the stuff in your little runner's pack. Take your mobile. If you get stuck, ring me or Trevor."

"Ring you? While I'm burgling? Are you serious?"

"Hey, this is a high-tech age!"

Caz rang the three doorbells again. And again, though she waited and listened there was no movement from inside. She came out of the doorway and walked smartly, positively, round to the side of the building. On the ground were specks of oil and the tread-marks of one or two larger motorbikes. She came to a locked gate, garage-wide and was over it in two seconds. She was committed.

Out of sight now between the nursery and the wall dividing the grounds from next-door she stopped. Her heart was pounding way worse than on an armed surveillance. She flicked open her phone and dialled Trevor Jones's number.

"'Ello?"

She whispered. "Trevor, me. I'm there now. Just thought I'd let you know. Anything happens to me, if I'm not kicking arse out of Brighton by the end of the week, remember where I was, OK?"

"I'll stay by the phone now, in case you want some help."

"Appreciated," she said. She clicked the Micro-Tac closed. Time to case the joint. She had the urge to giggle.

"Toilet windows are good, Caz, anything off the ground floor. Just stay cool and look before you leap. People are not that great at security, especially if the place doesn't carry lots of cash or goods. Who wants to break into a nursery and knock off a load of old toys?"

There was a small fanlight, not locked. Maybe she could get through it in a fire – a kid could without blinking – but she thought she'd look for something more her size. At the back, a conservatory; another fanlight open, but too small again and sliding doors. Frank and Trevor had said patio doors were usually easy but keep looking.

The fire escape beckoned and she could see at the top a side door to the penthouse flat. Once Caz had climbed ten feet she would be exposed. She thought about it for maybe two seconds. All she was worried about was a job – this was about the lives of children. She padded quickly up two floors. At the top she was half-hidden again by metalwork.

"Be patient, remember the gloves and don't be too quick to presume everything is locked. Even if it looks locked give things a little tug."

She tried the door. It was solid. With what she had it would be easy to break in but if she could she wanted to get inside without leaving a mark.

She tried the window. There was a little movement but again, it would leave a mark. It was better than the door though. She could break in, tidy it up. They might not notice for weeks.

A certain calmness had come over her and she squatted,

hidden, while she thought. Round the corner of the building she could see the white ornate railings of a balcony, pretty new; and balconies meant fancy double doors.

"Just don't start trying to be clever, Flood. You're not a cat burglar and you're not a cat. You got one life, not nine. You see anything open you can't reach, don't get clever and start climbing. Falling off roofs is not a good idea."

The balcony was maybe ten feet away and there was a drainpipe and a one inch, maybe two inch, ledge all around the house. Caz would hardly have to take a risk. She hopped over the side of the fire escape, put two trainered toes on the ledge and leaned. OK, maybe it was a bit more than two times five feet. She wiggled a bit and tried to make love to the wall. Her right hand could touch but not grip the pipe. But if she let go of the fire-escape . . .

It was the wrong time to remember it, but once, on Lundy Island, Caz had decided to scramble across the top of the cave at the butt-end of Puffin Gully. That time she had been facing out and halfway across she had frozen. There the drop had been more than this but into, if she was lucky, six foot of rock strewn water. If she froze here, fell here, she would be more than dead, they'd be able to slide her under doors. It would have been nice not to remember, but that wasn't how life was. She had remembered. Vividly.

To the brickwork she said, "Well, thank you for that, God." Then she let go with her left hand and did her Spiderman impression flat against the side of the house.

She stayed like that for not long, say two or three lifetimes and then, with her fingertips between the drainpipe and the wall she edged right. Six inches, she discovered was a lot of millimetres. She would never complain about Valerie again. It started to rain.

Now Caz was past the point of no return. She gently extricated her hand, so she could actually grip the pipe, slid round it like it was some kind of sex-tool and then pulled herself that way. Her trailing hand, she discovered, was loath to release the security of a grouted gap between bricks. Now she realised how much she ached. The light rain turned into serious pissing down.

She went for it, figuring God was taking such an interest

he'd already decided her fate one way or another. She wasn't conscious of the move but suddenly she was clamped with both hands to the drain-pipe and wondering about the integrity of the fixing bolts. Rain water was rolling down her neck and she wondered if falling off here might actually be a bonus. She decided that the best way for the second half was to do it quick and to think herself rubber. She started working her right foot along the ledge, then had to bring it back when she realised the real problem was getting the *left* one past the pipe. She managed it, roughly in the time it took to build a cathedral, then she started doing the splits again, reaching, reaching. Then suddenly, orgasmically, she was holding cold, wet, white metal. She pulled, squeaked, slid, and was on the balcony, sitting in a puddle. She had decided to use a chain-saw to get through this one if it was locked. God tossed some thunder over Caerphilly Mountain but Caz just laughed at him. Then she tried the door and *Open Sesame*, it rolled, it sailed, it oozed, it leg-parted, it slid magnificently asunder and she was in!

First thing, fuck! What could she do about footprints?

One-Hundred-and-Thirteen

There was nothing for it; not after all this effort. Caz took off her wet trainers, unhooked her running slacks and removed her socks, Then she undid her Goretex top, slid it off, peeled off her slightly damp T-shirt and used it to dry her feet. There was some sort of dizzy pleasure in all this but she hadn't quite worked out what it was. The best bit was putting the T-shirt back on. She tried to imagine the headlines had someone walked in just then: TOPLESS BURGLAR CAUGHT RED-FOOTED. Nah, no one would print it.

She put the wet shoes and socks on a newspaper while she sniffed around and now she looked properly, it seemed decidedly ordinary.

The three piece suite, black leather, wasn't cheap but was not too unconventional. In front of the long three-fat-people sofa was a hairy rug, cream and there was a 26-inch TV, a good Sony Video and on one wall a pretty B&O stereo system. There was a bookcase with a lot of videos, half TDK, the rest pre-recorded stuff, musicals, older films, Lawrence of Arabia. There were so many, in places they were two-deep. Behind, she found Batman cartoons, "Mary Poppins", "Chitty-Chitty-Bang-Bang", a few "Thomas the Tank Engines" and three "Fireman Sams". Nothing in the books caught her fancy. To the right was a Dell PC. She decided, as soon as she had done what she came to do, she would switch it on, take a peek, and play.

Then something occurred to her. She rang Trevor, very Welsh.

"'Ello, buttee. Just fort I'd let you know, like, I'm inside, see, and chuffed to ninepence, isn't it?"

"Do what you have t'do and get out of there. Aren't you scared?"

"Should I be?"

"Why do you think burglars shit on the landing?"

"You know, I always wondered why they did that."

"Get out of there, Caz."

"Yeah, yeah," she said. She clicked off again.

Caz pitter-pattered quickly everywhere. She found two cameras, one a Video Eight, about a grand's worth, the second one, also SONY much bigger, more professional with *PRO* on the side. The obvious question was why two cameras but that wasn't why she was here.

The bedrooms, ordinary apart from the black sheets; the kitchen nothing to report. The bathroom – she peed – straightforward, very clean. The hallway, nothing – oh, and no alarm system – the kitchen ditto, but there were lots of chocolate biscuits in a big pink piggy jar which she contemplated nicking as a trophy.

She wondered; was this what a paedophile's place looked like? But then she thought what *did* a paedophile's place look like? These were older men, so why the kiddie videos, why the fancy cameras?

There were a million answers of course and Caz remembered two things; the counsel of Jill Bartholomew and the research papers she had read. And these were brothers, four of them, and four nurseries, separate counties, one penthouse over each nursery, every one with a fire-escape, every one with a door down from the upstairs-upstairs to the ordinary upstairs, to the children. Men owning nurseries, involved in nurseries, living over the top of nurseries, taking pictures of naked, frightened little boys, she knew for sure in one.

She had work to do. She did it. She got ready to leave. Then she remembered the PC.

She still felt lucky.

One-Hundred-and-Fourteen

Chester, 16:33

Angel sat quietly in a tea-house near the walls. In front of him was the second half of a toasted tea-cake, a little cold tea. He had been so near and yet so far, but in the end he couldn't risk it. Even the phone call was risky.

"Mum, it's Jack."

"Hello, luv. Where are you?"

"Spalding."

"Are you going to the old farm?"

"No, Mum, I'm working, but I'm quite near there right now. Just thought I'd ring me old Mum, you know. You OK, Mum?"

"You know me, son. Fitzus Fiddles Strongzun Oxes!"

"So what's new?"

"Nothing much. Remember Mrs Arkwright, at number three? She died, and two days later Joe Arkwright keeled over halfway through bingo at Saint Winifred's."

"That's nice."

"Joe and Nancy dying? How is that nice, son?"

"They're together again, Mum."

"Tosh!"

"Oh, Mum, you know you're just being obstinate. For an atheist you make a good plumber. How come you still go to church if you don't believe any more?"

"Habit. To meet my old friends. Them that's left at least."

"I can't hang about long, Mum."

"I know, son. Things to do, right? Places to go?"

"Has there been any mail for me? Any phone calls? Have any old mates dropped round looking for me?"

"Just the parcel you said about. I put it in your bedroom."

He ached. "Listen, Mum. If I can, a couple of days, I'll try to make it over and see you, but I'm really busy since I became an Inspector and some of the cases, like this one, well, they're very, very secret and a bit dangerous. I don't always know where I'm going to be."

"I understand, Jack."

"I've stuck a birthday card in the post for Wednesday."

"Get away yer big softie."

"I've got to go, Mum."

"I know."

There was quiet.

"Mum?"

"Yes, son?"

"Are you going to church tonight?"

"As always."

"Then do me a favour, would you, say a big one for me? I could do with a good word."

"Jack, you said I was an atheist."

"Doesn't matter, Mum. It's like horseshoes, they're lucky whether you believe in them or not."

"OK, son. Bye-bye, son."

"Good-bye Mum."

One-Hundred-and-Fifteen

16:47

Caz switched on the computer. The fan whummed and the hard disk clunkered. She pressed the on-off button on the 17″ monitor. The screen un-blacked in time for her to see the autoexec commands running through. The last two were *cls* and *menu.*

Her feet were cold.

She got up and went to the door. For the first time since she'd been there, she was suddenly nervous. She dropped the latch. When she went back she read the screen.

1 Word Perfect
2 Accounts
3 D-Base
4 C-Serve
5 Net

She pressed 1.

One-Hundred-and-Sixteen

Caz pressed the F5 function key and the screen filled with obscure file names. Straight away she realised that a lucky-dip browse was hardly likely to produce gold dust and she pressed escape, then F7. When the menu came up, instead of selecting a number she typed *dir* *. and pressed Enter. She was in luck, one of the directories was PC-Tools. She typed *tools* and got *bad command* or *file name*, typed *dir* *. *bat* and got a list of batch files.

She typed *util*. While PC-Tools loaded she grabbed the box of floppies from her haversack.

She browsed the hard disk, looking for hidden files. The ones she found she converted, and saved to the floppy in a: drive. Then she copied all the Word Perfect documents. It took five minutes and a second disk. Then, using the utility software, she asked the PC to search for *..oyle..* There were four hits. She was so shocked, it was such a long-shot that she gasped. She copied these to the 3.5″ disk as well. Her skin prickled and buzzed as she typed *..yswy..* and clicked on Search; she was shaking. A hit; copied to the floppy. She removed the floppy and stuck in another. Then she tried *..Aber..* and found the same file. This time she actually looked and read; *at the Aberyswyth Hotel.* Suddenly Caz was scared. Now, rather than prickling, her skin crawled. The text meant little to her and there was no address, but her gut still churned and she felt very alone. All this from one chance remark in a house in Winchester! She had to leave, and now. Just one more thing. If she could just stop shaking. . . .

She came out of PC-Tools, typed *menu* and pressed Enter. When the opening screen re-appeared she selected 5 and pressed the Enter key again. She heard the rapid pah-beep, a brrrrzzz and then the bree of a modem connecting, then, as the screens changed, she wrote down everything she could catch. Then she searched until she found *"favourite places"*. There were six Internet web sites and she wrote down the names. Every time she breathed now she heard a different creak, a car braking outside, voices, people coming up the stairs, the locked door opening. If she didn't leave now she'd fill her pants.

One-Hundred-and-Seventeen

Caz gathered up her stuff, the wet socks inside the wet shoes, the floppies back in their box stuffed into the haversack with the newspaper. She had thought herself brave but she was getting more and more frightened, close to panic. She muttered at herself to keep calm, stopped once to slap her own face. She guessed the fear had to be some territorial thing; it wasn't Caz's tree, wasn't her cave.

She went to the window and looked out and down. The car-park was empty. Then she saw a car coming down the street, slowing, its right-hand indicator flashing. *Oh, shit*! P-lllease! Then it pulled into a driveway two doors down the street. *Jesus Christ* . . .

She looked out again. Nothing. Looked round the room. OK. She had never been here. PC off? Yes. Door closed? Yes. She felt sick now, close to throwing up. She lifted the latch on the front door, took a deep breath and slipped out, down a flight of stairs and into the nursery.

This was all so animal-basic now, so primitive. The house was taking over, the smells she could not smell, the presences she could not see or touch but permeated the walls. Not your cave, Flood. You are a violation. Here you are weak, alien, submissive. This is not your place, be gone!

The walls were spread with cutesy pictures, hand-paintings by staff or a guest artist; Snow White and the Seven Dwarfs, Prince Charming desperately seeking Cinders. Now they all looked manic, threatening. She went quickly down the stairs.

At the bottom, in the hallway, she waited the wrong side

of large white doors, the glass stained. Outside, as far as she could sense, nothing. God, was she scared!

There were two big locks; the types a double-turn made key-only. She tried them and prayed. Just like Frank had said, they turned, people get lazy. The door opened and outside it was grey, still raining. It looked like Heaven. In the porch she slipped her shoes on to bare feet. She checked her watch. It was two minutes to six. Give or take a heart attack, she'd just spent two hours the wrong side of the law and had taken about ten years off her life.

But she was OK!

She jogged from there and was swallowed up by the rain.

One-Hundred-and-Eighteen

Monday 06:25

Caz slipped out of her room and cantered out on to the A48, moving easily along the pavement. It was cold and damp but pretty nice for running. She felt strange, almost hung-over, and she hoped a few steady miles would help to clear her head. For sure it had to be all that tension. What she had done yesterday afternoon she had decided, absolutely she would never, *never* do again.

Frank's wife had been immaculate with dark, tucked-under hair. She looked like a piano-teacher, gracious and soft-spoken. When she had left, Frank had said to Caz, "These nonces, they talk to each other, use the Internet, exchange ideas, swap photos and names. A good search of the hard disk, you never know what might turn up."

But it was pure whim, a lucky instinct, to try for the fragments of names from Angel's flat. The shock, though, of so many hits! Suffer the little children; she was beginning to think God was on her side.

It had taken twenty minutes to get the use of a hotel computer on a Sunday night. She had called up the interesting files and printed them off, all e-mails or Word Perfect files. The rest of the stuff she put in a scrounged envelope and addressed it to Trevor Jones. She felt lucky still; but you never knew when luck might desert you.

She took a narrow lane away from the main road and reckoned she might well be on the route of the Empire Games Marathon: 1958, would that be? It was a nice flat fast course. So when did it stop being an Empire and become a Commonwealth?

She ran about seven miles, maybe eight, walking back in at half past seven rippling with the pleasure that LSD – long slow-distance running – brought. She had a quick shower, dressed and then went down for a full English breakfast, her promised reward for a night of no booze and a good steady run in the morning. By eight-thirty she was on the road towards Newport, this time in the car, picking up the motorway at Tredegar Park.

After the Brynglas tunnel she crossed the Usk, skipped the first exit then took the next, a dual-carriageway to Monmouth, another tunnel, then Ross-on-Wye and then the M50 and M5. By eleven she was approaching the south of Birmingham. Twenty minutes later she passed the junction with the A5 and headed foot-down for Chester.

One-Hundred-and-Nineteen

Chester

Caz sat quietly in a tea-house near the walls. She had eaten a toasted tea-cake and drunk some tea but half of her second cake and the remains of her third cup remained on the table. She was so near to Angel she could smell it, imagine him sitting there, wondering if he should visit his Mum. If he had been here it must have been tough to have been so near, yet so far, but she couldn't believe he would have chanced it. It would have been risky even to phone.

There was just one Sweet in the telephone directory; Caz had doubted her luck would be that good. The electoral register gave her two more addresses and when she dialled enquiries one had no phone, the other was ex-directory. They went to the top of her list. If Jack Sweet's mum was in a nursing home or rest home, Caz had a lot of work to do – if she was dead things would be trickier. But she wouldn't be; Caz knew this script.

She toyed with the little silver tea-pot and water jug, clinking the lid, wondering. With her searches, the slowness she had aimed for, stopping for lunch – on a whim she had taken back roads not the motorways, into the city – and generally feeling flat and inefficient, the time had just flown. She looked at her watch: 16:43, there was just time to make some calls to her other life and one to her new one, but she refused point-blank to be one of those yuppie sods who played electronic executive in the company of others. She dropped a fiver onto the table and left with her mobile phone in her hand.

Outside she ducked into a side-street. First she dialled Valerie. He was in a meeting. Yes, they'd tell him Caz had called. Nil-One.

Peter Mason. Not back yet. He'd gone to Winchester – the CPS or something. He'd probably not turn in, it was so late. Did she want to leave him a message? What? Right. Yes, they'd tell him Flood had called.

Nil-Two.

Trevor Jones.

"Oh, hi, Caz. He's at work. You want the number?"

"Please."

"And it's OK," Jenny said gently, "about him helping you. He told me what it was about. Here's the number."

One-Two at half-time.

"Trevor?"

"You *have* to call me at work, Caz?"

"Is it a problem?"

"Nope."

"OK. What's the score?"

"Your end work out all right?"

"Well, now I know why burglars shit on the landing, but yeah. There's some stuff in the post to you, paperwork and some computer disks, should arrive tomorrow."

"What do you want me to do with it?"

"Get it to Frank, ask him to see if there's anything of importance there. There are web sites, Internet stuff and the dial-out was into the continent so it may be net porn."

"Why didn't you take a look while you were there?"

"Landings, Trevor, y'know, crap and landings? I was there an hour and a half and *literally* shitting myself."

Trevor laughed. "That's a long time Flood. But everywhere else went smooth as silk. There was some real heavy stuff in Reading."

"Everyone knows the time, et cetera?"

"Yes, Caz."

"Thanks, Trevor. I'm glad, you know . . ."

"Glad what?"
"Glad you're clean."
"Fuck off, Flood."

One-Hundred-and-Twenty

The house, driving past with it on the left, had been built one side of the war, more likely the recent side. It was largeish, with huge bay windows and a display of mock Tudor black against the white stucco near the roof. Coming back the other way Caz saw the stained-glass roses in the top lights, the heavy set of the green front door, the slight ache in the woodwork, the cracks in the front path. A long-lived-in-house, occupants older.

She parked almost outside and pulled out her copy of *Outlander*, opened it and pretended to read. She had figured three houses max either way and opposite, but most likely just the house directly across the road or one of its two neighbours. She looked carefully, pointedly, cone-specific, and then less carefully – the corners of the eye better at detecting movement. After ten minutes she decided if there was an observation team on the house, they were *very* good. She grabbed a clip-board, stepped out of the car and walked up to the door of Mrs Sweet's neighbour, a canvasser.

She rang a bell which she couldn't hear, waited, then rang again. When there was again no answer, she scribbled something on her pad and walked next door; selling double-glazing was never easy.

No car in Mrs Sweet's drive, a weed or two pushing up through the cracks.

She rang the doorbell, one of those illuminated ones. The drrr-ingg felt like it sounded in empty rooms.

The sensation of maybe being watched by coppers was extremely strange. If there was a team, and Caz had missed them – if there was an arrest – Mrs Sweet would need to be looked after. If there *was* a team, then there'd be at least one WPC, in case. Caz wondered if she'd be anything like her or more like Moira.

There was no movement in the house. She rang again. Then there was the faintest shift in the weight in the air, someone on the stairs.

Caz scribbled again on her pad.

"Hello?" A quiet voice, but not timid, just cautious.

Caz opened the letter-box. "Mrs Sweet? Could I have a word?"

"My boy says not to open the door to strangers."

Go for it . . .

Caz had her warrant card pinned open on her clip-board.

"I'm a police officer, Mrs Sweet. If you look through the letterbox you can see my ID."

She turned her board and held it up slightly.

"I was hoping to have a word with you about your son. I'm a friend of his."

She could see eyes bobbing in the slot.

"You're a friend of Harold's?"

Fuck! "No, ma'am. A friend of Jack's."

The eyes came closer. "Well, you'd better come in then."

Caz heard the clack-rattle of a chain. The door opened.

Mrs Sweet smiled.

"Would you like tea?"

One-Hundred-and-Twenty-One

Caz wasn't sure whether Harold was Jack, was a brother, or was Mrs Sweet's presumably dead husband. But this was the right dear old Mum, she knew the moment she stepped inside the front door, even before she saw the classic passing-out parade picture on the wall, the row of helmets, thin sproggy faces, hands on knees in the front row. In the sitting room, more photos: Angel Sweet, Jeanette, and their boy; innocent, yet doomed as if spirits called him.

"Milk and sugar, dear?"

Caz was somewhere else. She heard herself say yes.

"One lump or two?"

"What?"

"Sugar, dear."

"No, thank you."

She heard clinking china and, ludicrously loud, the sh-luppered pouring of tea from pot to cup. From out the sound she remembered her Gran's Herefordshire farmhouse and the chu-lirupp that never spilled. Time and practice, rep-etition. Gran had a gravy spoon too, so often used and scooping that over the years it had lost a half-inch of its rubbed away tip and more amazingly, this metal had been eaten by Gran, by Grancher Jones, by their daughter, and by Caz, their daughter's daughter. Time, repetition, children. Hey, Bubbles . . .

"His name was Robin." Ethel Sweet said. "When he was very little his cheeks were red and Harold called him Robin Redbreast. But he was Bubbles for me. We lost him, you know."

It's not hard to let go Caz. Let go, see Robin now, feel it all. Listen to the music in the house, the laughter on the stairs, the deep brown voice of Harold Jackson Sweet.

Smell the Sunday lunch; oxo, cabbage steaming – a little pinch of bicarbonate of soda for softness – New Zealand Lamb, a nice fat leg, cooking slowly overnight. Fresh mint being chopped acrat-attattat as Ethel, repetitive, learned, double handed, dices and turns, dices and turns, acrat-attattat on the breadboard. Smell it!

Gravy made in the meat tray, the juices, the cabbage-water, full of iron is cabbage-water, add in the flour and stir, watch the lumps, you do better than Harold; Harold is impatient.

The caramel ring of "and from BFPO seventeen", Cliff Michelmore, Jean Metcalfe, Two-Way Family Favourites, mix in the Tate & Lyle sugar, the Sarson's Vinegar, a good bit of lamb has to have a nice bit of mint. "Strangers in the Night," "Spanish Eyes", Harold sings "Volare!" Jack says he has a girlfriend, a girlfriend, can you believe it? That's Jack, Caz, not Robin. She is really pretty mum, she won't go out with me, but I'm going to marry her.

Jack, Jack. Robin is a million light years to come.

Someone has poured you tea.

This is Robin.

"Grandad, Graneeeee!!"

"Hello, little fellah, come and show me your gun. Hiyah, son, hello Jeanette, your mother's in the kitchen, go and say hello. Say, little fellah, you shot any bears yet?"

"There aren't any bears, Grandad! Not forever! Can we go down the garden and look at the birds?"

"Have you been good for your Mum and Dad. Cleaned your teeth?"

"Yes!"

"Then I think we might just manage a couple of minutes."

"Mum! Grand-dad's taking me to see the birds!"

"Yes, love."

And now just you, Ethel, a bit of chicken Sundays is it?

One-Hundred-and-Twenty-Two

"I'm on my own these days. I lost little Robert, and then my Harold. Then three years later we lost Jeanette. Then Jack had to move down south. He's a Chief Inspector, you know."

"Yes, I know."

"The hardest bit – little Robert – the hardest bit is not knowing. Jack said, he *always* said, that there was no point in having hopes, we should get used to the idea of what had happened. But not ever hearing it, not knowing, well it's hard to say he's gone, isn't it?"

"Yes."

"Were you a friend of Jack's? Did you say? He rang me yesterday. From Spalding."

"The Aberyswyth Hotel?"

"Where, dear?"

"The Aberyswyth Hotel?"

"There's no Aberyswyth Hotel in Spalding, dear."

"My mistake. I don't know what I'm thinking of. It's just that Jack was always going on about a place called the Aberyswyth Hotel."

"I don't think so, dear. I know we never went to any place of that name, or to the town, even. And I don't think Jack did, either."

"I must be getting mixed up. He said something about a man called Doyle who owned the place."

"I don't think I know any Doyles, either, my dear."

Caz managed a light laugh. "Not to worry, eh? Jack was

always going on about holidays and hotels and little places in Wales. It's just like me to get myself all confused."

"We had the same holiday most years, our little chalet on Lake Bala but it's hardly a hotel, and it's a long way from Aberyswyth."

Caz sipped her tea.

"You didn't say why you had come here, dear. Were you hoping to catch up with Jack?"

"It would be nice, and it's nice to meet up with you and see young Robert's picture. Jack told me about—"

"It's OK, dear. We can say it. Robert disappeared. Three years and ten months ago. He was just nine."

"Could I ask? Where? How?"

"Jack and Jeanette had bought a new place in Frodsham. Jack was working in Manchester then and Frodsham was sort of in between there and here. It's a nice place, old Cheshire, safe."

Ethel paused and when she went to drink a little tea, her hand tremored slightly.

"Harold bought Robert a new bicycle, for Christmas. Well, we both bought it, if you know what I mean, but Harold chose it from the shop. Robert was thrilled! They all came down for the weekend right after Christmas, and we looked after Robert while Jack and Jeanette had a little holiday. They went away for three days to the Isle of Man. They were away when it happened."

She paused again, aging as she took a breath.

"We were always so very careful... Don't speak to strangers, that sort of thing. Robert was nine and was very sensible but he looked like a little cherub because of his looks and he seemed younger. That day he went off on his bike, just round the close."

"He just disappeared?"

"Yes. No one saw anything. They never found Robert or the bike. We had to ring Jack and Jeanette. We were very upset and that was when Harold had his first turn. A week later he died. That was the worst week of my life."

One-Hundred-and-Twenty-Three

Somewhere, somewhere. Don't give up!

Caz spoke softly. "Ethel? May I call you Ethel? This feels a little silly but, well, I have a feeling that – didn't Jack tell you about us?"

"Us, dear?"

"Jack and I."

"I'm sorry, dear?"

"Jack and I. We're very good friends."

"That's nice. Jack needs a good friend."

"I'm hoping we'll get married."

"That would be nice."

"It's just – well, the thing with little Robin, I need to understand. I want to help more, be closer. Jack, he's, well, *distant* sometimes."

Ethel smiled and looked up at the wall. "That's just the way he is. Even as a boy he had his own little world. Robert was like it too."

"I just want to know. To help, Ethel."

"I'm sure, dear. But how?"

"Oh, Ethel, I don't know. I just sometimes think, the pain is still there for Jack and I wish, I wish . . ."

"If you had known Robbie, my little Bubbles, that would have helped, but he's gone now, somewhere better, so Jack says. Would you like some more tea?"

"I would, Ethel. Could I use the toilet?"

"Of course, dear. Top of the stairs, left and left again."

Caz smiled and Ethel Sweet smiled back. "Left and left!" she said, "I'll put another kettle on."

"Got it," Caz said.

The first bedroom was Ethel's; a double bed as high off the ground as Caz had ever seen, sheets, wool blankets and a silky quilt on top, a long solid bolster, a single white pillow in its centre. The floor was once-polished floor-boards and there was a rug beside the bed.

The second bedroom; another double-bed, blanketed, quilted the same as the other room and Caz just knew this was where Jeanette and Jack slept, maybe where Jack slept. Nothing in the cupboards.

The box room had a single bed, a Manchester United bedspread, Manchester United posters on the wall, a red and white football scarf. At a small desk a computer, too new to be Robin's. Beside it, an external modem. Caz went into the lavatory, washed, made noises and went back downstairs.

When she went back into the lounge, Ethel was waiting.

She said, "He bought it the day Jeanette died. For months he was locked in there."

Caz feigned bemusement and Ethel flared.

"Child, please! I am seventy-four years old, that's all, seventy-four, I am *not* senile. Now you were walking around upstairs, you went in every bedroom. Don't you think I know? I have lived here twenty-eight years. I know what going to the toilet sounds like. Now I know you care for my son. I can tell that even when you're lying to me, but please respect me in my own home. Tell me what it is you really want."

One-Hundred-and-Twenty-Four

"Well?"

The woman Caz had left downstairs was a little white-haired old dear, sweet enough, but adjunctive, artefactual, part of Jack Sweet's description. This one was her feisty sister, sharp light in the back of those rheumy eyes, the body stiffer, taller, harder, the white hair now proud rather than quaint. Caz was in shock.

"Well, I—"

"You care for my Jack?"

"Yes, I—"

"Then tell me the truth, and let a mother help her son."

So Caz told her.

One-Hundred-and-Twenty-Five

"Jack is a good man, Mrs Sweet. He's a very good policeman and he works very hard. He's single-minded and he's not easily put off. I think he's been investigating Robert's disappearance and has finally got somewhere. He's my Detective Inspector but we are very close. He took some leave and I think he's come back up to Cheshire to – find someone. I've taken leave too. I want to try to help him, find who he's looking for and stop him doing anything stupid."

"Stupid?"

"Taking the law into his own hands."

"Why is that stupid?"

"Well, his career, his—"

"Do you mean, he might find the man who took Robin?"

"Yes."

"And then what?"

"I don't really know, Ethel. I would just like to be with him if he finds who he's looking for. Whatever he does then, I want him to think carefully about it, that's all. I'm on his side."

"You won't stop him?"

"You don't think I should?"

"He's my son. He'll do the right thing. No."

"Then I won't stop him."

"Look at me," Ethel said. Caz looked into her face.

Ethel asked again. "Jack's decision?"

"Yes," Caz said.

One-Hundred-and-Twenty-Six

Caz switched on the computer: a Compaq 486 next to an older Canon Ink-Jet printer.

"I'll leave you then," Ethel said. "I'll cook us something."

Caz reached out and touched her arm. "Thank you," she said.

There was a beep, then a double beep. Caz looked.

PASSWORD?

She tried *Angel* and pressed Enter. The screen cleared with a final beep. She typed *dir* *.

There were no games, no fancy screen savers, just DOS, Windows, Word Perfect and a couple of directories with names she had never seen. But there was the modem; and that had to be for something so Caz guessed at Internet. She typed *dir *.bat* to check the batch files. Then she heard Ethel shout. Would a fish-pie be OK?

She shouted back. It would be great. She pressed another key.

One-Hundred-and-Twenty-Seven

There were more passwords. She tried *Jack*, she tried *Harold*, *Sweet* and *Bubbles*. She Re-tried *Angel*. The first level she broke through using *Bunny-Notts*; the final one by typing *Skeggy* after both *Skegness* and Ethel's maiden name had failed. That got her access to the pictures, to a man called Doyle, to a European network of evil, and finally, *finally*, to the Aberyswyth Hotel.

The pictures hurt her, reviled her, made her ashamed; of what she wasn't precisely sure. But worse, more terrible than all this, she realised exactly what Angel had been forced to do, the sewers he had trodden to find his way to the Aberyswyth Hotel. The jokes he had cracked about juicy chickens, the e-mails he had read; the things he had had to say, the slow sickening steps he had taken to infiltrate into this seething world of monsters.

You want girls, Jacko? Twelve and under? Lolitas huh, Jack? Ten a penny! Eleven years old, sure, you prefer Thai or Filipino? If Filipino is OK I can even guarantee you a real nice tight one, brand-new, you're the first up. Ten years old? Nine? Yeah, yeah, we got regular trips into Bangkok, a coupla good Travel Agents in the know, absolutely no problem.

What about videos? So what's your fancy, Jacko? Shit, Jacko, we got a Brit diplomat on the books, we move the stuff anywhere, easy. Snuff? The snuff we got is real. Blondes you want? But gotta be boys? I guess so. And real young. How young is young, Jack, only I got all ages. Nine, ten? That's not young, Jack!

Caz drew in slow breaths. She ached. She felt as if she had run for days, stayed awake for nights; a huge black cancer pulsed in her gut. She looked at the wall, the red-shirted footballers, little Robin's heroes, the handsome, the rugged, the smart haircuts, the blue and brown-eyed. She pointed a finger and for a second she hated men, then hated the evil that could crawl in among men, not these men.

And she thought of downstairs, Ethel Sweet; just another Mum, cooking the fish-pie; and upstairs, for a couple of thousand pounds was a conduit straight into Hell. And there were other upstairs too; one on the road to Caerphilly from Cardiff, another she knew, in Brighton, in lofts, in sheds, in back-rooms. Pathological, deliberate evil, half understood, covered up, ignored, much not illegal; shifty, shifting, shiftless, but calculating. Thieves, users, abusers; men to whom tiny bodies were nothing but an extra resistance that a touch of KY could cure. She wanted every last one dead and not just easily dead but slowly dead, horribly and obscenely dead.

And some of all of this, the sex-tourism, the cruel pictures, the fuck-stories exchanged, the leering, dribble-mouthed chatter about the more talented rent-boys, some of this, some of this, against the other, it came close to being understandable, not excusable, but something else – something else when compared to savage rape, when compared to abduction, the drugging, and the cruelty of depraved man after sick, evil, brutal man tearing into a helpless boy's body, until used up, shattered, his very spirit forced from him, he is cast out. Until then at some unmarked plot, a point somewhere, someone formally kills him, buries him in a shallow grave; then goes home, showers, put on a clean suit and goes to work.

It takes a long time to get this close, Jack, but when we party friend, we party. So you fancy a weekend at the Aberyswyth Hotel?

One-Hundred-and-Twenty-Eight

18:42

Caz went downstairs. As she reached the hallway, Ethel Sweet emerged from the kitchen. There was a sparkle in her eyes. Her hands smoothed down the front of her pinnie.

"Oh, hello, dear. The fish pie—"

She stopped when she saw Caz's face. Caz took her hand.

"I can't stop, Ethel. I can't stop. I need to be somewhere."

"Is it Jack?"

"It's Jack," Caz said.

"He's not in Spalding?"

"No, Ethel."

"Will you come back?"

"I'll try."

Caz kissed Jack's Mum and left quickly, turning to appear to shake a hand then waving and striding to her car, clipboard prominent. She still had no idea if the house was under observation, but she was terrified that right now, some over-bright DC would pull her and stop her getting to Angel on time.

She got in the car, calmed herself and prepared to drive away, even adjusting her mirror and her seat-belt for any audience and for herself. She started the MX5 and then saw Ethel Sweet framed in her bay window. The look was odd, a tragic joy. Ethel knew this was the end of it all. Perhaps not a happy ending, but at least an ending.

She drove out on the Roman Road until she caught the A55 ringroad, swung left and went north on that until she hit the M53. Ten minutes later she was heading east towards Manchester on the M56, Thornton-le-Moors to her left, beyond there the Mersey, grey, uncaring, mud-banked, cold. She had to force herself to stay below eighty miles an hour. Frodsham appeared and disappeared on her right then the blip-lit stacks of Runcorn's chemical works, plumes of fawn smoke on her left. She was by-passing Warrington and heading over the M6 and into Manchester. She had never felt so sick, so useless.

19:59

When the M56 met the M63 Caz took that and headed north-east towards Stretford. Near junction four she saw the floodlights of Old Trafford and she thought of the roar as little Robin's United heroes ran out red-breasted on to the pitch. She had murder in her heart.

When she reached the M62 she travelled along it, following the signs for Leeds, then swung onto the M66, off that at junction two and down onto smaller roads. She was looking for a hill, a moor, a reservoir.

It was dark now, rain slowly falling, the night's filth slapping right and left across the windscreen, the Mazda headlights spinning off the road into a horseless, loveless black. She slowed right down and now the fear grew. She was searching, searching.

The sign she had been looking for she found just before nine o'clock, stuck up from a dry-stone wall, hanging in the wind off a thick post. She flashed a torch to make sure, saw the three legs of Mann and turned. Ahead of her, lighter then darker between folds of now relentless rain, the farmhouse, amber to the night, a few cars outside in front of a barn.

One-Hundred-and-Twenty-Nine

Caz drove past the farm – there were four cars – found a turning and squeezed off the road. She got out, was soaked in seconds, went to the rear of the car, and lifted the boot. She grabbed what she could; a roll of rope, a crowbar, the long torch and her can of Mace, then she stepped into the road and back toward the farm. In the front of her waistband was her mobile phone, and in the back, against her spine, her riding crop. She had walked thirty yards when the sweep of distant headlights sent her into the ditch. She was on her knees in muddy water as the car approached, slowed, stopped thirty yards from her, reversed, and then turned into the farmyard on full lock. Three men got out and dived from the rain into the house. This was now nothing short of ridiculous; even if Angel was one of those inside, it meant, at the very best, odds of three to one; and it could be worse.

The easy thing now was to do a quick nine-nine-nine. She could stay out here and the worst danger was catching pneumonia. Or she could back-track to the car for that matter. Or . . .

Caz thought of little Robin.

She climbed out of the ditch and ducked along the road. The rain lashed, but its noise was welcome. This wet, she had to be squelching. At the six-bar gate she dropped down and listened. She could hear nothing except the rain. She ducked and moved again, this time the width of the drive, into the deeper shadows by the barn. She looked towards the house and tried to think. All that came to her was how wet she felt, then, *you could die here, Flood.*

Caz pulled out her Micro-Tac to phone, then thought again. Was she really going to call from here? She looked behind her at the tall doors of the barn. Inside she would have a little more security, high up she'd have extra seconds. She opened the door pulling at its base, and slipped through on her hands and knees. Rain drummed on the corrugated roof.

She stood up and pulled the door to. Then she sniffed. Potatoes? She used the small touch on tight beam, thinking of the cracks under the door, and swept the back of the barn. Potatoes? You could say that – there was a diagonal slope of them going right back into the roof, more than she had ever seen. It reminded her of beef mountains and wine lakes. She had her first idea.

To her right was a ladder and at the top end a half-floor, a minstrel's gallery above the doors and halfway round the sides. She went up there, found a door the size of a window, unlatched it and pulled it inwards. She was exposed, but in deep darkness, and she knew people never looked up. She opened the mobile phone and switched it on. The rain was so loud she didn't hear the log-on beep. She tapped out a number and pressed send, lifted the phone to her ear.

The rapid blee-blee-blee-blee of no signal.

She pressed stop and then send again.

She was looking down into the yard.

Blee-blee-blee-blee.

Stop. Send,

Blee-blee-blee-blee.

Shit and corruption, Custer. No cavalry.

One-Hundred-and-Thirty

Try not to think about what could happen, Flood.

Piss off, are you mad? I know what these animals are capable of!

Then slip away, Flood, drive to somewhere the phone will work. Dial up the locals and call for back-up.

I can't, I can't, Angel is in there! There might be a child in there!

Then get help, Flood. You're a woman, not the bloody SAS.

She looked down into the yard; just cars, darkness, rain, the cast of yellow light from three lit rooms. But no faces looking out, no bodies passing; it was as if she had dropped into a silent movie, the rain a white noise, invisible when she was active, manic and drumming if she stopped to think. She tried not to think. Fuck!

She slapped herself. Tried the phone again. Nothing's impossible . . .

Blee-blee-blee-blee.

Oh, thank-*you*, God.

OK. OK. OK.

She looked out again. Nothing. Tried the phone again.

Blee-blee-blee-blee. *Just checking . . .*

OK. She took a deep breath, got up and climbed down the ladder. With the larger torch she wandered, looking for weapons. All she found was a pile of hessian sacking and the few thousand tons of spuds. She tried a sack with a few large potatoes dropped in to the bottom; a weapon of sorts. Then she weighted a second and third sack, switched off her torch and went into the rain.

One-Hundred-and-Thirty-One

If the barn door creaked Caz didn't hear it, the rain, the trees, the drumming on the roof, was more than enough to mask anything.

Except a car alarm.

She dropped down behind the line of cars; their variety was chilling. On the far end a Jaguar XJS; on this end a Range Rover; in between a Renault 19, a clapped-out Ford pick-up, a Sierra.

She could hear Jill Bartholomew now: *All walks of life, Caz, they don't look like monsters, they'll be everything from the unemployed to managing directors. But remember, they are resourceful.*

She took out a couple of potatoes.

Hey, tell me about it Jill!

The exhausts were still warm and as she pushed and twisted, pushed and twisted, the potato lodged more and more on, farther, deeper inside. She did it carefully, trying not to rock the cars. It took ten minutes. One of these would be Angel's car, but there was no way of choosing. Now she thought she would see what else she could find. She stood, crouched, her head below the horizon of the cars, checking for the tiny red-yellow bleeps of any alarm systems. The expensive ones would have alarms, but she was hoping their owners felt they were far enough away from Manchester and hadn't bothered.

Then one light went off in the farmhouse; another went on. Then flash as the front door opened and the blue floodlit bloop of security lighting, bootsteps crunching across gravel, then slapping mud.

One-Hundred-and-Thirty-Two

Caz froze. She was the driver's side of the XJS, the passenger side of the Renault. There were six paths for the man to take; one of them was directly through her, over her. She grabbed the long torch. Jesus, if he was leaving, he'd try to start his engine and . . .

The footfall went to the right, Caz spun on the balls of her feet, still low down on her haunches and looked under the back of the Renault. It was a tallish man, light brown hair, at the rear of the Range Rover, tailgate up. He came away with a long box, the lid undone, what looked like wires protruding. The back slammed and then Caz heard the breeleeeep!! of the car alarm being re-set.

She looked up at Heaven and smiled. The man walked back to the house, there was an exchange of deep voices and the door closed.

The Range Rover wasn't Angel's; and he wouldn't have bought or hired the XJS. She didn't see him driving a pick-up and the car with the 3 guys, even though she'd been ducking away out of sight, she was pretty sure had been a Sierra. God seemed to be back on the job so she decided. It was the Renault 19. She wiped her face, un-crouched and looked through the passenger window for an alarm. No light. She went round to the back and took out the crowbar. Then she had a thought, dropped down and worked the potato free from the exhaust. Then she had another thought. She went to the driver's door. Yes, unlocked. Inside, in the ignition, the keys. Angel's car for sure, set up for a fast exit.

She slipped in. Sat. She was invisible unless the security lighting came back on.

Caz waited. No one came out, there was no football-field sudden blue light. Now she was acting, actually doing something, it was easier. She checked the car. In the back a Nike Sports Bag. She leaned over to pull it into the front and check it out. It was heavy.

One-Hundred-and-Thirty-Three

Caz was about to get out of the car when she noticed the small microphone above and in front of her head; an in-car cellular. She looked down into the passenger well and found the handset. More power, and a better aerial – it was worth a try. She looked up at the house, down at the car keys and quietly turned the ignition. The phone be-deeped. She looked at the house again.

It had stopped raining. The sudden silence buzzed. Caz could hear the car's heater fan and switched it off. Again she looked up at the farmhouse. Then she lifted the handset, tapped in a number and pressed Send. She heard half a crackle and a shaky dial-tone. Then someone answered. She wanted to talk normally but she found she was whispering. She sounded hoarse. She hadn't realised how dry her mouth had got.

"Trevor, it's me, Caz."

"It's a shitty line Flood."

"It's a *wonderful* line, Trevor. I need you to write some stuff down, OK?"

"OK."

"I'll tell you where I am. What I'm doing. You don't hear from me in twenty minutes you dial Brighton nick, and Manchester Central, nine-nine-nine, and tell 'em what I'm gonna tell you now. I'm in the wilds somewhere north of Manchester and it's deep-shit country."

"So tell me."

"OK," Caz said. "First some names, some car numbers . . ."

One-Hundred-and-Thirty-Four

Caz slipped out of the Renault with the Nike bag, gently closed the door and moved back behind the row of cars. Now it wasn't raining she felt wetter. She kept low and jogged to the barn, then retraced her earlier steps, out of the range of the security lights. When she got to the gate, she crossed the driveway, cut into the bushes and worked her way round to the side of the farmhouse.

Most places had a sensor on the front, a sensor on the back. You got richer, and or more paranoid, you put sensors on the sides too, or compromised with wide-angle ones on the corners. Here there was enough light to see that the side of the house was clean. Caz slipped out of the bushes and across a few feet of space. Nothing happened.

She stopped to breathe long and deep a few times. It calmed her and gave her a spare belly-full of oxygen; an old Jiu-jitsu trick. On the corner of the house she paused, and looked up for the sensor and the light. They both pointed out at least fifteen feet. That tallied with the Range-Rover guy. He had been well away from the house before the yard had lit up like Christmas. She rounded the wall and edged along to the first dark window. She listened. Nothing.

The next window was lit and she thought she heard voices. She could hear classical music, very low, either quietly playing in the room or drifting there from elsewhere in the house. Through curtains she could sense movement but see nothing. This just got worse. What was she supposed to do, go up to the door and ring the bell? Then she heard Angel. "Fuck you!" he said. Then he screamed.

One-Hundred-and-Thirty-Five

Caz went to the front door and rang the bell. It was like she had switched the world off. The music stopped, the house stopped, there were no screams; only the imagined echo of the bell. She pressed it again. Water plopped on to the doorstep. She smiled and the rain started up again. Then she felt someone approach the door. She grabbed two good breaths. Then the door opened. She smiled again.

"Hello," she said.

The man's mouth dropped open and he went to speak, but as he did, Caz looked down. So did he, and she shot him in the knee with Angel's pistol.

Caz would have preferred it if he hadn't screamed. The silenced report was just a little "phoot" and she might have got one more before it got difficult. She kicked him, very hard, in the throat, stepped over him and brought the sack down hard on his back. She doubted he'd be unconscious but she hoped she'd pissed him off.

Then she felt neat, turned, and shot out the windscreen of the Range Rover. The alarm duly obliged with flashing indicators, headlights and a distracting wah-wah-wah. She screamed, "*police*!" and ran past the room she knew was occupied.

She slapped through a door, a kitchen, empty as she fell, rolled, came up with the pump-action and faced back down the hall. As they came out she shot into and along the floor, taking two of them down with wounds below the knees, pellets and splinter spray. One appeared to have fainted, the other started to crawl over him.

Caz rose as the other door slammed. She heard furniture moving; That was actually good from her point of view. She went up to the crawler and smacked the back of his head before rolling him over.

He gibbered. She put the shotgun in his mouth and pushed. He gagged and then he vomited. Caz pulled the gun away, waited, then pushed him back flat and pressed the gun up under his nose. The noises he made were animal and pathetic, pleading, mewing. She so wanted to kill him. She pushed the gun again and he flinched.

"Now listen, you evil fuck. You have half a chance. Tell me who is here and where they are, or I'll kill you now. If you turn out to be wrong, I'll come back and kill you anyway."

She pushed again and it squealed again.

"One chance," she said.

She pulled the gun back and looked at him. There was blood on his teeth. He was trying to talk but heeing as if an asthma attack was imminent.

"Hi, hi, carn . . ."

"OK," Caz said calmly. She put the shotgun up to her shoulder and aimed.

"Seven!" the man said.

"What?"

"There were seven of us and Jackson. We were all in there."

"The room you came out of?"

He nodded. Caz nodded. "Right," she said. "If you want to stay alive, start crawling out the door now. I'm going to torch this place!"

He looked. She waved the gun. He started slithering away, his blood slugging down the hall behind him.

"Hey," she shouted after him. "You forgot your friend."

He just kept crawling, smearing. Caz could smell his piss.

One-Hundred-and-Thirty-Six

Caz had to step on the thing to go past him and out of the front door. She went back into the rain, to the window of the locked room. She couldn't tell for sure, but she thought maybe the windows were openable. There was no way she could be certain but then it wasn't her who had put up a barricade. It could always come down. What worried her was a second exit. She ran back inside, stomping over the leg-shot men.

She leaned back against the wall and called out.

"This is the police! You have a man in there. Let him speak!"

"Flood?"

There was a smack of something on flesh, a grunt, and then Caz thought she could hear Angel laughing.

"Are you in there, Doyle?" Caz shouted. "I want Jack!"

Someone shouted back. "Jack, you call him? What's he worth?"

Fuck this. Caz checked her shells and started blasting the door, aiming high. Inside there were shouts, someone screamed and she thought Angel let out a long arrrggghh.

She was surrounded in smoke, her ears ringing. When she stopped there was a splintered hole about two foot wide. There was a crash as a cupboard was pushed against it. Someone was shouting, "Come on! Come on!" and someone else was shouting back at the voice, "They're fucking stuck, I tell yer!"

Angel was laughing then she heard him. "Way to go, Flood!"

There was a sickening thwack and he went silent. Caz reloaded.

She ran outside again: There were faces at the window. She raised the shotgun and they disappeared. She let two shots go anyway and the glass, some of the frame, exploded. It was pissing down again and she screamed at the men inside, exactly what, she didn't know. One of the wounded guys had slithered down the front steps. She almost shot him, then she bawled at him to stay still.

She ran over.

"The names of the guys inside! Now!"

"Doyle, Lipper, Green and Smith!"

"Right. Now you stay still, or you're fucking dead."

She ran inside again, heaving now with lust. She fell against the wall. The third man was trying to get even lower, pressing himself into the floor. He had pissed too.

"Doyle?"

"What?"

"You must know I'm not the law by now. I just want Jack. Now are we going to do a deal?"

"A *deal*? Fuck off, lady. There's five of us in here. We're all armed and the first person to catch a bullet in the teeth is your man, Jack."

It made Caz stupidly angry. She turned to let loose a couple more shells. Then she stopped herself. "Yeah, yeah. Doyle, if you lot were tooled up, you'd've used them by now. You're hiding in there, shitting your pants. Now stop fucking me about."

"What sort of deal?"

"I want Jack."

"And we just give him to you?"

"A swap."

"For what?"

"For staying alive? Let Jack out, I'll throw you the gun."

"And I'm the mayor of fucking Salford! Do me a favour, woman!"

"I'm going to the window!" Caz shouted. "Any furniture moves and I'll torch the place, you and Jack, the lot of you."

She was becoming calmer. Now she had to sound angry.

She stepped into the rain. Up to the window.

"OK, Doyle, I'll toss in a dozen shells. You give them to Jack. Let him come to the window. I'll empty the gun in front of you. Then we swap; Jack for the gun. We'll have thirty seconds to get away, that'll be enough."

There was no answer.

"Doyle?"

Still no answer, just the rain.

"Doyle?"

"Doyle?"

"What?" Something in the voice . . .

"Do we have a deal?"

"It's not that great."

"If you're holding out for better, Doyle, you're dreaming."

Then she heard it, the wardobe, gently lifted, moving. She ran. She slipped once in the wet, then she was inside again, one of them climbing out through the hole. She ran behind, slammed the back with the barrel. He slid soundlessly to the ground. She glanced, saw the taped mouth. *Angel*! As she pulled it away there was a crash of glass. Angel slumped. She was torn. But his eyes said go.

She ran again, out into the rain again, heading for the gate. They would have to go out that way. The night was hateful now, whaling, slashing, vicious now, the bluelight bright, the RangeRover still screeching, blinking. She ran and something sharp hit her across the eyes.

One-Hundred-and-Thirty-Seven

Caz was in water, terrible pain. She felt a boot thud into her side, another into her head. For a second, a bright light, a moment's sleep and then more kicking, but this hardly hurt. It was raining, she thought, and there were four men there, a gun – a gun? Pointing at her. There was a gate, white. Then she heard a car – the screech of tyres on gravel, and the man held her chin and spat in her face and then there was a shout and the man raised the gun and his face was bright white light, and there was a very loud bang in her ear, a dull thud, and the men were gone and the man was gone and it was raining, raining, and a car was . . .

One-Hundred-and-Thirty-Eight

It was raining, raining and Caz hurt, oh, shit, she hurt. There was a farmhouse, lights, she went for help. In the drive there was a man, blood on his legs, in the porch, another man, the same. In the hall a man sat up, little blood, his eyes staring. She had been here before.

She checked the man. No pulse. She could hear rain. There was a door, blackened, shattered, a gaping hole. The man in the porch was dead too. Outside on the gravel, dead too. This had something to do with her; she could almost remember. There was a car against a post. She'd been in a crash?

She walked that way. There were two men on the ground, one twisted awkwardly, the other long and thin, peaceful almost, but there was something wrong with him, his head, black marks like diamonds across his broken, plasticine face. He had no pulse. And no pulse from the rag doll on the floor either, and against the wall, the car between his legs, one above the bonnet, the other horribly smashed, the sixth man. He had no pulse.

> One, two, buckle my shoe,
> Three, four, shut the door,
> Five, six, pick up sticks,

Wasn't there a seven, wasn't there an eight? She felt sick now, and she felt a little bit cold and in the car . . .

In the car was no-one. There was no-one in the car. There were a lot of cars though, over there, and—

She went that way. Big doors, open. Someone inside. And blood.

The one man is sitting in potatoes. He wears a dinner-jacket and he is holding his leg and crying. The leg is pumping blood and Doyle, you think Doyle, he has a fist pressed there, trying not to die. The other man has red all over him, you think Angel, and Angel is trying to crawl towards Doyle. You hear yourself say "Angel!" and you remember who you are. You are Caz Flood, a police officer.

Angel stops, he can't go any further. You look at the man Doyle and he says, "Help me, for God's sake help me!" and then you know everything again.

You go to Angel, dear, sad Angel. You can hear Doyle begging in God's name for help. In the name of God, help. And you turn Angel over and he sees you, tries to recognise you, and some little flutter of life comes back to him, his breast is red. He smiles, a weak child's smile a falling asleep listening to a fairy-tale smile, a tuck-me-in-tight-Daddy smile and you know you're crying and you don't care.

And you pick up this good man. He is heavy, you are sick, but you make it together to the pile of potatoes and the worthless thing there, pleading, bleating, begging for its life and you're both there now and you help Angel hold a potato and you help him, lift his arm, and you help him as he drops it feebly into the face of this thing called Doyle, this weak creature Doyle. And now you hold Angel. He has been dead a long time but he had to wait to let his soul go. And you are crying but he is happy and you think of a woman called Jeanette, a mother called Ethel, a tiny, tiny little red-breast Robin and you hold this angel on your left breast, tight inside your left arm, and he sleeps and while he sleeps you pull potatoes down with your right hand and slowly, slowly, slowly, you cover the thing called Doyle and your Angel sleeps, you sleep, and way way off on the horseless loveless moors you hear sirens, imagine lights.

Christmas Eve

Jimmy Bright, green trousers, red top, his cloak black and gold, his black eye-mask slipping, playing with his Duplo Zoo.

"He won't take it off," Tom Bright says. "I told him Batman made the bad Sarah go away. Now he insists he's his right hand man."

"All's well then," Caz says.

Carol speaks. "He's much better now, much better. But really, you didn't need . . ."

"The forty-five pounds wasn't mine," Caz says.

"He's thrilled with it all, anyway," Tom says. Caz smiles.

"And this is for the two of you," Caz says. She touches the thin scar above her eye and passes across an envelope.

"We didn't buy you anything," Tom says. "We couldn't think. We thought something extra special for the wedding . . ."

Caz smiles again. The package sits there.

Jimmy Bright's dad looks up. "Is this what I think it is?"

"Press cuttings," Caz says. "The demise of the Acorn & Tree Tops Group; gone into voluntary liquidation, I hear. It's still not certain there will be any charges, but the scandal, child pornography being found in four nurseries, well, the press were bound to hear about it. People withdrew their children in droves. And then there was the Brighton fire, suspected arson. Julian Treece looks implicated. The evidence is circumstantial, mainly, but the Crown Prosecution Service will run with it."

Tom has undone the envelope. There is something else.

"And this?"

"Coroner's report – don't ask. Something that happened just north of Manchester. Seven paedophiles and one man dead. Three deaths from carotid strangles, another two from multiple injuries after being struck by a vehicle, a third, multiple injuries, then strangled. The seventh, the man Doyle, loss of blood, resulting from a road traffic accident."

"The man, the other man?"

"A man called Jack Sweet. I knew him as Angel. A bobby like me; a good copper. He worked on your son's case briefly. He was undercover when things went wrong. They shot him."

"I'm sorry."

"I'm not," Caz says.

Notes

In the process of writing this book I spoke to child protection officers, the social services, national child agencies and to a very senior psychologist. To these I owe much. They care.

Cruelty to children is common. At least four children die every week as a result of abuse or neglect. In England alone, in 1991, 45,200 children were listed on child protection registers. Almost half of these children are listed as of grave concern to the authorities. Of the 23,000 others, at least 5,400 are listed as being victims of sexual abuse.

98% of sexual abuse is by males. Paedophiles seek to work where they have regular access to children.

Much sexual abuse goes unreported and where it is reported and investigated, conviction rates are low.

All the crimes fictionalised in A Wild Justice are based on actual offences.

Children do disappear.

There is no complete national database of missing persons.